The Sundial

Return to
HQ Store

Maarten 't Hart is one of Holland's best-selling writers. He has written more than ten novels, several collections of short stories, and many volumes of essays. His work has been translated into a number of languages.

Praise for *The Sundial*:

'An extremely well-written suspense' – *Playboy*

'A bizarre, enjoyable detective story with a great storyline' – *De Morgen*

'An extremely lively novel . . . a believable thriller complete with murder and attempted murder' – *NRC*

'Reading Maarten 't Hart is pure pleasure. *The Sundial* is a great story' – *De Groene Amsterdammer*

'The irony sparkles, the dialogues are sometimes so absurd that they are side-splittingly funny . . . compellingly suspenseful - *GPD*

'A suggestive novel. In genre terms a whodunit, in terms of content more a diary of a writer with a preference for transvestism' – *Algemeen Dagblad* (four-starred review)

'Above all, it is evident the pleasure of the author in projecting himself into the world of a woman who disguises herself as another woman' - *Trouw*

MAARTEN 'T HART

The Sundial

Translated from the Dutch by Michiel Horn

Arcadia Books Ltd
15-16 Nassau Street
London W1W 7AB

www.arcadiabooks.co.uk

First published in the United Kingdom 2004
Copyright © Maarten 't Hart 2002
First published by Uitgeverij De Arbeiderspers, Amsterdam as *De zonnewijzer* in 2002
Translation © Michiel Horn 2004

A catalogue record for this book is available from the British Library.

ISBN 1-900850-88-5

The publication of this book has been made possible with the financial support from the Foundation for the Production and Translation of Dutch Literature.

Typeset in Minion by Basement Press
Printed in the UK by J W Arrowsmith Ltd, Bristol

Arcadia Books distributors are as follows:

in the UK and elsewhere in Europe:
Turnaround Publishers Services
Unit 3, Olympia Trading Estate
Coburg Road
London N22 6TZ

in the USA and Canada:
Independent Publishers Group
814 N. Franklin St.
Chicago, IL 60610

in Australia:
Tower Books
PO Box 213
Brookvale, NSW 2100

in New Zealand:
Addenda
Box 78224
Grey Lynn
Auckland

in South Africa:
Quartet Sales and Marketing
PO Box 1218
Northcliffe
Johannesburg 2115

Arcadia Books is the Sunday Times Small Publisher of the Year

Acknowledgements

The translation of the last stanza of 'Le chat' by Charles Baudelaire is by Cornelia Schuh and Michiel Horn. The translations of two passages from Arthur Schopenhauer, *Die Welt als Wille und Vorstellung*, are by Michiel Horn. The translation from the Russian of the poem by Osip Mandelstam is by Robert Tracy, © 1981 by Princeton University Press. The translation of a passage from Rainer Maria Rilke's 'Herbsttag' is by Michiel Horn. The translation of the four lines from Johann Wolfgang von Goethe's *Faust*, Part One is © David Luke, Oxford and New York: Oxford University Press, 1987. The passage from George Watt, 'Datura fastuosa, Criminal Purposes' is taken from *Dictionary of the Economic Products of India*, Calcutta: Government Printers, 1889-1896. The translation of seven lines from a poem by Johann Hoheisel is by Cornelia Schuh. The translation from the Dutch of 'Come and Stand Amazed You People,' is by Klaas Hart, © 1987 by CRC Publications, 2850 Kalamazoo SE, Grand Rapids, Michigan 49560. The translation of four lines from '*Mondnacht*' by Joseph Freiherr von Eichendorff is by Cornelia Schuh and Michiel Horn.

1.

Rose was dead, and I didn't know what to wear. If only it were winter, I thought, then I could put on my long black coat. Whoever heard of anyone dying in the summer? Granted, it was a Dutch pseudo-summer, with chilly, clammy days. Since the beginning of June the western European monsoon had ruled. All the same, a winter coat wouldn't do. So what would?

How peculiar, when my best friend had died, to be grimly, almost angrily, grabbing one item of clothing after another from the closet and tossing it on the bed. When three-quarters of my faded miserable wardrobe lay displayed, I sank dispiritedly into a chair. 'Why, for God's sake?' I snarled at the door. I knew I would have to get up soon. If I kept on sitting there, I would slowly turn to stone. In the funeral home, as soon as my gaze had fleetingly passed over the transparent lid on her coffin and I had seen her still, bluish-pale face, an ashen despondency had settled over me. As long as I kept moving I could keep it at a distance; if I sat or lay down, I sank into mineshafts unfathomed even by the poet who had written Psalm 130: 'Out of the depths have I cried unto thee, O Lord.' At least *he* had still been able to cry!

'Death, death, dying and the dead,' I muttered, a line of poetry by Du Perron, and I got up again. Resolutely I reached for the jacket of my black Vertigo suit. It had been my first choice. Because Rose had given it to me, though, I had thought it was out of the question. Go to a funeral in clothes that used to belong to the deceased?

Indisputably and by far the most beautiful suit that I possessed, also deepest black, so eminently suitable for a solemn occasion like this one. But the hem of the skirt just barely reached my kneecap, and the jacket was nipped in at the waist: rather provocative, was that all right at a funeral? Fine, then I would have to compensate by putting up my hair. That would at the

1

same time allow me to hide the fact that it was long and that the ends were split. I couldn't delay a visit to the hairdresser much longer. When I had put on the suit and saw that I had become just a bit too heavy for it, I muttered: 'If I'm going to wear this, I've absolutely got to put on dark stockings.' Did I have a pair of dark tights without runs? In the bottom drawer of my dresser I found two pairs, each with a run in one leg. Ruthlessly I took a pair of scissors to each damaged leg. This left me with two mutilated pairs of tights, each with one unblemished leg. Whether they looked exactly the same and had the same sheen I wasn't sure, but what else could I do? I had no time to go out shopping. Besides, the stores were closed on Monday morning. Before I put on the two pairs of tights I donned gloves. Pulling up stockings without gloves would mean another run right away.

Then I had to face the handbag problem. I had a cheap black patent leather purse. Did that go with such an expensive suit? But what choice did I have?

On the subject of my shoes too, I conferred with myself at length, but in the end I stood at the bus stop, in the chilly summer rain, wearing black high heels. Because I was just standing there, that searing despondent feeling showed up as it was bound to, and when at last an articulated bus came sliding to a halt, I was barely able to get on. Then I had to transfer at the station. Fortunately the bus to the cemetery was already standing there.

As we approached Rhijnhof, the weather suddenly changed. Playful little clouds pushed the monsoon greyness towards Germany. At the very moment I got off outside Datura Florists the sun even broke through. I looked a bit of an idiot with my black umbrella.

In the corridors of the crematorium we were held back. The previous funeral service seemed to be running late. I ascertained that the designer suit looked enticing. Or are men simply more susceptible when they are in a cemetery or crematorium? Whatever the reason, they were giving me the once-over.

As I directed my high heels towards the large swinging doors of the main hall, an aged necktie-wearer accosted me.

'Did you know Rose well?'

'She was my best friend,' I snapped.

'Unbelievable,' the man said, 'dead just like that…and still so young.'

'Next week she would have been forty-three,' I said. 'She was a Leo. In those dumb little astrology books they always say that Leos have such beautiful postures, walk bolt upright, act courageously. That fitted her to a T, as if she'd been created to prove those astrological retards right…'

I stopped, feeling a bit shocked at myself. Why such a flood of words directed at someone I had never seen before? And in such a sharp tone too.

'As you say,' the old man said amiably and imperturbably, 'she always looked great. And beautifully upright, just as you say, bolt upright…'

More in the same vein followed, but I didn't hear it. I thought: would Thomas be here? I did not spot him among the people standing in line in front of me. When I turned to look behind me, I found myself face to face with one of his former colleagues. Although younger than Thomas, this man had been appointed to the Chair of Pharmacology several years ago on the basis of some startling research on blood pressure-reducing medication. Thomas had been bitter, of course. At the time he had first taken out his rage on me, then had applied for positions elsewhere, had even left the country. Don't look back, I told myself, anything is better than a failed childless marriage like that.

'Hello there,' said the Professor of Hypertension, 'do you know whether Thomas is coming too?'

'I was just wondering that myself,' I said, 'but maybe he doesn't know that Rose has died.'

'But haven't you phoned him?'

'No,' I said brusquely.

I was taken aback myself by my bitchy tone. He turned to his wife, who looked ready for an Easter parade dressed in her daffodil-yellow suit, and said in an aggrieved tone: 'It was supposed to start at one, and now it's already ten after.'

'It doesn't matter a damn to Rose,' Marjolein mocked him, 'and your eulogy has been printed up, so why should it bother you if things start a few minutes late?'

'Right on the dot, that's my motto.'

'Just like death,' Marjolein said.

'Why do you always have to be so difficult?'

'Who's being difficult here? Not Rose, she can't, she's lying there quietly in her coffin, so who's complaining about ten teensy-weensy minutes…?'

He wanted to say something in response, but the doors swung open, and we were allowed to go inside. Her coffin stood at the front. I took a seat in the second row. The slow movement of Mozart's first Haydn quartet sounded from the speakers. Not too heartrending, I thought, very fitting, I had made a good choice there.

After everybody had found a seat, one of those undertakers strode to a lectern. He said: 'Professor Wehnagel will speak,' and stepped away. Eduard, at one time a substantial man with a big belly but now retired and looking old and shrivelled up, tottered towards the lectern, took a sip of water and said: 'We have gathered together to say farewell to Rose Berczy. As most of you probably know, Rose was of Hungarian origin. Her father and mother escaped from Hungary in November 1956. She was born the year after. She was an only child. All her family were murdered during the Hungarian Uprising. Her parents passed away, one soon after the other, during the 1980s. Now, still far too young, she has herself passed away. In the noontide of her days, as the old book says, she had to go to the gates of the grave and was deprived of the residue of her years.'

He paused, took another sip of water. 'It seems like yesterday that she applied for a job as research assistant in our department. She had two competitors, but she stood out right away. She was such a stunningly attractive girl. I still remember thinking: don't judge by appearances, please. And I also thought: a girl with nails that long can't possibly be a careful worker. Going straight against my inclination, I decided to pick one of the other two. Neat, grey, mousy girls, those other two applicants. When I had spoken to all three of them, and didn't have a clue whom I should take, I had them all come back for a second interview. I asked the first mousy girl: "Can you balance a ten-cent piece on its side?" The girl got a ten-cent piece out of a small purse and tried desperately to stand it on its side. If you've ever tried it, you know it can't be done. The second girl also tried to balance the ten-cent piece on its side, but Rose looked at me, looked at me... I can still see how she fished a ten-cent piece out of a red purse...I recall clearly how disappointed I was, thinking: would she also try...but she took a box of matches out of her handbag, deftly clamped the ten-cent piece between the box and the sliding cover and stood the box on its end. "There you are," she said, "a ten-cent piece on its side." There was no escape: I had to take her.

'I could not have made a better choice. For two decades I've worked with her. If my research has received any attention, it is thanks to Rose. Because of her thoroughness, her detective sense, her shrewdness, we in the Department of Pharmacology have been able to do fantastic research. How we shall miss her!'

He moved away from the lectern, walked over to the coffin, stroked the wood with his right hand, said tremulously 'Farewell, Rose' and then sat down.

Once again the undertaker strode through the hall. She had to leave in the noontide of her days and was deprived of the residue of her years, I thought, where is that from? I was surprised to find I was not sufficiently well versed in the Bible to know it at once.

'And now Professor Mentink has the floor.'

After getting a little nudge from his daffodil-yellow spouse, Bas Mentink trotted up to the lectern. On the way there he pulled his eulogy out of the inside pocket of his suit jacket, which had the same dark-grey colour as those refuse cans that have come into use recently. Even before he had unfolded all the pages his high bright voice cut through the hall.

'I knew Rose for a good twenty years. We started in the laboratory at roughly the same time, I as a medical student who was doing a minor in Pharmacology. I didn't know yet I would stay there permanently. I wasn't able to call on her for help with my research immediately. She was working fulltime for my mentor, who spoke a moment ago, but we saw each other daily. When she had time to work for me as well, how I learned to value her dedication, her industry, her conscientiousness! It is almost impossible to comprehend that she is no longer with us.

'When I arrived at the lab on the morning of that fatal day she was already hard at work. "Today looks like a beautiful summer day," she said, "at long last." "Yes," I said, "as far as I'm concerned you can have the afternoon off to go to the beach." "I'd love to," she said. Who could have guessed that on the beach at Katwijk that afternoon she would get sunstroke so seriously that it put her into a coma? If it had been noticed in time it might still have been possible to save her. But she lay there all that time, with the sun beating on her head and back. Even when a swimmer finally discovered that she was in a coma…even then, as I say, nobody could have thought…that very same evening…that she was going to pass away in the hospital that evening.'

The high voice died away, as the sun that had killed her shone exuberantly into the hall through the high windows. Mentink swallowed some water, got hold of himself and repeated: '…that she was going to pass away in the hospital.'

With his right hand he wiped the drops from his lips.

'Rose, what are we going to do without you? No one can ever replace you. You were the sun of the department. You were fantastic. Incomprehensible that you never got married. Plenty of admirers, but evidently you weren't interested in a husband, in children, in the security of a family. After all, you were married to your work. You were amazingly alone; you had no relatives. You did have a lot of friends – an entire hall full of them as we can see today. We shall all miss you terribly.'

He too walked over to the coffin, muttered something unintelligible and returned to his seat.

There we sat, in that warm, sun-filled hall. No one said anything, and I thought: maybe there should be some music now, but I had only asked for two pieces: Mozart to begin with, Beethoven at the end. The undertaker came to the front and asked whether anyone else wanted to say a few words. He cast an angry glance in my direction, it seemed as if he wanted to say: isn't it your turn? I went through the whole order of service for this solemn occasion with you; you were going to say something too, weren't you?

If I go up there, I thought, I might get two words out before I start sobbing.

Outside we heard the clear chattering laugh of the green woodpecker, the cooing of the Turkish turtledoves, the whining song of the greenfinch. It was midsummer, after all, and for a few moments more we sat in the sparkling sunlight that had killed her a few days earlier. In that amazing silence – two, three minutes at most – I thought: all the five billion people that now walk the earth have to be buried or cremated, one by one, and it seemed as if there would hardly be time or opportunity for that, given such an enormous supply of the potentially dead. I died a thousand deaths thinking of the logistics of those billions of funeral services. All those eulogies, at least three or four per funeral – because only two eulogies, it was now clear, seemed distinctly shabby – at least fifteen billion eulogies, where in Heaven's name would they all come from?

The slow movement of Beethoven's last string quartet sounded softly from the speakers in the hall. That too was acceptable as funeral music, did not choke you up, hurl you into depths from which you could not possibly cry out.

We were conducted from the hall into a reception room with high windows and potted palms. Since Rose had no family, there was in fact no one to express condolences to. But you can't go home from a funeral without expressing condolences, so Bas and I took our places, side by side, between two potted palms. Bas said: 'My predecessor ought to join us,' but he turned out to have left already. 'That doesn't surprise me in the least,' Bas said. 'It has hit him hard, he was terribly upset; standing here shaking hands and chatting, he clearly didn't feel up to that. And his wife is ill, maybe that was another reason for wanting to get home quickly.'

So there the two of us stood, side by side. Everybody seemed openly pleased that they could express their condolences to someone and made eager use of the opportunity. It always amazes me how relieved people are at the end of a funeral service. After a while, over the cake and coffee, a reception like that can get really quite jolly.

'Do you know where in the Bible it says: "In the noontide of her days she had to go to the gates of the grave, she was deprived of the residue of her years"?' I asked Bas.

'Are you sure it's from the Bible? He mentioned an old book.'

'What other old book could he have been referring to?'

'How should I know? But the Bible...yeah, that's probably it, well, what does it matter where it's from? In any case it was very suitable...in the noontide of her youth she had to go to the grave, she was deprived of the residue of her years.'

I wanted to say: not 'youth' but 'days'. However, he was now occupied with some condoling guests.

When we had shaken all the proffered hands Bas said: 'The job is done, I think, we can go and mingle with the crowd.'

'Someone's still coming,' I said, but he didn't hear me and quickly moved off.

A fragile, red-haired, alabaster-skinned girl approached me. She shook my hand, mumbled something unintelligible in which I thought I recognized the word 'participation' and immediately headed for the exit. I walked over to Bas. I wanted to ask him: did you recognize that girl? He was talking with his wife. From the sound of it there was more strife and trouble. Bas's wife turned away angrily, saw me, cast a disdainful eye over my stockings and then my miserable handbag, took a step in my direction and said: 'What a stunning suit you're wearing.'

'Thank you.'

'Too bad they didn't have it in your size,' she said.

2.

I can't get used to the warbling of today's telephones. Give me the old-fashioned ring. That muffled bleating, as if there were a castrated billy goat down in the basement – whoever thought that up?

When the telephone began its eerie chirping, at 8:30 in the morning a few days after the funeral, I was startled half out of my mind.

'Leonie Kuyper speaking.'

'The office of Notary Graafland here, I'll connect you with the notary himself,' a light soprano said.

A soft click, then a jovial voice: 'Do I have the pleasure...am I speaking with Mrs Kuyper?'

'Yes, you are.'

'Excellent! Very busy this morning?'

'No,' I said surprised. 'I was going to the hairdresser today, but that can wait.'

'Can you drop by my office? It would be best to g...start on everything at once. We could make a proper appointment for several days from now, but if by chance you have nothing in your agenda I don't have anything in mine, and we could at once make a start on this and that...you are the sole heir, you alone are named in the will, in brief: you inherit the lot. I want to g...g...discuss matters with you.'

'I am the sole heir?' I asked, astonished.

'Yes, you are...yes, not so long ag...g...it hasn't been long since Mrs Berczy made her will, and in it she made you her sole heir.'

'Sole heir,' I repeated.

'Exactly,' the notary said in a pleased tone, 'it would be g...g...very nice if you and I could have the opportunity to talk about this and that. Would you be able to drop over?'

'Right at this very moment? Is that really necessary?'

'Necessary? What is necessary? Life isn't necessary. But please come...we can deal with the formalities in short order...consult with each other...the issue is: do you want to accept the inheritance? There are a number of strings attached; why not think about it in the car on your way over here?'

'I don't have a car.'

'Doesn't matter. Bicycle also fine, or taxi. Or ride on shank's mare. Or come on horseback, for my part. Or on a donkey. So long as you find your way over here, my office is at 40 G...G... Galig...Galigaangr...gr...gr...gracht, in Gr...Gr...Groen...'

Is it permissible to finish the word in which a stutterer has got stuck? I don't think so, yet I said 'Groenhoven', almost tripping over the word myself.

Cycling over there, I hardly thought about the inheritance. Mostly I thought: you can't pronounce a 'g', so of course your name is Graafland and you live on Galigaangracht in Groenhoven.

From his jovial voice I had built up a picture of Graafland. How wrong I was! The voice turned out not to belong to the tall, somewhat stooped fifty-year-old I had vaguely conjured up at the other end of the line, but to a stocky, athletically built, very boyish-looking man with merrily sparkling eyes above a ridiculous moustache. He wore a camel-coloured jacket with a hound's-tooth check and a wide, bright-green tie.

'So...so...you are Mrs Kuyper. Please have a seat. I'll g...g...I won't waste any time. Mrs Berczy wanted to leave everything to her pussycats. You can do that in America, not here. Then we discussed the possibility of establishing a foundation. Its directors could then appoint someone to look after the cats, but, well, terribly complicated all of that. Finally we reached a simpler solution. Leave everything to a trustworthy, dependable, solid person who would assume the task of pampering the cats. Then your name came up. So you are the sole heir; anyway, you g...g...get the picture. On the way over here, did you consider whether you'll accept the inheritance?'

'You mentioned there are quite a lot of strings attached.'

'Quite a few. You see, Mrs Berczy...oh, you're bound to know all of this already, you must have spoken with her at length. You've already been taking care of her cats since her death, I assume...'

'I cycle over to her apartment every day.'

'Exactly, I thought so, g...marvellous, but did you also speak about moving in there on account of those cats?'

'Live in her apartment? She did once or twice say to me casually "Would you take care of my cats if anything happened to me?" and I said yes, that went without saying, but I didn't know... I mean...you don't expect...she was in her early forties.'

'Am I to assume from this that you're pulling out?'

'I'm not pulling out, Mr Graafland, but I didn't anticipate...'

'So you did not exhaustively discuss matters with each other. Those cats, she was crazy about them, anyway, you'd know that better than me. She wanted more than anything else that, after her death, the cats should stay in their familiar environment...her will was directed towards that end. She has left everything to you, provided you will move in there and provided you follow in her footsteps, as it were, assume her role, copy her, pamper her pussycats the way she used to. For the cats it has to seem as if everything is still the same, as if their mistress were still alive. You would...you could...with a whiff of her perfume and dressed in her clothes...just a suggestion... *Ach*, you know, looking after pussycats, that's really not so bad. Now if it were ferrets or pythons...and moreover, she lived in style.'

'Yes, her place is beautiful, but do I inherit the apartment too?'

'Absolutely, and mortg...g...g...gage-free. She had already paid it off. You're in clover. But of course there are sky-high estate taxes... For that reason she had taken out a substantial life insurance policy. Whether it will be enough...house prices in Leiden have g...g...risen so much in the last few years. So I don't know yet. All that still remains to be seen.'

With his knuckles he drummed a lively little march on his desk. He rummaged through a document-filled folder, looked at me and asked: 'You live on a side street of the Burg...gr...gravenlaan? You won't want to leave there?'

'Oh no, not at all. I live in a dreary little rental apartment. I ended up there after my divorce because when my husband ran off I couldn't pay the mortgage on our house all by myself.'

'Well, well, so moving won't be a problem.'

'Not in principle.'

'Excellent, so you could move in right away and start by renting, for example.'

'Renting? But who from? Didn't she own the apartment?'

'You'll be renting from the estate, Mrs Kuyper.'

'From the estate?'

'Yes, from the Berczy estate, so in the strict sense from yourself. But fine, before all that has been sorted out, has been more or less tidied up from the point of view of administering the estate, we'll all be at least a year older. You'll have paid a year's rent by then. Rental apartments are always worth about sixty percent less than owner-occupied condominiums. So lower estate taxes too. At least, if the taxman falls for it. And if not...you can sell some of her common shares...take out a small mortg...g...gage if need be...it won't be all that bad.'

'Small mortgage? That takes me by surprise, rather... I don't get...I don't understand... I'm beginning to stammer, oh God, how could I say such a stupid thing? Please excuse me.'

'Oh, not at all, I've stuttered since I was in diapers...not possible, you say? A bit later, then, since the playpen. I function reasonably well nevertheless. Flourishing practice. Leg...g...g...gal documents are a problem sometimes, but you can always compose them in such a way that there's no "g" in them. That way it goes... Hey, did you hear that? All at once it goes fine; suddenly they come out properly. Kind of crazy. All those 'g's. With a bit of luck no problem until lunch. Because of you, because you commented so frankly and openly on my stutter...good, yes, it goes fine...good grocers give goobers to great grey gorillas...'

I stared at the muscular little man in astonishment. His sparkling eyes beamed at me. Without stuttering, he summarized what he had said earlier. 'So you are the sole heir, Mrs Kuyper. You can accept everything without worry. There are no debts. Her estate is substantial. Unfortunately you are not related, so estate taxes are no joke, but that has been taken care of as well. She carried an impressive amount of life insurance. And she had a prepaid funeral contract, so that has been covered. The only thing is, you've got to move in there and take care of the cats.'

'I don't quite understand... I... How come she had made a will already? How did she come to arrange everything in such detail? Was she...did she think that she didn't have long to live? It doesn't smell right. You don't go to the notary when you're not yet forty-three, do you?'

'A mistake lots of folks make. They think: there's lots of time, I'm still young, all my life is ahead of me...oh, oh, how silly. You can pop off just like that, for no reason at all, you can be gone between breakfast and lunch. A will...you can't make one soon enough.'

'I find it strange, very strange.'

'I don't. She was one smart lady. When she bought her apartment I did the property transfer, I said to her: "Mrs Berczy, give some thought to your last will and testament," and now I'm saying it to you as well. I'm at your service...doesn't cost a lot. And you'll be prepared for anything. Really, you can't do it soon enough.'

'While still in your diapers, I suppose.'

Graafland burst out laughing and then said with a start: 'I haven't offered you anything yet.'

'Doesn't matter,' I said.

'A cup of coffee?'

'Please.'

He switched on the intercom and shouted: 'Margreet, could you bring us two cups of coffee?'

Nervously he drummed on the desk with his fingers, he said: 'All kinds of things enter into it, an inheritance like this. Internal revenue department, assessments…have you got an accountant?'

'No,' I said, 'why should I?'

'You could use her accountant. He's well informed about her affairs and has a hotline to my office, so together we can pull you through it without any nonsense, if you like…or you could look for another notary and another accountant.'

A soft knock at the door, it swung open, and through it appeared an arm, pushing a small table with a tray on it.

'Ah, yes, the coffee,' Graafland said and shot out of his chair,

'Sugar? Cream?'

'A few drops of cream,' I said.

He handed me a small package of creamer and said in a jolly tone: 'Watch out. It's remarkably flammable.'

'Flammable?' I said, surprised.

'Never seen it?'

He opened a second package of creamer, shook it into the palm of his left hand, reached with his right hand for a lighter that he flicked on, tossed the creamer in the air and raised the lighter. For a split second there was an enormous flame that immediately went out.

'A great show every time.' He grinned.

Full of amazement I looked at the little fellow. Was he really a notary public, this stuttering pyromaniac? He looked at me, as pleased as Punch. 'If now you think you'd rather do without the creamer,' he said, 'I can also offer you canned condensed milk.'

'To be honest, yes, please.'

'Marvellous! Set fire to the creamer, and people don't want it in their coffee any more. Easy to understand. But it's impossible to grasp how so many people, often without even having made a will, can shovel all kinds of things into themselves without a worry or a care, not knowing what's in those things, not knowing how flammable they are, not knowing how gr...gr... Oh no, not now, no, no, great ghouls dig graves...ha, it's all right.'

He sat down again and stirred his coffee.

Do you have any children, Mrs Kuyper?'

'No,' I said curtly.

'I do. Three of them. Nice kids.'

He sipped twice.

'There are a couple of bequests, so you won't get everything. Big bequest to SPCA, big one to the anti-fur foundation, Respect for Animals.'

'Respect for Animals?' I said, utterly astonished, 'but she had two fur coats herself, a light-brown muskrat jacket and a mink...'

'Yes, she was wearing it when she was here for her will...yes, beautiful fur...yours now...it'll look great on you too.'

'Yes, but leaving money to an anti-fur foundation, while she herself...'

'Not all that strange, is it? Feelings of guilt...gorgeous coat...guilt feelings bought off. It's the thieves who support the church welfare fund. It's the paedophiles who donate money to the orphanage.'

He slammed his cup down on its saucer.

'What do you do for a living?' he asked.

'I do some translating, and I substitute as a French teacher now and then,' I said, 'but I haven't got a regular job.'

'Would you feel like working here two half-days a week? Margreet is leaving on the first of September.'

'Here, Mr Graafland? What would I do?'

'Reception...you welcome people, make them feel at ease...you're good at that. Thanks to you my g's emerge effortlessly, for that reason alone...think about it for a bit...you may need a small mortgage...you could use a job...'

'She didn't already have a mortgage?'

'She had paid it off, as I told you before.'

'Paid off? With what money?'

'I don't know. She was single, had a good salary, could salt a bit away.'

'Paid off, how could that be?'

'The apartment was dirt-cheap when she bought it. Since then prices in Leiden have gone up like mad, but at the time...'

He looked at me dreamily and whispered: 'Why not come and work here, two half-days, you've got something special...an inheritance like that...nice it has come your way... *Ach*, I have to get back to work, a transfer of property

13

in a little while...don't hesitate to phone me if there are any problems. Come, I'll show you out.'

Not only did he walk me to the front door but he also went out into the street with me. He pointed at the rain clouds and sang: 'Where is our summer, our beautiful summer?'

'It was gorgeous for *one* day,' I said grimly, 'and that was the day Rose got her sunstroke.'

'Sunstroke. You rarely hear of that, do you? People dying of sunstroke.'

'They got to her too late,' I said.

'Come on,' he said, 'it can't have been just sunstroke... She lay in the sun so often, for hours on end...of course there must have been something else the matter, heart problem, what do I know? Small cerebral haemorrhage, you can think of a whole bunch of things...sunstroke, well, never mind, what do I know? I'm not a pathologist. Did they check her out properly? Who did the autopsy? Let it be a lesson to you, Mrs Kuyper: before you know it you could be done for, honest, it can happen just like that. So give some thought to your last will and testament...I'm at your service.'

3.

As if by special arrangement, Rose's condominium was located halfway between Galigaangracht and my dreary apartment. Every day since Rose's death I had gone there on my bicycle at the end of the afternoon to supply Tiger, Ober and Lellebel with their luxury cat nibbles. Now, on the way home, I could not bring myself to cycle past without stopping by, even though it was long before their dinnertime. Was it my destiny to go and live there? I could hardly believe it. Such a beautiful, light-filled apartment, in an elegant, red-brick building, with double-glazing and the most modern security features, a sweet little TV screen in the hall, for example, which showed who was at the main entrance when the doorbell rang.

Down below I first took the mail out of the mailbox. There was a proliferation of magazines aimed at cat-lovers: *Whiskers*, stencilled; *The Pussycat News*, printed; *Puss 'n Boots*, in gleaming black and white; and *Majesty*, a glossy, expensive journal.

When I got upstairs and entered her hall with its mini-TV screen, I inhaled the sharp cat smell. Of course I had smelled that odour before, I had always taken it in when I went to Rose's place. It seemed stronger now – a nasty penetrating cat-pee smell. Or was I simply imagining it? Did I have to change the litter in the litter boxes again? A good thing the boxes could be put out on the covered balcony. Just imagine if they were in the kitchen, or in the bedroom or bathroom!

Was this my destiny, to become a cat lady? I certainly didn't dislike cats. Yet it had never occurred to me to acquire a cat myself. That unmistakable cat odour had always slightly nauseated me, wherever I had smelled it. And now I would have to live in that smell, oh my God! Still completely dazed by Rose's unexpected death, I had hardly asked myself what would eventually happen

15

to the cats. All I had thought was: I'll look after them as long as necessary.

Tiger was the first to greet me. Beautiful cat, gorgeously spotted pattern, who regarded me unflinchingly with a look straight from Baudelaire's poem:

Je vois avec étonnement
le feu de ses prunelles pâles
Clairs fanaux, vivantes opales
Qui me contemplent fixement.

With astonishment I see
The fire of those pale pupils
Bright lanterns, living opals
That contemplate me fixedly.

Ober I saw only when I entered the living room. Coal-black, with a white triangle under his chin. Lellebel, of course, was nowhere to be seen. She always hid under a bed or on top of a cupboard. You rarely saw her.

'I'm coming to live with you,' I said to Tiger and Ober. 'I can move in right away, I can leave my own miserable possessions at the curb for the refuse truck. But…all these clocks…why did Rose have so many clocks? Would you mind if I got rid of a few?'

An old-fashioned cuckoo clock hung above the living-room door. Right next to the large window was a big Friesian wall-clock, ticking away deafeningly. Too bad it had escaped those burglars who specialized in stealing them. Sell it? Unthinkable. But all those digital clocks, with their red fluorescent numbers, could I not get rid of them? In the living room the intrusive, fire engine-red numbers shone in the bookcase as well as on the display below the television screen. In the kitchen blue numbers glowed on the microwave. I walked into the bedroom, where I saw a clock radio with red numbers and an ultra-modern alarm clock, also with red numbers. As well, there was an older alarm clock that ticked in a nasty irritated way. I picked it up, took it into the bathroom and put it on the counter next to the sink, where it doggedly kept on ticking. I looked into the small room where Rose put up her guests. It seemed at first glance to be clock-free. I returned to her bedroom. Carefully I lowered myself into the tall armchair that stood at her dressing table. I had always coveted a dressing table like that, but frugal Thomas had been dead set against it, and in the tiny place I was renting there was no room for one.

I leaned forward, pushed a switch. Yes, indeed, all those little lights came on. But I kept hearing the thundering ticking of the clocks and smelling the cat odour. I jumped up, feeling angry. I closed the bedroom door and returned to the dressing table with its comfortable armchair. 'Not long ago I saw a physicist on TV who said that time does not exist,' I said to Tiger, who had followed me in and nestled down on the bed. I didn't know whether I approved, but Rose had almost certainly tolerated it. 'That idiot said I should follow in Rose's footsteps,' I muttered to Tiger, 'I should copy her, crawl into her skin, put on her clothes, use a whiff of her perfume…good idea, then I'll smell nice, then maybe I'll manage to accept all that dumb ticking and your awful pee smell. And the fact that you're lying there on her bed, cool as a cucumber.'

I looked at the large colour photo of Rose that hung next to the dressing table. Had Rose hung a photo of herself there so that, when she was applying her makeup, she could see how it should be done? Or had she simply been vain? I regarded myself in the illuminated mirror. I looked at all the high-priced cosmetics, arranged there so neatly and temptingly. She had often quoted Dolly Parton: 'There's no such thing as natural beauty,' and she had said to me: 'Never skimp on makeup. Always buy what's most expensive. Only the very best is good enough for your tender skin.' How could I ever have afforded these hideously expensive creams on my miserable translator's fees? Now I had the opportunity to try out various things, and feeling curiously light-hearted, knowing for certain that Rose would have approved, I began carefully to make myself up with her treasures, while the notary's remarks were still buzzing in my ears. At first I was not yet fully aware of what I was doing, but as I progressed the realization grew that I was trying to summon her up. The process had been set into motion when I had worn her suit to the funeral service. That way I had been able to keep the all-consuming despondency at a distance. Sitting at her dressing table worked even better. If I could summon her up, crawl into her skin, then she was not definitively dead, only provisionally: then she could come to life again.

'I must get my hair cut the way Rose did,' I said to Tiger, 'that would be easy, after all, my hair is longer, I can have a lot taken off, it can be changed to her style…maybe a bit of a rinse and then…'

The thought occurred to me that, to move closer to the goal, I could put up my hair right away and wear one of her jaunty berets.

After I had made myself up and put up my hair and put on a white beret, all the while peering at her photo to gain inspiration, I took a light-blue summer suit from her closet. It fitted me, but, like the Vertigo suit, it would look better if I lost a few pounds. 'There's no alternative, I've got to go on a diet,' I said to Tiger, and he meowed encouragingly.

I stood in front of the mirror, looked at myself, saw that it was good, provided I could make her bolt-upright posture my own. And it would be better if I copied her hairstyle too.

For a long time I stood there, looking in the mirror at Rose's shadow, constantly asking myself: why am I doing this? Am I doing this on the notary's instructions or on my own? It could be duty or compulsion or insanity. I recalled I had once read that men in mourning sometimes put on the clothes of their deceased wife. Maybe it was something like that. I couldn't say.

I tried to assume her facial expression. A bit mocking and cheerful and often a bit condescending. How horribly difficult! I lacked her heavy, half-closed eyelids. Wait, what if I applied false eyelashes from her ample supply? When after some serious effort I had managed that, I actually seemed to have got a step farther along.

Once I had her hairstyle, surely it would be easier to imitate her facial expressions. A mocking look, I could manage that all right, but it wasn't me. I threw up my hands the way she had always done when expressing herself critically about a mutual acquaintance. Not at all bad, now her finger-pointing: also a characteristic gesture. That was reasonably successful, but I realized at once that when doing this she had always stretched her hands, with their extravagant witch-like talons, out wide.

I stared at my hands for a while. If I crawled into her skin, as was apparently notarially required, did I also have to adorn myself with vulgar fingernails? For as long as I had known Rose, twenty years or so, she had worn her nails long and polished. Every once in a very long while I would ask: 'What's with those fingernails?' and she would reply: 'I think they're attractive,' and then I would say: 'Attractive? Aren't they a tad vulgar?' and she would reply: 'You mustn't avoid what's vulgar or common, that's part of life too. If you try to put it out the front door, it will march in through the back.' Now that she was dead I felt guilty that I had occasionally expressed myself critically about her extravagant fingernails and had often looked at them with disdain.

By way of penance I opened a drawer in the dressing table. Yet more cosmetics. I pulled out a second drawer: a small opened box containing at least half of the one hundred Curve Oval artificial fingernails that, according to the label, had once comprised the contents. Also acrylic powder and a small bottle of fluid.

'Let's go,' I muttered. 'No harm in trying them on. I can take always them off again. Prove all things; hold fast only that which is good, to use the words of St Paul. All things? No: no drugs, no incest, no bungee jumping, no sadomasochism.'

One thing I have learned in this life: first read the instructions. All the same I cast only half an eye on the folded sheet of paper in the box: read only that, before attaching the nail, you first had to file the surface of your own nail. The glue held better then because it could grip the roughened nail.

What a finicky job it turned out to be, applying artificial nails. I had seen Rose do it a few times. Attach the artificial nail to the top of your own nail. Fill up area between cuticle and bottom edge of nail with smelly acrylic. Although I should therefore have known better, I at once made a typical beginner's mistake. You've got to do the nails of your right hand first. If, as you are naturally inclined to do, you begin the wrong way around, then you're stuck with a left hand with bothersome long nails that get in the way when you start working on your right.

In the end, after a lot of tinkering, I got it done. Two hands equipped – what am I saying? – *armed* with long, oval, pointed, somewhat curved nails. Rather vulgar, enormously alienating, fascinating in a creepy sort of way. One thing was certain: my fleshy hands looked less lumpish.

'Now I've still got to paint them,' I heard myself say almost with relish. 'Where is the nail polish?'

The little bottle was on the dressing table, right in front of my nose, so at first I looked right past it. It was a disgusting colour: purplish red, with a hint of blue mixed in. Never mind, it was the colour she had been wearing those last few weeks. I had no choice.

And as if I hadn't learned a thing, once again I started with the nails on my left hand. 'Even a donkey doesn't stumble over the same stone twice,' I snorted when I had completed my left thumbnail.

When at last I was through and my nails had dried I made the throwaway motion with my hands, and then I extended those talons with the satisfying sense that I had taken a big step in the right direction. Equipped with Curve Oval, I could not help looking different, more like Rose, I had distanced myself a bit from my own accommodating, rather docile nature, had surrendered some of my saint-like patience. At the same time I felt like bursting into tears. But if I began to blubber, my – no, *her* – makeup would run. I sensed the tingling in the corners of my eyes, felt the tears itching to flow forth. I raised my hands, bent my fingers, dug the Curve Oval nails into my palms and got myself under control.

19

Then I heard the front door. Was someone coming in? But who, for crying out loud? I slipped back into the living room, my heart thumping like a frightened rabbit's, put my hand around the door and pulled it carefully toward me. In the meantime, the intruder had progressed into the hall. All he saw of me at first were my Curve Oval fingers, clenched around the door. A strangled sound, as though somebody was choking off the plaintive cry of a tawny owl. I threw the door open. Bas Mentink stood there in the semi-dark hall. Of course he saw me too. I was still wearing that beautiful white beret and the light-blue designer suit. He looked at me the way Saul at Endor must have looked at Samuel. 'And he stooped with his face to the ground, and bowed himself,' says the Word of the Lord. Bas also stooped with his face to the ground; he also bowed himself, but he did not straighten up, he bowed ever deeper and then smacked down on the vinyl tiles.

'Did I faint?' he asked after he came to.

'Not really,' I said. 'You were out for at most five seconds.'

'I sometimes pass out if I squat down and then get up after a while. It seems to be not altogether risk-free. In no time at all millions of brain cells die.'

He got up, looked at me and said: 'I thought you were Rose, I saw her fingernails, so… Jesus Christ, I was scared shitless.'

'That figures,' I said, 'but, after all, who would drop into her apartment unannounced?'

'You're here too, aren't you?'

'I'm looking after her cats.'

'That's what *I* came for. In the lab a few moments ago I thought: my God, her cats…'

'You have a key?'

'Yes.'

'Who else has a key?'

'I don't know.'

'That means I'll have to change the lock.'

'Why would you?'

'It's not a pleasant thought that everybody can walk in here just like that.'

'Come off it, everybody… I doubt there's that many other people…say, how come you've disguised yourself as Rose?'

'Notary's orders. It's in the will. I've got to follow in her footsteps. Because of the cats. So that everything stays as much as possible the way it was, and Tiger and Ober and Lellebel will think Rose is still puttering around.'

He looked at me as if to say: she's demented, she's come down with Kreutzfeld-Jacob disease.

'Rose put it in her will that the cats must stay here and that I've got to take care of them.'

'And that is what you're doing?'

'You can see that, can't you? I've already started.'

'Yes, her cats…they were her children, but still, I…so you're moving in here? Is that all right?'

'According to her notary, it is.'

'I'm flabbergasted. When I tell that to Marjolein…'

'Why would you tell that to Marjolein? She doesn't need to know, does she? She hates me enough already.'

'If I don't tell her, she'll find out some other way.'

'Would that matter?'

Again the uncontrollable urge to start howling crowded in on me. Even though I didn't care for him all that much, I wanted most of all to put my head on his shoulder and have a good cry. He kept on looking at me, and I said: 'Come on in, I'll make us a cup of tea.'

'No, I'm on my way back to the lab, I only came to make sure the cats hadn't died for lack of food and water.'

He stepped from the hall into the sunny walkway. I closed the door behind him, put the end of a chain into a small catch. I walked back to the living room, sat down by the window, sang softly: 'All creatures that on earth do dwell, sing to the Lord with cheerful voice.' How comforting those slowly passing white clouds are. And they keep on coming past, and you know they will still be going by after your death, after a nuclear war, after the extinction of the human race. Granted, maybe not for all eternity, but certainly for millions if not billions of years. How much that consoled me!

I wrenched carefully at Curve Oval. The nails did not yield. I walked to the bedroom, got the instructions. They said nothing about taking the nails off. I wrenched again. They seemed to have fused with my own fingernails. How in God's name was I ever going to get them off again? Was I condemned to keep on wearing them? This much was certain: with those nails I had been able to evoke her so skilfully that, when he saw them, Bas had passed out. I had been able to perpetuate something of her presence on this shabby globe even after her death, and that gave me an obscure sour satisfaction.

4.

I couldn't bring myself to spend the night in Rose's apartment. First a new lock on the door, then I would think about it again. I phoned a locksmith. 'No, ma'am, not that soon, not a chance, we'll need to book beyond the weekend. Monday we're closed. Tuesday, August 22, that would work, eleven a.m.'

On Tuesday morning, on the way from my rented hole to her apartment, I cycled by one of those shops where they equip women with artificial nails all day long, working under fluorescent light. I entered the store. A nail stylist was filing her own nails and did not stop. Can that be healthy, I thought, to sit there all day, filing artificial nails with your head bent over? No question: you'd be filling your lungs with a load of the gunk they use to make those suckers and to glue them on with.

The stylist looked up for a moment. I asked: 'Have you maybe got something I can use to get these artificial nails off?'

'Glued them on yourself, did you?' she asked tartly.

'Yes,' I said guiltily.

'You should have had that done by a pro,' she said.

She cast a glance at my nails.

'What did you stick them on with?'

'With Etos *Extra Strong*.'

'That contains cyanoacrylic, too bad, they're stuck on good and proper. I can't help you.'

'Is there absolutely…?'

'In a pinch you could dissolve them in acetone, but I must warn you: it'll turn into an awful mess.'

'So I'll have to walk around with these forever? I'll have to be buried with them?'

She took my right hand, tapped one of my artificial nails with one of her own and said with authority: 'This curved model sticks on much tighter than a straight one because it fits better over your own nail, you won't get it off even with glue solvent; we used to carry it but not anymore, we had a storm of complaints.'

'I stuck them on as a joke. Seems they won't come off again.'

'Yeah, if only you had come here. This kind of do-it-yourself job...but why would you want to take them off? You're not exactly endowed with slim fingers. These nails really do make your hands look a whole lot better.'

'Could be, but they're a real pain. You can't do up your buttons any longer, you can't pick up anything you want just like that any more. And on the toilet...'

'Yeah, wiping your bum, that's a real chore with long nails,' said the stylist. She actually had the nerve to smile. 'How long have you had them?'

'Since last week.'

'Good Heavens, that's no big deal, honest, just stick with it, you'll get used to it, and what you can't do with your fingertips you can do with your knuckles, like keying in your PIN code, for example. After a while you won't know any better, and you won't ever want to change again.'

'Quite possibly, but...'

'Come on, stop complaining; you can always cut them off when your own nails have grown a bit.'

'That could take a while. My nails grow so slowly.'

When I left the shop it began to drizzle silently. It was the kind of chilly sneaky rain that makes you think, optimistically: this won't get me wet. But I *did* get wet, and I shivered as I cycled to Rose's apartment, thinking: what nonsense, of course these nails will come off, she was pulling my chain, that nail-filing nasty. Although the late-summer dog days had just barely come and gone, the heat in the apartment glowed gently. How eerily comfortable. Nothing enslaves like comfort, but nobody knows this any longer because comfort is taken for granted nowadays.

Once again I paced back and forth between the living room and the bedroom. Once again all those ticking clocks and glowing red, hateful, silent numbers drove me nearly wild. I pulled the cord of one of the small digital clocks out of the outlet. The nasty little numbers died at once.

'That's better,' I muttered, but as I continued my path across the noise-reducing floor covering, the idea hit me that I ought to undo this bold interference with the status quo. What gave me the right to criticize Rose beyond the grave, as it were? By the way, could you say that: beyond the grave, when somebody had been cremated? All right, what difference did it make; this much was certain: when I visited Rose I had never had the nerve to say 'Do you really need to keep all these awful clocks around?' Now that she was dead, I did dare to say it. Ugh, I was such a coward.

The locksmith rang the doorbell. He unscrewed the cylinder, inserted a new one, gave me the keys, and I paid him. This made the apartment seem a bit more like home, and as I went back to the living room I thought even the cat smell had become more bearable.

The phone began to chirp. What should I do? Pick up the receiver? I hesitated, but the insistent sound would not stop. Gingerly I put my hand on the white designer phone. I quickly picked up the receiver and immediately put it back. Thank God, the insistent sound stopped at once. To compensate for not actually having answered the phone, I walked over to the digital clock I had disconnected and put the plug back into the outlet. Furiously blinking zeroes appeared on the display. Plus angry little dots between the zeroes. How could I end that non-stop blinking? At the top there were several black buttons with English terms below them: snooze, hour, min, time, alarm, as well as an on/off knob. But before I was able to depress one of the buttons with my knuckles the phone started buzzing again. The word 'Secret' appeared on the display. I lifted the receiver and said suspiciously: 'Hello?'

'Fred here. Is Rose available?' a man's voice barked.

'Is Rose available?' I echoed in astonishment.

'Yes, is Rose available,' the man snarled even more disagreeably than before.

'Rose is dead,' I said.

'Tell me another one.'

'It's true. Rose is dead.'

I heard the man breathe heavily. Before he could get anything else out, I said: 'She was cremated last week, on Monday.'

'Listen, lady, you can't bullshit me. If Rose was dead, we'd have known it by now…we'd have seen a death notice somewhere at the very least.'

'I don't think anyone placed a death notice. *We* didn't do it, and she didn't have any relatives. I don't think anybody hit on the idea of a death notice.'

'Lady, I don't believe you. I saw Rose a little over a week ago. She was alive and kicking, the very picture of good health. And now you're trying to tell me she is dead?'

'She died as the result of sunstroke.'

'Sunstroke? Died of sunstroke? Come off it. No way I'm going to believe that, not even for a second. If she really is dead, something is rotten in the state of Denmark. Sunstroke: get real.'

'Wednesday two weeks ago, when the weather was so gorgeous, she became ill while on the beach, went into a coma and died in the hospital late that evening.'

'Gorgeous weather Wednesday two weeks ago? You see that you're lying through your teeth? Me and my buddy had to go to the Veluwe that Wednesday for a small job. On the way we didn't see even *one* ray of sunlight, not a speck of sun; the weather was just as crappy as today.'

'It was gorgeous weather on the beach at Katwijk.'

'Oh yeah? You were there yourself?'

'No.'

'Then I'd try to find out if there was a gap in the clouds over Katwijk that day for the sun to shine through. Sunstroke! Rose dead of sunstroke. Jesus, if you really believe that you must be dumb as all get out.'

'But what else could it have been?'

'How should I know? I wasn't there.'

'Honest, the doctor…'

'The doctor? What kind of doctor? One of those youngsters, still wet behind the ears, right? Fresh from the lecture hall. No experience to speak of. Doesn't look past the end of his nose. Hasn't got a clue. So he has a stab at it and writes "sunstroke" on the death certificate. God almighty. Rose dead, I can't believe it, this evening we were going to…this evening we had…what are we going to do without her? Sunstroke. Come off it! If there was no more than a watery sun in the sky she was out tanning on her roof deck. If anybody was used to the sun, it was her. You know what she said to me kind of as a joke the last time I saw her? "Fred," she said, "I think somebody wants me dead." So I said to her: "Kid, on Hogewoerd alone there's at least two guys who'd love to push me off a construction-site scaffold, but I'm still alive."'

'Where did you know Rose from?' I asked.

'None of your business. I don't think Rose would like it if I told you. Me and Rose and a couple of other regular guys belonged to a nice little club… I don't want to say any more. Rose dead, it isn't true, it can't be true.'

I heard his rasping breath. Then he said: 'Are you maybe the…? She mentioned someone who was going to…she was going to give her cats to that person, if she died unexpectedly. Is that you?'

'Yes, it's me.'

'Then I'm sorry I said the things I did, but Rose…Rose…no, dead, that can't be true. If it *is* true we'll miss her terribly. Take care.'

He hung up. I sat there for a while with the white receiver in my hand. With my free hand I rubbed my ear to get rid of the after-sound of that harsh grating voice. How on earth had Rose got mixed up with a jerk like that?

The zeroes and dots on the clock-face kept blinking. I hit 'hour', I hit 'time', but the blinking went on. Again I hit 'hour', again 'time', thinking: how stupid, simply repeating senseless acts without thinking. For the second time I pulled the cord out of the outlet. It seemed less inappropriate to disconnect one of her digital clocks now that I knew Rose had been involved with a construction worker.

Outside the wind suddenly rose. Thin poplars swept wildly back and forth. A forked streak of lightning shot down from a light-blue cloud, and right after that came the sound of thunder. Then the rain pelted so heavily against the windows that it seemed as if the angels were trying to douse a fire. Tiger jumped on the windowsill and tapped on the window with his left front paw as if to say: can you cool it a bit? I joined him at the window and stared at the disturbed sky, stared at the complicated arrangement of aluminium tubes on a piece of industrial land on the opposite side of the street. It looked as if the aluminium construction had been designed by M C Escher. The tubes were wrapped around each other, lost themselves in each other, reappeared unexpectedly from behind tall cranes.

It was sunstroke, of course it was, what else could it have been?

What if the sun *had* barely shown itself that afternoon? What if the autopsy *had* been superficial and careless? 'I think somebody wants me dead,' she had said jokingly to that awful Fred. That must have meant *something*. But what? It seemed ridiculous to think that someone had wanted to murder her, worse, had murdered her so cunningly that Wednesday afternoon that it looked like she had died of sunstroke. After all, it happened often enough that you thought: if I could murder someone without being caught, then I would…but it never came to anything. There was a saying: if looks could kill, but would all those unsavoury characters you met in the street actually dare to kill you if they could do so with their eyes? Besides, sometimes you thought: that person would just as soon bump me off. For instance, Marjolein wanted me dead for sure. And maybe I felt the same way about her.

Looking at the rain that came flooding down, giving the big living-room window a free wash, I felt once more like a little girl on a Wednesday afternoon in summer, when I didn't have to be in school, feeling blissfully happy to be standing at a window in my parents' home, looking at the down-rushing rain and listening to the gurgling eaves.

5.

'Two weeks ago Wednesday? I can't possibly remember. Was it sunny that day? Sounds unlikely. It's been such a crappy summer. I might just as well shut the place down. I've got only two men working, the rest I've had to send home.'

'Maybe you could tell from the turnover if...'

'Turnover? My dear lady, I haven't got any turnover at all, just look at the condition of everything. The rain oozes off my tables out there all the damned day long, it's just like they're standing there blubbering.'

'You don't remember either that an ambulance drove on to the beach at the end of that afternoon two weeks ago?'

'Lady, that happens just about every day, if I have to start paying attention to that... Christ almighty, it is possible, now you mention it, I think some woman did pass out, middle of the afternoon...end of the afternoon...yes, that's probably it.'

'In that case, do you remember whether it was sunny at the time?'

'The only thing I remember is that damned siren. But I seem to recall we had a reasonably good afternoon's business a couple of weeks ago, so that was probably the day. I can still see it...a lot of people showing up out of the blue, milling around when they lifted that woman onto the stretcher...so it must have been fairly crowded on the beach. Well, crowded, sometimes you just can't figure out where all those folks have suddenly come from. But fine, let's say it was actually half-decent weather that afternoon. Better than what we're having right now, this sucks big time.'

'Do you have any idea who discovered that this woman was unconscious?'

'No, not a clue.'

'She had rented a deckchair from you?'

'She must have. Where else? Maybe Flip knows more. He's checking the chairs at this moment.'

The manager of The Sailor's Horse went over to a pair of those swinging half-doors you always see in fake saloons in Westerns, pushed them open and yelled: 'Flip!'

A skinny pale young man with almost snow-white hair emerged from the catacombs. His eyelids blinked uninterruptedly. He peered at my nails.

I have to get rid of them as soon as possible, I thought, but how?

'You remember that woman fourteen days ago?'

Flip looked as if to say: what woman?

'The one who was carried off by the ambulance,' clarified the manager.

Flip nodded his head demonstratively.

'Was it decent weather that day?'

Flip nodded.

'Who found that woman? You?'

Again Flip moved his white head, this time from side to side, muttered something incomprehensible and made as if to walk away.

'You little jerk, stick around, this lady lost her best friend fourteen days ago, and she'd really like to know what happened here. Am I right, lady?'

'Yes,' I said.

'Good, then I'll ask it another way: Flip, do you know who found her friend?'

Flip straightened himself, pointed resolutely to the nearest buildings.

'Well, it does seem like we're making progress. So she was found by someone from Katwijk.'

Flip held up two fingers.

'She was found by *two* guys from Katwijk. Which ones, Flip, which ones? Would it maybe suit you to make a statement in good Dutch?'

Flip was silent.

'Do you remember?'

Flip nodded.

'Bit by bit we're getting somewhere. Now the trick is to pry loose the names of those two guys. In that case, Flip will have to open his trap, but if there's one thing Flip hates to do, it's talking. Oh, our Flip had such rotten luck, he'd much rather have been born deaf and dumb. And so we all have our cross to bear; well, boy, come on, let's have those names.'

Flip stared out to sea, looked back, mumbled something I didn't catch.

'Well, it's not easy to hear, but it's clear enough all right, I'll give him that;

your friend was found by the Mastenbroeks. I should have been able to figure that out myself. One ray of sunshine, and they're out there, heavily marinated in suntan oil, baking on their air mattresses, the woman especially. If you walk back that way along the boulevard you'll come to a little white church, you can't miss it. Turn off there, and you'll come to the apartment building where the Mastenbroeks live. Don't ask me what number, I don't know, just look at the nameplates down in the entrance hall, it's almost impossible to miss.'

With a heavy heart, I walked back along the boulevard. I had no idea what I was doing there. Was I carrying out an investigation? Into what? I just want to be sure you really did have sunstroke, that nothing else happened, I said to Rose in my thoughts.

In the hall of the apartment building I located a nameplate with small Gothic letters that spelled out 'Mastenbroek'. Cautiously I pressed a white button. Almost immediately a man's voice asked over the intercom: 'Who's there?' I gave my name and added: 'I should like to ask you something, may I come up for a moment?' There was no answer, but the door opened. An elevator took me to the sixth floor. Along a wind-swept walkway I proceeded to the Mastenbroeks' front door. It stood wide open, but there was nobody to be seen. Slowly I entered the hall. A deeply tanned man emerged from the living room and came towards me. He reeked of stale cooking oil and pickled herring.

'Come in so I can close the front door,' he said nervously. 'There's a nasty draft here, especially when everything is open. Then the door will blow shut with a bang.'

After he had closed the front door behind me and came back into the room he said a bit tentatively: 'My wife has just gone shopping, she should be back shortly.'

He pointed at the sea and said in a tone of voice that sounded almost apologetic: 'What a view, eh, Mrs Kuyper? Never boring, constantly changing. Every moment you see a different colour, grey, blue, white, you name it. Sometimes it's green too.'

'Sea wind does seem to be really bad for paint and wood,' I said. It's strange how incredibly tactless I can be when I feel ill at ease.

The man seemed to shrink, looked at me in dismay and said: 'Not at all, no truth to that, maybe if you live right on the sea, but not here. At most, the window frames need a bit of extra maintenance, but to us that's more than worth it. Will you have something? Coffee, tea, a soft drink, or a small sherry – your call.'

'No thank you, I must be going in a moment, I just wanted to ask you…two weeks ago you seem to have been the first to see…notice…discover that there was something the matter with my friend Rose.'

Something flickered in the man's eyes. Then he said in a curiously embarrassed manner: 'Who told you that?'

'Flip.'

'Flip? I don't know any Flip.'

'I don't know Flip either. He works at The Sailor's Grave…oh gosh, I mean The Sailor's Horse. He looks after the deck chairs.'

'Oh, so that's Flip. That pale-looking little shit.'

How was I supposed to respond to that? I nodded a coward's nod, thought: dammit, this embarrassed-acting weirdo is giving me the creeps, what's keeping his wife?'

He said: 'All afternoon long we were broiling there right next to her. It was warm enough…out of the wind it was quite nice, though it was not exactly tropical. She lay there quietly, getting a tan. She was wearing a very nice pair of sunglasses and a damned good-looking bikini. The contrast with her brown skin was great. I took…I…when my wife took a nap I quickly filmed Rose…I could show you, but…'

He walked indecisively around the room.

'Was she a very good friend of yours, Mrs Kuyper?'

'Yes, she always said we were like two sisters.'

'Sisters? I'm quite sure I've never seen you before. She was always lying there by herself. Didn't you ever feel like going to the beach with her?'

'To the beach?' I said surprised. 'Me, to the beach?'

'Why not?'

'Jellyfish, scary animals you can step on, sand between your toes, and…and…I don't tan, I burn.'

'Oh, so that's why.' He regarded me sceptically. 'Whenever my wife took a nap, I filmed Rose secretly. I've got quite a few little bits of tape with her on it. That week I got her too. And I got that ambulance real good, my wife knows about that, even though she'd already gone home by then, I mean, there was such an uproar, I didn't have to do it secretly…my wife would have thought it odd if I had left my camcorder in its case. So I could show you that bit right now, but on the other hand…if my wife gets back in a few minutes, and I'm here playing a tape to a complete stranger, right away she'll go off the deep end…so no can do, I'm sorry, but no can do. Two things I *can* do…have you got a VCR?'

'No,' I said.

'Too bad; well, then I'm not sure what to do.'

'Rose had a VCR,' I said. 'We could…' And then I thought: dammit, this weirdo in Rose's apartment, never, and I clammed up.

'Well, how about that?' said the man. 'If we make an appointment to meet there, I'll bring along the cassette I've got her on, and we can look at it in peace and quiet.'

'I don't know whether that will be necessary, Mr Mastenbroek. Just tell me exactly what happened two weeks ago. She lay there sunbathing all afternoon?'

'Yes, until she began to breathe heavily.'

'Did anyone else come by during that time? Did she talk with anybody? Did she leave at some point to get something? Something to drink or an ice cream?'

'Not as far as I know, all afternoon she lay there on her beach towel without moving. I think she was sleeping all that time…or rather, snoozing. Midway through the afternoon she started…yeah, how shall I put it…to snore? That kind of sound, it seemed like she couldn't get enough air…like she was trying desperately to gulp air… I've got some really good tape of that, complete with that sound, you really should see it. And also how strange, how cramped up she was lying there then, yeah, I got that beautifully on tape, I was able to take it from close up, because my wife had already called it quits and had gone to put the spuds on.'

'Piet,' a voice called.

'Jesus, that'll be her, there she is already, Goddammit…'

Taking big steps, he moved to the living-room door and hurried along the hallway of the apartment, pulled the front door open and shouted: 'We've got a visitor.'

'A visitor?'

'Yes, a friend of Rose's. She came here…she was eager to know what happened two weeks ago.'

'What's to know? She lay there sunbathing, started to breathe heavily, was lifted into an ambulance and was gone, that's all.'

'I thought maybe I can show her that videotape; what do you think, darling?'

'Show her that videotape? What in Heaven's name is the point of that?'

The woman entered the living room. She was very blonde, but her roots were dark. Her hair was in a ponytail that popped out of the back of a fire engine-red baseball cap. She wore rust-brown Bermudas, a long white T-shirt hanging down over them. Her nails were longer but less curved than mine. They were painted with a dark-red polish that was peeling off. How vulgar that looked. All at once my own hands looked a bit less tacky, thank God.

She took off her sunglasses, made a pass in my direction with her nails, got hold of herself and said ultra-sweetly: 'So, you're a good friend of Rose's. How come I've never seen you on the beach with her? Don't you like the sea?'

'I don't like sunbathing,' I said.

'Oh, well, deep down my husband doesn't either, right Piet? *Ach*, that Rose...'

'*Ach*, that Rose,' echoed her husband.

'We've got to go,' the woman said. 'We're supposed to be at the Zwarthoeds' place at four-thirty.'

'So we are,' the man said meekly.

He accompanied me to the front door and took me some distance along the walkway. 'If you'd like to see that video, tomorrow morning my wife will be at Quasar,' he whispered.

'Quasar...?'

'Yes, some kind of physiotherapy. For her figure. She'll be gone for a couple of hours. But I can also come over to your place. Whatever you like. At the end of the day, it's the last thing you can see of your friend, of Rose. And if not...I'll wait to hear from you, I'm in the phonebook, you can call me any day before nine. She's still in bed then.'

On the way back I had to cycle along the boulevard for a bit. To my right the sea lay glistening silently. Even the breakers were quiet. When I was getting divorced and was desperately unhappy, I had allowed Rose to persuade me to join her and go to the beach a few times. I had never dared to tell even Rose why I later hadn't wanted to do that anymore. In a book by Mensje van Keulen I had read: 'I remember the first moments with my son and that one strong association: the sea.' At the time that remark had caused me an unbelievable stab of envy. Why her and not me? Why had that never been given to me: those first moments with my son? Maybe then I would have had that strong association too. Oh, how dearly I wanted to know whether that would have been true. But I had been denied what so many other women were allowed to experience, often more than once.

Was it childish that I therefore preferred to avoid the dunes and the surf and the beach and the shrieking seagulls?

6.

The next day I was punished because I still didn't dare to spend the night in Rose's apartment. If I had been there when someone rang the bell that morning, I would first have checked the small monitor in her hallway to see who wanted to get in down below. If I had seen Piet Mastenbroek, I would simply not have opened the door.

As it was, he saw me coming from a distance when I turned my bike into Grimburchstraat. I saw him too, but I didn't realize at first that it was him. He was on the sidewalk on the other side of the street, hopping up and down like a sick sparrow. Then with both hands he seized the bars of the fence that separated the industrial area with the Escher-tubing from the Grimburchstraat sidewalk.

When I got nearer and recognized him, he let go of the bars and tried to smile ingratiatingly. He failed, but nevertheless his baboon-like grin had something endearing to it.

'Well,' he said, 'there you are, Mrs Kuyper, I saw you before you saw me. This morning I thought: I'll take a chance. Of course I don't know where you live, but I managed to figure out a long time ago where your friend lived. And I thought to myself: some time or other you're bound to drop by there. And yes indeed, here you are. That's just fine, I brought my tapes…I got quite a lot of her…yeah, when you've got a hobby…you film one thing and another, you edit as best you can, you play around with it till you've got a real movie. It's nice to have something to do when you're on long-term disability.'

Was it to be my fate, on this sunny, though windy summer day, to look at videotapes in the apartment of a departed friend in the company of some unknown creep?

'I want to get to work, Mr Mastenbroek,' I said as briskly as I could. 'I've got to clean up her apartment, feed the cats, run errands...what would you think of leaving the cassette...?'

'The *cassettes*,' he said, 'there's four of them.'

'...of leaving the cassettes with me. I'll take good care of them. I could look at them at my leisure this evening. The conditions aren't right for sitting in front of the TV anyway. Much too bright.'

'The shades can be closed, right?'

'Yes, but...no, I should...I'd rather...'

'Do you know how to use her VCR?'

'Why wouldn't I?'

'Well, not to make a big deal of it, but these VCRs...honest, it's no disgrace. They're often terribly complicated these days; in Katwijk they've got courses on VCRs for pensioners because it...with all of those buttons on the remote and, don't forget, on the machine itself, altogether more than a hundred buttons sometimes... I mean, I'm at home with that stuff, I've become acquainted with it, I could help you find your way through.'

'Put the cassette in, hit *play* and...'

'Sure, that's the way it used to be, but nowadays, honest, it could be quite tricky.'

'If I can't manage to get them to play, I can always call on you.'

'Sure thing, you can count on that, but...'

'Just give me those tapes,' I said as resolutely as possible. 'I'll try to manage by myself. If that doesn't work, I'll let you know.'

'Fine by me,' Piet Mastenbroek said in an aggrieved tone, 'as you wish. In any case I should make my getaway soon. I've got to be home before Corinne gets there. But maybe we could, over a cup of java...if I just could put in the tape from that week for you, I'll make tracks right after, pretty well have to. I looked at it again yesterday evening. More than worth it.'

'Let's go,' I heard myself say. Why couldn't I be more resolute? Something like this would never have happened to Rose. She would have said briskly: 'My dear fellow, just give me that cassette,' and he would have given it to her without further argument.

So it happened that soon afterwards I was in Rose's kitchen, pouring hot water into one of those marvellous Danish pressure-operated coffeemakers, while the creep was in the living room, noisily occupied with her window shades and her VCR.

When I entered the room with the coffeemaker, he had already installed himself, with the remote, on the handsome couch. He said: 'You look like your friend.'

'Others have said so too.'

He hit a button. The TV came on. He hit another button. The VCR began to run. The beach at Katwijk showed up on the screen. Flags hanging down, deck chairs decorated with seahorses. Rose came constantly in and out of view.

'You have to agree,' said the man, 'you've got much the same posture, if you had a hairdo like that you could easily pass for her.'

'I'm not nearly as tanned.'

'Can be easily fixed. Ultraviolet lamp.'

'I don't tan, I burn.'

'Get yourself a good sun-block.'

Attentively I peered at the monotonous pictures. The creep ingested his coffee with idiotic little sips. I prayed he would leave as soon as his coffee was finished.

'You find it dull?' he asked.

Dull? I saw Rose lying on her beach towel. She wore her idiotically expensive Ray-Ban sunglasses. Where were those glasses? If I put them on, I would look more like her. Would I then be able to shake off a weirdo like Piet Mastenbroek more easily? How fervently I longed for that at that moment!

Nothing happened. Rose lay there. There seemed to be next to no wind. Now and then a minuscule cloud passed in front of the sun.

'Does it go on like this much longer?'

'No,' said Mastenbroek. 'I only taped ten minutes or so, the only thing that mattered was to have another piece with Rose on it… I've got so many of those pieces…I ought to connect them all, it'll be a movie about a woman who, year in, year out, sunbathes in the same place.'

'Did she actually know that you were filming her?'

Mastenbroek acted as though he hadn't heard my question. I took a breath in order to repeat it, but he was ahead of me.

'All those years, you'll see she hardly changes, hardly gets older…'

Stubbornly I said: 'Did she know that…?'

At that moment a shadow passed over Rose. Another small cloud?

'Did you see that?' I asked.

'What?'

'That shadow.'

'Shadow?'

'Back up a bit.'

Obediently Piet rewound a piece. Rose reappeared on the screen, and I said: 'Oh gee, what a long way back we are now.'

'Shall I fast-forward a bit?'

'No, please don't, let's just watch.'

I peered at the quiet, pretty well immobile scene, watching carefully, meanwhile thinking: what a strange fellow he is to have been secretly filming a sunbathing woman, year after year, how creepy, what to make of that? Or was it innocent? Should one simply regard it as a bizarre hobby?

Then I called out: 'There it is again. What's that?'

'I think somebody walked by very close to her. That's what it looks like. It's the shadow of a sunbather passing by, I think. Hold on, now I know what point it's at, I'll reverse a bit; we'll run it frame by frame, we'll be able to see…'

We studied it a second time, and it did strike me as more than likely that the shadow of a passing sunbather had brushed over her.

'But how come we don't see shadows like that more often?'

'Why should we see them more often?'

'Did just one sunbather walk by? There were a fair number of people on the beach, right?'

'There's bound to have been more than one person walking by, but you don't see anything because they… I mean, this character must have just about stepped right over her.'

'But then you must have seen this person.'

'I don't remember anything.'

'But you were holding the camcorder…you…'

'I was not. I'd hidden the camcorder under some towels in a beach chair. The lens was peeking out between the folds. It wasn't anybody else's business that I… I mean…'

Then the shadow brushed over Rose a second time, this time going in the opposite direction.

'That's him again.'

'Yeah, you're right.'

Almost immediately the picture vanished. After a few fiery stripes, and then that extraordinary flickering that looks like a heavy snowfall in Siberia, the beach came back into view. It was later in the afternoon. The shadows were longer.

Rose was being filmed from closer up. She lay stock-still on her beach towel. I heard a very nasty, curiously rasping sound.

'Do you hear that?' Mastenbroek said excitedly. 'That's it…it's just like she can't inhale properly, like she's trying to suck up air.'

'Isn't anybody doing anything?' I asked in despair.

'What were we supposed to do? I had already alerted the lifeguard, as far as I know the ambulance had been called for, listen, there it is.'

The nasal ominous signal of the ambulance drowned out Rose's rasping breathing. It drove suddenly into view. Two men in white clothes got out quickly, one of them opened the rear doors of the ambulance and pulled out a stretcher, while the other was already bending over Rose. Together they lifted her onto the stretcher and shoved her inside. The doors were slammed shut, and almost at once the red and white vehicle drove out of view. It was bewildering to be sitting in her living room and watch how fast everything had happened.

'Look,' said Mastenbroek, 'this is where I zoomed out.'

'What a lot of people.'

'You can say that again.'

I looked carefully at all those curious sunbathers. Maybe among them were people I knew. It was hard for me to verify this. Almost everyone wore sunglasses; almost everyone wore one of those silly baseball caps with idiotically large visors. Almost everyone was all but naked. All those gleaming, beautifully tanned bodies – it seemed as if they were interchangeable, as if they had been cloned from the same bronzed ancestors.

I couldn't understand what all those people were doing there. They kept hanging around even after Rose had been taken away. It seemed as though the main event hadn't taken place yet, as if people were standing there expectantly, killing time with small talk while waiting. The bright sunlight protected them, kept them anonymous. Nevertheless, it seemed to me as if one of those sunbathers, a slender woman, looked familiar. She stepped out of view.

'Back up a bit, please.'

Piet obeyed. Again the ambulance came driving into the picture, and quick as lightning Rose was removed from her spot, again all those sunglasses and baseball caps and naked brown backs appeared on the screen. Again the slender woman appeared. She was one of the few who were in street clothes. She also wore big sunglasses and a straw hat.

'Rewind, and then one frame at a time, please,' I said.

'At your command.'

'That slender woman looks familiar,' I said as I walked toward the screen.

'But who is she?'

'Don't ask me, I don't know that beanpole.'

'Could it be the alabaster-skinned girl?' I muttered.

'What did you say, Leonie?'

'Oh, I asked myself whether it might be the same girl I saw at the memorial service. Could you rewind once more, Piet?'

Damn, I thought, I'm using his first name and he's using mine.

Again the slender person came into view. Was it her? Hard to say. The alabaster-skinned girl who had expressed her condolences was red-haired, almost certainly had a sensitive skin, and so couldn't spend much time in the sun. Was that why she was wearing all her clothes as well as such a ridiculously large straw hat? Was that the reason she was wearing sunglasses that could double as a mask?

'It could be her,' I said.

'Why are you so interested in all this?'

'That's just the way I am,' I said airily.

Piet tried out his baboon grin again. How remarkably endearing! Even a creep like him turned out to have something that made him seem appealing.

'I must be going,' he said, 'otherwise I'll be home late, and I'll catch… I'll leave the other tapes with you, so you can view them when it suits you, it's very simple, you hit "play"…'

'That's what I said, didn't I?'

'Yeah, but this is a fairly old machine, the new ones…'

And then he left, thank God. In the hall he said: 'Nice place. I wouldn't mind living here myself.'

When he had gone I walked into her bedroom. That's where I knew the plastic bag was that the funeral director had given to me. 'They gave it to me in the hospital,' he had said in a businesslike manner, 'her beach things should be in it.'

That turned out to be correct. From underneath her white bikini I dug up the Ray-Ban sunglasses. I put them on, walked over to the mirror. What I had suspected was indeed the case: with those glasses I did get closer. I felt like weeping. It was so strange: as soon as that dejection caused by her death presented itself, that curious, almost obsessive desire to identify myself fully with her immediately became so strong that it took my breath away. It made me feel ridiculously weepy, but it did keep that searing despondency at a distance. I opened her closet and took out a pair of white summer pants and a white jersey embroidered in gold thread.

As I was pulling on her pants I thought of our dominee, our minister. In his sermons he had more than once said: 'Sisters, don't hanker after men's clothing; trousers on a woman grieve the Lord so greatly.' How grateful I was to him for that! Because of that comment, I always felt a heathenish pleasure whenever I put on a pair of pants.

A moment later I stood in front of the mirror, in her white sandals, dressed in her pants and jersey, her sunglasses on my face. Now her hairdo, I thought, and heard myself sigh and wanted to weep again and fortified myself by balling my fists, whereby her oval, weirdly purple nails came into view. I'll have to polish them again, I thought, they're a dreadful nuisance, I can't decently button anything, I can hardly wipe my bum, I can't wash myself properly, I can't pick anything up, and I can't type, but I must learn to live with them, I must, I must, I must. In any case I can, if necessary, use them to scratch out some video-creep's eyes.

7.

With a heavy heart I crawled under her goose-down duvet for the first time that night. When I woke up the next morning, feeling surprised, I hummed a couple of lines from near the beginning of the Psalter: 'I rest and go to sleep and rise, for God will keep His own in His protection.' It was amazing to have slept so well in a strange bed. Perhaps because it was so much quieter in Grimburch Estates than in my dreary rented quarters? There I kept hearing the melancholy slurping of the furnace all night and the gurgling of water going down the drain whenever one of my neighbours flushed the toilet.

I regretted not having a car. What I most wanted to do was to move the few possessions I valued from my place near Burggravenlaan to Grimburchstraat right away. As a condition of my rental I had to give three months' notice. Maybe the same thing would happen to me that had happened to a former neighbour. 'I went to the municipal rental office to give notice,' she had said. 'Some bureaucrat said to me: "Are you moving in three months or do you want to leave at once?" "Is that possible?" I asked. "Yes, it is, because we have quite a lot of asylum-seekers who have to be given priority help, so we're really keen to get hold of apartments." "I can be gone next week," I said, and then he asked: "Are you taking your curtains and carpets with you?" "That was my intention, yes," I said. "*Ach*," he said, "it would really help us if you left a few things behind. You'll get reasonable compensation, and then some asylum-seeker can move in at once. Otherwise a family like that has to be outfitted with new things at municipal expense." So I left my old rugs lying there and left the curtains hanging, and beyond that I left behind as much old stuff as possible, cane chairs, a table, a bed, the whole kit and caboodle...including a lot of kitchenware and such. At one go I was rid of all that junk, and I got a nice bit of pocket money into the bargain.'

I too would leave my household belongings behind if they were wanted. I was allowed to begin afresh. I had the chance to try to become a different person in a new environment, someone more stylish and elegant, maybe even more charming, and hopefully more assertive.

Thanks to her death, I thought, and I looked through the bars of the fence at the Escher tubes, glistening deceptively in the drizzle. Then I seemed to hear her say: 'You don't think you'll make me happier by sitting there in sackcloth and ashes, do you? I've said it so often: dress a bit more smartly. When you stand in front of a mirror, there's no need for you always to think: ugh, how attractive I look, how can I camouflage that as quickly as possible? Come on, I'll make you up a bit, we'll go shopping together, we're the same size, we'll buy two of something unbelievably attractive, we can be twin sisters... I so badly wanted to have a sister.' When she said that it was as if I heard myself saying: I so badly wanted to have children.

That was the way it had begun, she herself had set into motion what had now settled in me as a secret obsession. Now I had to identify myself with her, now, with notarial authorization, I had to crawl into her skin, as a futile but determined protest against her death. Softly I sang a verse from Psalm 17: 'My footsteps hold fast to the ways of your law; in your paths my feet shall not stumble.' The words seemed somehow to apply to the situation I found myself in.

As I sang, Tiger, who was sitting on the wide windowsill, washing his left front paw as if his life depended on it, looked at me with surprise and then meowed plaintively. Did he not care for psalms? Ober approached noiselessly, looking up at me with concern, and I said: 'But where is Lellebel?' They stood there and watched the way cats watch: with those mirror-like, questioning eyes – *clairs fanaux, vivantes opales* – in which the daylight is reflected. How I would love to know what's going on in their heads at a moment like that.

'I'm coming to live with you,' I said to the two cats, and they contemplated me attentively. 'It's too bad I haven't got a car, otherwise I could...I would...' Tiger held out his paw to me then jumped gracefully down on the rug and walked over to Ober. Of course it's impossible for a cat to tell you anything, but it seemed just as if Tiger, as he posed himself belligerently next to Ober, said to me: 'Dimwit, Rose has a car, why not use *it*?'

'But where did she park it?' I heard myself say softly.

Of course I got no answer, so I tried another question: 'Where are her car keys?'

That elicited no answer either. Had I not I seen those keys recently? Where? Just try to remember where you last saw some object. When you put something down without thinking, a day later you won't have a clue where you left it. If you don't take extreme care to put back scissors and needles and knitting needles and tools and keys in the same place after using them, you can regularly go crazy searching for them. 'I could find it blindfolded if I only knew where I put it,' my mother used to sing as a sort of recitative. Rose very likely had a set place for her car keys. That was no earthly use to me as long as I didn't know where. I had seen them yesterday: that I knew for sure, but where, in God's name? In any case they were in the apartment.

So I started out on a fruitless journey through the immense living room, the luxurious bedroom, the guest bedroom, the Siemens-equipped kitchen, the hall. Where had I seen those keys?

When I had gone through the apartment three times and finally installed myself by the big living-room window, gazing at the grey clouds, I said to Tiger, who had followed me in my wanderings: 'Even if I were to find those keys, I still don't know if I can use her car. How would it be with the insurance if I got into an accident? Wouldn't the car have to be registered in my name first? Do I in fact inherit it?'

I went over to her telephone directory, looked for a number, keyed it in, heard a girl's voice lisp, songlike: 'You've reached the office of Mr Graafland, how can I help you?'

'Would I be able to speak with the notary for a moment?'

'He is in a most important meeting, he can't be disturbed right now, uh…uh…hold on a second, he's right here beside me, he heard your voice, he'd like to talk with you. He's going into his office, I shall connect you.'

I heard mysterious clicking sounds, followed by: 'Well, well, Mrs Kuyper, what a pleasure…you wanted to tell me that the job…'

'Oh Heavens, Mr Graafland, I've hardly even thought about it yet, I just wanted to ask you something. Her car, do I inherit it as well?'

'Of course you do.'

'Can I use it right away?'

'Why not?'

'Suppose I have an accident, the insurance…'

'You won't have an accident.'

'I haven't driven for years.'

'As long as the car is not yet in your name, it's like you were borrowing it from her.'

'Can you borrow something from someone who's no longer alive?'

'G…clever question. Never had anything like this to deal with before. I would drive the car without worrying about it.'

'First I'll have to find out where it's parked.'

'Isn't it in the parking area of that building where she lived?'

'She had her own parking spot here. Right near the entrance. I'm sure it's not there. Otherwise I would have seen it.'

'Maybe it's still parked in Katwijk.'

Even before he had finished speaking, I knew where I had seen those keys the day before. In the plastic bag from which I had dug up her sunglasses. Why had I not immediately hit on the idea that her car was still in Katwijk? Was I that big a dope?

'Are you still there, Mrs Kuyper?' the notary asked.

'Yes,' I said.

'How's it g…g…how are you doing? Have you moved in yet?'

'No, that's what I need the car for.'

'What do *you* think: would it still be in Katwijk?'

'I'm sure of it.'

'I don't think they tow away cars there, except from the boulevard by the sea.'

'She certainly wouldn't have parked it on the boulevard; it's probably in some back street where you can park free. Not because she was frugal, but because she couldn't stand having to be back before the time printed on the ticket…'

'Yes, right, so it could be quite a chore to find the car. You could always phone the police, of course.'

'I may end up doing that, but first I'll go and have a look for it.'

'Happy hunting. Everything all right with the pussycats?'

'Yes, all three in fine fettle.'

'Excellent. I'm not really sure whether the will obliges me to check if all its conditions are being met…*ach*, what nonsense, have you found the cat-care instructions?'

'Yes, I already knew what they were; they were several years old. For use when she went on holidays and I had to look after her cats. The document was in a kitchen cupboard.'

'So it contains everything she wanted you…'

'I should say so, it's almost like a manual. On Saturday I've got to prepare whiting for them. Fresh from the market, bought from Klaas Hartevelt. I'm not allowed to buy it from the other fishmongers; their whiting might not be fresh. Nor am I allowed to give them Whiskas, it makes them throw up, they only get that super-expensive Sheba. I've got to provide them with saucers of milk and refresh it regularly. Ober has to have a piece of papaya now and then, he's crazy about that, and Tiger loves water with a dash of Pokon plant food dissolved in it. They have to be brushed daily. There are elaborate instructions for emptying the litter box…'

'Oh, you don't really need to follow them to the letter.'

'My view is that I owe it to her to follow them strictly.'

'That's very noble-minded of you.'

'Noble-minded? That's got nothing to do with it. If I don't observe…if I depart from her instructions…what I mean is, I've got to empty the litter box and put new filler in it just as often as she did. She didn't care for bad smells, and neither do I.'

My reluctance to alter Rose's instructions had nothing to do with Graafland. It was due to my wish to follow in her footsteps as closely as possible in all respects, including where her cats were concerned, however exaggerated I had once thought her boundless dedication and perfectionist care to be. After all, what I thought didn't matter. What mattered was that Leonie Kuyper should merge into, should transform herself into, Rose Berczy, or if that was too ambitious, into Rose Berczy's sister. Compromises were to be avoided wherever possible.

As I sat in the empty bus to Katwijk, a thought kept buzzing through my head: sooner or later you get tired of everybody. Sooner or later you're happy to be released from anyone's company. But you can never really escape from your own company, even if you're fed up with yourself. Even when you sleep, you're shackled to yourself. I couldn't remember ever dreaming I was someone else. It was indisputably an illusion to think you could escape from yourself by following in somebody else's footsteps, by crawling into their skin. That old grouch Schopenhauer was right when he said: 'To our amazement we learn that we are not free but subject to necessity, that in spite of all our good intentions and reflections we cannot change our conduct, that we have to obey, from the cradle to the grave, the same character that we ourselves condemn, and that we must, as it were, play out the part we have assumed, right to the end.' However true that might be, the last clause offered an escape hatch. What Schopenhauer mentioned was a part that had been assumed. But what was to stop one from changing parts? Now that Rose's death had offered me the chance, playing another part struck me as an admittedly risky but exhilarating experiment. What did I have to lose? At most something of myself. Gradually I had seen everything there was to see about me. If I were someone else, I might be able to avoid myself.

Once arrived in Katwijk, I stayed away from the boulevard. Her black Saab would not be parked there, and I would smell the sea there, one litre of whose surface water, Thomas had told me more than once, contained on average ten billion viruses. But I smelled the sea too in the streets and alleys behind the boulevard, and I walked on dejectedly. At the time of my divorce, when I had clung to Rose like a koala bear and had often driven to Katwijk with her, I had even lain sunbathing next to her on one of her enormous beach towels. I still felt ashamed that in my despair I had pushed myself so blindly on her. To console me she had said: 'You can have my car; you'll have freedom, you'll be distracted, and I can buy a Saab.' I had driven her hand-me-down until it was completely shot. After that I hadn't been able to afford another used car. I had not regretted that. Freedom? Always stuck in a traffic jam and always on the lookout for a parking spot, one that invariably cost a lot of money: that was supposed to be freedom?

At the time she had always parked her car on Varkevisserstraat. 'What's in a name?' she had said. 'Apparently, the fishermen here think: one day we'll catch *varkens* – pigs. Varkevisserstraat is so long that you can always find a spot somewhere along it, and the name is so silly that even I won't forget it. So I'll always know where I'm parked, which doesn't do any harm.'

Never again would she deliver herself of a remark in that way, so light-hearted and carefree and cheerful. In view of her tendency to stick to familiar routines, it seemed to me most likely that on the fatal Wednesday she had parked her Saab on Varkevisserstraat. Starting at the little white church, I was able to find the street: first along Duinstraat, then around the corner. Nothing seemed to have changed since the time when Rose and I had first strolled in the area on beautiful summer evenings some fifteen years ago now. I walked along the street until I reached Schelpendam and then walked back again. It couldn't be parked much farther away. She had parked there on a weekday; it couldn't have been *that* busy. I looked intently at all the parked cars. No Saab. Again I walked past all the parked cars and again and again, as though I could make it appear if I kept on walking long enough.

'Are you looking for something, ma'am?' I heard a voice behind me. I turned around, looked into the face of an inquisitive old man.

'A black Saab.'

'A black Saab? A while ago a black Saab was parked here for several days.'

'Are you sure?'

'Ma'am, I've got nothing to do with my time, I just sit at the window all day, twiddling my thumbs, and well, that way I'm bound to see the occasional thing. I spotted you walking back and forth and I said to my wife, Miep, I said, I'm going outside for a sec, there's someone walking back and forth, maybe I can help her with something.'

'Can you recall the licence number?'

'Twenty-five was in it…it so happens I was born in 1925, so that's why I remember that number, but those letters, stupid of me, if only I'd written them down, I thought about it at the time. The only thing I remember is that the letters were the same, only turned around.'

'NJ-JN-25 is what it was,' I said, 'so it probably was the car I'm looking for. And if so, it was first parked here on Wednesday, August 9.'

'Could well be. It was parked there over the following weekend. Monday it was there all day long, by Tuesday it was gone, but I didn't see anyone driving off in it. It could have happened late in the evening, it could have happened overnight, it could have happened at the crack of dawn, I just don't know.'

'Thanks a lot,' I said, 'you've been a big help.'

I considered going to the Katwijk police, but that didn't appeal to me. First I wanted to confer with Graafland. Could the Saab have been stolen? In Katwijk, where the churches are still packed on Sunday?

Once I got home I phoned Graafland. I hoped everyone had left for the day, so that I would get the answering machine. Then I would be able to report briefly that the Saab had probably been stolen and wouldn't have to answer difficult questions, such as why I hadn't gone to the Katwijk police.

I got the answering machine and after the beep I left my message.

8.

'You wish to change your hairstyle? I can readily understand that. What you've got now, a Florence Nightingale cut like that, simply doesn't make the grade these days.'

'I'd really like to have it cut this way,' I said, showing him the colour photo of Rose I had taken off the bedroom wall.

'You want that style? Are you sure? But madam, it doesn't suit you. You have a...may I say it? You have a fairly round face, you don't want to look like Princess Irene, do you?'

'No, I want to look like the woman on this photo.'

'Yes, but this woman...'

The hairstylist carefully ran his finger over the beautiful portrait of Rose. He said: 'This woman has high cheekbones, you...*d'accord*, perhaps you have them too, but your cheeks are fuller.'

'Then I'll have to diet.'

'The question remains whether that would make your face narrower. To be honest, I advise against it, nothing will come of it. True, you don't have ten thousand wrinkles yet like Her Royal Highness, but nonetheless...come, I'll put you into the computer. It will give you something to think about.'

Moments later I stared with fascination at the transformations my head was undergoing. Time and again the stylist hit the keys and I appeared in view, but each time with a different hairdo.

'You see,' he said, 'you can go in any direction, all you need to do is say the word. You have a wide choice...honest, the possibilities are endless, why tie yourself down, why must you absolutely have the hairstyle on this photo? Yes, this fine lady looks like a duchess, but it would not...*évidemment*, it *is* possible, but wait...no, let us work through the existing repertoire first.'

And so I passed by as a raven-black superbitch, as a bleached-blonde nightclub hostess and as a vamp with luxuriant dark-red hair. As a simpering girl, a femme fatale, a mean witch, a sweet 1950s matron, a severe schoolmarm. It was unbelievable what I got to see. What your hair looks like, the way it falls, its curl, determines who you are. What would Schopenhauer have said of that?

Naturally, there are lots of limitations, boundaries imposed by the quality and possibilities of your hair. Wigs allow you to escape from those limitations. As a woman you can have a thousand faces. As a man too. To make up for the fact that his hairdo gives him fewer options, a man has all kinds of moustaches and beards available to him.

'Watch,' said the stylist, 'now we'll see if I can introduce your friend's hairstyle...I don't think it will be altogether easy, wait, perhaps *tout simplement* with the scanner...'

His fingers tripped lightly over the keyboard. Was this slight little man with his Flemish accent an ordinary women's hairstylist? He seemed more like a computer nerd.

Rose's face loomed up out of a pale-blue light. Why did that hurt so much, even though it was simply a reproduction of the photo I had brought with me? There it came again, that spell cast by Psalm 130, that searing despondency. The abyss opened, and everything seemed so terribly pointless.

'Now we shall blur her facial features and insert yours in their place,' said the computer nerd.

I had printed photos on occasion. When you did that, you saw a face take shape in the developing tray. Now I saw the reverse, saw her face disappear, fade, dissolve.

'And now...yes, yes, it works...do you see now...? Ah, well, it's better than I expected, but really great...you wouldn't look to best advantage, wait, let's...'

'No, no,' I said, struggling to extricate myself from the depths of misery.

'Good,' he said. 'I still wanted to play with the shape of your face, see what you might be able to do with makeup...but I'm fine with this. Why not let this sink in first?'

What I saw was quite simply breathtaking. Whether Rose's hair suited me was hardly the point. More important was that with her hairstyle I resembled her amazingly. Her hair, that's what did it, it would change me into her sister more effectively than her clothes or her extravagant nails or her false eyelashes or her earrings or her makeup. As I stared at the silent picture a couple of lines by Hendrik Marsman came to mind: 'That one, as the other she sometimes sees, thinks to herself, is that not me?'

'You know what?' said the hair artist. 'I shall print out some things, *coiffures* that flatter you, you can take them with you, look at them at your leisure when you get home, and then you can choose what you like best. You'll see... I'll also print you out with your friend's hairstyle. Show it to your partner, your acquaintances, honest, each and every one will tell you that you don't look your best with that style. Yes indeed, nowadays there's a lot to consider when a woman goes to get her hair cut. Oh, oh, the possibilities one has these days, I couldn't even dream of that years ago when I first went to work with the curling iron as an up-and-coming young hairstylist.'

When I was back in her apartment and had refreshed the milk in all the saucers, I suddenly remembered that she had often said: 'Where in God's name do you get your hair cut? Come with me to my hairdresser in the Songbird district of Den Haag some time. She styles hair like an angel, even though she's quite mad. But what difference does that make? Better mad than sad.' I had always fended her off. Stupidly, as it turned out, because what could have been simpler than going there and saying: 'Cut my hair the way you cut Rose's.' How strange that I now wanted almost obsessively to do what I had always rejected during her lifetime. Perhaps there was a secret logic hidden in that.

I looked through her telephone directory until I found an address on Tureluurlaan in Den Haag. I entered the number and got a connection almost instantly. 'Salon Marquise,' a cheerful voice said. After I had explained who I was and what I wanted, the woman at the other end of the line said: 'Well, well, a friend of Rose's. I so much wanted to attend her funeral service, but I bruised all my ribs that morning, that can happen, the kind of day that everything is against you. This morning I fell downstairs, wham, just like that, I had to cancel all my clients for today, and now I'm moaning and groaning because I hurt my tailbone something fierce, so I have to stay on my feet and might just as well be cutting hair, but I can't very well go call my clients all over again, so why don't you come over, and I'll have all the time in the world for you, and we can have a really good chinwag about Rose. To think that she is dead now, I can't bear the thought, what time should I expect you?'

'I think it'll take me an hour, hour and a half to get over to your place. Where do I find Tureluurlaan?'

'Right by the woods, if I stick my hand out of the window I can pull the leaves off the trees. When you get to Sportlaan you turn off almost at once towards the sea. Right after the playing fields. Then into Kwakstraat, through

Draaihalsstraat, then Snorstraat right to the end, it's easy, and then left, and left again…you can't miss it.'

There was virtually no wind. The sun shone from a clear blue September sky as I cycled parallel to Highway A44, along polders outlined by ditches in which the water barely rippled. At Den Deyl I had to cross the highway and proceeded along an empty two-way bicycle path on the sea side of the A44. Along it roared an uninterrupted stream of cars and trucks and buses that were tailgating each other in terrifying fashion, while I had the broad bicycle path all to myself.

A car horn sounded. I looked left. A black Saab raced by. Had *it* honked? But why? I peered at the receding licence plate. Was that the number I had been looking for in Katwijk last week? Was I now suffering from delusions?

I entered Den Haag, passing the offices of the Dutch Touring Club. A bit farther on was Madurodam, the miniature town where hundreds of young children strolled in the golden sunlight among the replicas of buildings from all over the country. The curious distortion of perspective, which turned the children into giants, made me feel as though an enormous claw seized me by the scruff of the neck and smacked me down, impressing on me once again what I had missed out on.

Quickly I donned her sunglasses. It scarcely helped, I pedalled like a maniac, shot onto a bicycle path, didn't even know whether I was headed in the right direction, ended up in groves of luxuriant green and thought: do I need professional help? But a psychiatrist wouldn't be able to tell me anything I didn't know already. That I am hopelessly screwed up because I've been seeing my girlfriends become grandmothers, one after the other. That for this reason I am now engaged in a crazy endeavour. Then I thought of what Rose used to say when she noticed that the sight of one of those old-fashioned baby carriages – which you rarely saw any more these days, thank God – got me all upset. 'Act your age, keep in mind that there are SS20 missiles with multiple nuclear warheads aimed at us. Whoever gives birth these days is irresponsible.'

I reached the Songbird district, rode through Poelsnipstraat, Haakbekstraat, Steenloperstraat, arrived at Snorplein, was evidently in the right neighbourhood. I kept on pedalling. There was no one to be seen; the September sun shone generously.

Snorstraat, what had she said, did I have to go through to the end? Glory be, a fellow human emerged from a house. 'Excuse me, do you know where Tureluurlaan is?' 'Sure, go this way, then around the square, and there it is.'

A minute later I halted in front of the last house on Tureluurlaan. A large billboard on slender poles adorned the front yard: Salon Marquise. I chained my bicycle to one of the poles and rang the doorbell. A frightening bark could be heard inside, the front door opened noiselessly, and behind it a huge white quadruped looked at me so threateningly that for a moment I thought: it's a polar bear.

The predator snorted, then beat its tail against a gold-lacquered banister. Apparently it was wagging its tail in welcome and I was free to enter. Womanfully I stepped past the animal and went up the stairs with their gleaming banister.

'Is anyone there?' I shouted.

Left and right along a long landing there were open doors. At the end of the landing, in a room with a mirrored wall, I saw a bewigged Styrofoam head standing on a dressing table. I walked that way and then saw the mirror image of a woman I oddly enough could not see in the flesh.

'Good afternoon,' I said.

'Oh, I beg your pardon,' said the mirror image, stepping out of the reflection and appearing right behind me.

'Please sit down,' she said. 'Yesterday…I had these funny clients yesterday, two hookers from Geleenstraat, they got here at the same time but didn't want to be in this room together, so I put one in the living room, closed all the doors, oh, the things you see here sometimes, they always tap their heads when they want to say someone is loony, but they'd do better to tap a bit higher…it's the hair, that's where the lunacy hides out. So you want exactly the same hairstyle as Rose…yes, I get it…you've already applied her nails, a big box from Wagenstraat, I sent her there. You want to be her double, what a gas, I'd love to try that out too, but fine, I don't have her posture, hold on, I'll get you something first, what can I offer you, coffee, tea?'

'A cup of tea please.'

'It's too bad, Rose dead just like that, my son told me.'

'Your son?' I asked, astonished. 'How did your son know that she had died?'

'My son always knows everything, my oldest, that is, I have two, one is psychotic, the other is neurotic, and both of them are chaotic…oh, children, family, they're really the very worst thing…my oldest…drugs…a revolving-door criminal.'

'Revolving-door criminal?'

'Yes, don't you know that term? There he goes into prison, here he comes out again. And yet, even though he's neurotic and on the armed-and-dangerous side, at bottom he is awfully sweet, Rose was crazy about him, and he about her, even though she was twenty years older…when she first came here he was still playing with his Dinky Toys on the landing. Later on things were different, well, I kept out of it, I used to think: maybe she can keep him on the straight and narrow, but it turned out to be just the opposite, he introduced her to a really classy club near here, in the Flower district. Well, never mind. She's gone now, what was I going to do again? Oh yes, make a cup of tea. Do you put anything in it?'

'No, thank you,' I said, 'I'm on a diet, I've got to lose weight, otherwise I…'

'On a diet? That's no use, you know. Whatever you lose you gain back double.'

'All the same, I've already lost a couple of kilos,' I said proudly.

'Oh yeah, so what are you doing without?'

'Nothing, as far as I know. Since Rose died I've been constantly on the go. Moving, lifting boxes, taking them over to her place by bicycle, for an entire week; everything had to be out of my old place before September 1, I think that's the reason.'

'I don't believe it for a moment, exercise…they make so many claims. In my experience, it's no use. Have you been eating less since she died?'

'No, why would I?'

'Why wouldn't you? You're sad, aren't you? People who are grieving haven't got an appetite. Or *aren't* you grieving? I am, you know, I can't bear it that she's dead. Oh dear, your tea, I'm such a hopeless case.'

She left the mirrored room. Was I eating less? Not as far as I knew. At most I was eating differently, because when I bought whiting for the cats I usually got some sole or bass for myself. Did eating more fish make people thinner? Did grieving make them lose their appetite? Could be, but every time during the last few months that another friend, proud as a peacock, had phoned to tell me that she had become a grandmother, I had bought big bags of potato chips at the supermarket. I had snacked on them while lounging in front of the TV, feeling utterly miserable. 'And that's no longer possible, because with these dumb nails I can't get the chips out of the bag any more,' I muttered as I studied my Curve Oval in amazement. Was I losing weight because I could hardly pick up chips with claws like these? And didn't touch peanuts any more either? Might this be a helpful hint for women who wanted to diet? Glue artificial nails, preferably long and curved, on to your fingers, then you can't deal with chips and beer nuts and peanuts any more. And I thought next: I spend less time cooking because it's so damned hard with these nails; my cooking isn't as good, so I eat less.

The hairdresser returned, carrying a cup of tea, then strapped me into a sort of straitjacket so that I couldn't take a sip and began to cut my hair, slowly but skilfully, with something that resembled nail scissors.

'I can't talk when I'm cutting,' she said, 'and you can talk if you like, but when I'm busy I can't listen either, so it would be best if we both played mute until I'm through. I always rinsed her hair at the end, because of the grey she was showing in places, should I do the same with you? It's not really necessary, I don't see grey anywhere... Still, maybe not a bad idea, you'd get her hair colour at the same time...'

A marvel was taking place in the mirror. Rose's hairstyle appeared, but only very slowly: completing the transformation took almost as long as performing a Bruckner symphony. Sitting there, looking at myself and listening to the bizarre babbling of a woman who couldn't talk when she was cutting but was apparently able to chatter on tirelessly, a dull lethargy came over me. I barely heard all the things the hairdresser reeled off.

At last I came to when, having completed her labours, rinse included, she said in a satisfied way: 'It's getting there very nicely. Good thing my son isn't here. The way he used to go for Rose...he'd really take a run at you. Poor girl, all of Rose's stalkers will go after you now, take good care...there were quite a few. I always thought she'd be strangled some day...she was just the type for it, to get strangled.'

She pinched my neck and said in a honeyed voice: 'Nice word, "strangled", I read it in the paper the other day, I immediately saw it in my mind's eye. Creepy guy, handsome type, wearing black leather gloves, clamps his fingers around your neck and there you go...in stages, because it seems to be quite tiring to strangle someone. Now and then the strangler has to pause in order to regain his strength and the victim comes to...so now you're the next candidate on the list, but what does it matter? You've got to die of something. You'll be gone, your family won't ever bother you again, just think of that, what a delight.'

She seized my neck with both hands as if she wanted to throttle me. 'Come out of that chair, let me have a good look, walk down the landing.'

I walked down the landing. She said: 'You've got to straighten out more. Rose always walked bolt upright.'

'Everybody says that,' I said.

'To be frank, I never trusted that, I always thought: she has a tendency to stoop, she must be wearing a tight corset under those clothes. You should have a good look through all her stuff. She's bound to have used some kind of armour. Made to measure. With billions of stays. I mean: so weirdly upright…I'll bet it was phoney. Just like her nails and her eyelashes.'

9.

When I walked into her apartment, close to six p.m., I was exhausted. 'Never eat when tired,' the founder of macrobiotics once said. Probably the only intelligent words ever to leave his mouth. I had been governed by them even before I had heard what he said. This time I would do so too, because I was so tired that the strong odour of cat almost made me faint. Does fatigue sharpen the sense of smell? I must have been going into my period: when I am premenstrual my sense of smell always improves.

As I went into the kitchen to make a pot of tea, the cats rubbed against my legs and purred. Even Lellebel showed herself briefly, with her black-and-white speckled paws that made her look as though she was wearing fishnet stockings. As soon as I tried to pet her, though, she shot away skittishly.

The sun entered exuberantly through the living-room window. I struggled with the blinds for a while. After that I struggled with the VCR. Why had I not paid attention while Mastenbroek was operating the machine? Why did I keep blindly pushing the buttons on the remote with my knuckles? The only solution was to use the manual. But I didn't have the faintest clue where Rose kept her manuals.

So I grimly kept on pushing the buttons, and yes, indeed, Mastenbroek's first tape started running at last. Blue numbers hurtled past in a small window. Now to get the picture on the screen. I zapped from a football match to a talk show to a quiz show. Was there nothing else on?

A veil passed down over the screen, only to be hauled up immediately. Rose came into view. She lay there peacefully in the sun. Aside from her, I saw only sand and bright sunlight; the scene was surrounded by deep black shadows. The sound of the breakers could be heard faintly. Or was that the sound of the cassette? For ten minutes I peered at her bronzed body. She hardly moved at all, only brushed away a fly about halfway through the video. As she did so her silver nails glistened brightly in the sunlight.

After those ten minutes came another ten minutes of Rose on an enormous beach towel. Was this a year later? She seemed unchanged, only she wore a somewhat more daring bikini, and her nails were longer and crimson.

How puzzling and disturbing it seemed that a diffident man like Mastenbroek had videotaped ten minutes of a sunbathing woman, one year after another. Did he have tapes of other sunbathing bikini-wearers as well? But perhaps it was no more puzzling or disturbing than my own mad desire to crawl into her skin. In his essay 'The Art of Being Happy' Schopenhauer wrote: 'The imitation of another's characteristics and idiosyncrasies dishonours a person far more than wearing another's clothes.'

She had started the whole thing, she had got it going, she had constantly dragged me along to expensive shops where she would most of all have liked to buy two of the same outfits. Oh, those forays into expensive stores on Sunday afternoons! We would enter, and right away some saleswoman would come up to Rose and ask: 'Ladies, how may I help you?' In spite of the plural, it was Rose alone to whom such a smartly dressed person had spoken. Everywhere she went she was treated like a grand duchess. And she allowed herself to be treated that way, as though she was a princess of the imperial blood who had surfaced recently, no, the tsarina herself, in fact. If a saleswoman was particularly eager to sell her something, Rose would reject it so decidedly that the woman almost seemed to shrink. Oh, how I had envied that ability to act superior. Not only did you inspire awe and respect that way, but it also didn't matter whether people liked you. You turned it around: everyone you met wanted to be liked by you, the tsarina.

A dead ordinary research assistant. All the same: superior. Oh, to be that way: superior, in control all the time and in every situation. That bitch Marjolein would never have dared to say to Rose: 'What a stunning suit you're wearing, too bad they didn't have it in your size.' One devastating look, and the sentence would have died on the vixen's lips. Someone like Rose was never offended, humiliated, ridiculed. It was illusory to think that I, as her look-alike, could appropriate that sovereign inviolability, but it was worth a try.

Meanwhile the silent images were gliding by on the screen. We had reached year three. 'Her bikinis are becoming flashier, and her nails ever longer, and the colours more daring,' I muttered, 'but those are the only differences.'

Had the moonstruck Mastenbroek wanted to appropriate her superiority too? Or were other urges at work? Was it simply lust? But in that case surely he wouldn't, year in year out, have done nothing more than shoot ten minutes of film of the woman he desired? This much seemed clear: he was crazier than me, and by being crazier he effectively gave me licence to crawl into her skin. There were as many kinds of madness as there were human heads. Didn't you hear about the most bizarre excesses every day? The most astonishing insane wishes and desires bubbled up uninterruptedly out of the human psyche. Fortunately only a negligible percentage of them were ever put into effect, thank God. On the front page you read about the most depressing actions, many of them crimes; but a man who year after year secretly used his camcorder, cleverly hidden under beach towels, to put a woman on tape, someone like that never makes the papers. He himself thought his action commonplace enough. Otherwise he wouldn't have lent out his cassettes so readily, would he? Unless he had an ulterior motive.

I shivered for a moment and stopped the VCR. The worst tiredness had ebbed away. I was still a bit saddle-sore, but that didn't need to keep me from conducting a search for her as yet hypothetical made-to-measure corset with a billion stays. Strange that I hadn't thought of that myself, that I had needed her hairdresser to give me the idea.

At the back of her closet I found four girdles, all of them fairly supple but nevertheless equipped with stiff stays. Or were they made-to-measure corsets? When I undressed and encased myself in one of those straitjackets, I had to overcome a feeling of embarrassment. At the outset I had also been bothered by it when I put on her clothes. In the meantime it had passed, but now it returned quite forcefully. Would something like this have bothered her? I doubted it. Then it shouldn't bother me either, right?

Soon it became evident that this mysterious cross between girdle and corset corrected my posture in exactly the right way. Bolt upright I walked around her bedroom. When I relaxed, I felt the stays stab nastily into my back. I certainly could not call it pleasant, but the effect was spectacular: thanks to this instrument of torture, I now owned her posture too.

Once again I removed from the wall the beautiful photo I had earlier taken along to the Flemish hairstylist. She must have been vain: otherwise she wouldn't have displayed such a dazzling photo of herself. Or was my Calvinist background playing me false?

I leaned her photo against the mirror and seated myself at her dressing table. Constantly peering at the photo, I tried as closely as possible to make myself up like the tsarina. For the second time this proved to be terribly difficult. I kept having to use those nifty little cotton swabs to correct mistakes.

Even so, especially thanks to the fact that my hair had been cut so skilfully to resemble hers, a look-alike appeared who could pass muster. And now that my hair no longer covered my ears I saw that I had no choice left: I would have to start wearing her dazzling earrings. At least a dozen of them lay displayed on a ledge at the side of the dressing table. From an early age that kind of glamorous accessory had repelled me, but unfortunately not her.

When I picked up a sparkling wagon wheel and clipped it to my ear, it immediately fell off. No surprise there, I thought, it weighs a ton. How would she have attached the clips? Among the earrings I noticed a small plastic bottle of glue. I looked at it. Carefully I applied a small drop of glue to the inside of the clip. Then I attached it. This time it stayed put. 'So that's how,' I grumbled, and I attached the other earring with a drop of glue as well. Something else learned; another secret unveiled.

I barely had the earrings on when the doorbell sounded its three-note tune. Fear gulfed through my body. Stupid scaredy-cat, I berated myself, what a ridiculous reaction. If I were ever going to shake off the odium of servility, I had to begin right now. I must boldly walk to the door and open it without a trace of timidity. I crept into the hallway. There was nothing to be seen on the mini-TV screen. The person who had rung the bell was already upstairs, standing at the door. I peeked through the small peephole in the front door. Expecting to see the baboon grin, I saw a travelling-salesman type instead. I opened the door.

'Good evening, you're home after all, I thought you were away for I haven't seen your Saab for a while, I live five penthouses along, we sometimes run across each other in the elevator, Wijnmeulen is the name, my cat's gone missing, could it perhaps be on your deck?'

'Not as far as I know,' I said.

'May I have a look?'

'Go ahead,' I said.

Did the yuppies in Grimburch Estates live in such isolation from each other that this man didn't know Rose had died?

With small, affected-looking steps he shuffled through the hall and the room to the door I myself had not opened yet. I had not yet steeled myself to go out on the roof deck.

'Nice summer evening,' the man said, 'just the sort of evening to go out and bask in the sun and snuggle up to the wife, but the cat…well, he saw his opportunity and took it.'

He unlatched the door, stepped out on the deck, called 'Pooky, Pooky', came back in and said: 'He's not here, I'll try the other neighbours.' Then he was gone, leaving me with a feeling of triumph, behind which that miserable weepiness loomed up.

I put on Rose's tailored red leather jacket, grabbed my handbag and went out onto the walkway. I was the only passenger in the elevator. Once I was out on Grimburchstraat, the low evening sun shone unmercifully into my eyes. I took her sunglasses out of my bag, put them on, walked down Grimburchstraat and crossed a broad arterial road. I went into Digros – fortunately the supermarket was always open until eight – and bought some grapes and Gouda cheese for dinner.

When I got back to her apartment – would I from now on have to say 'her penthouse'? What an idiot that neighbour was! – about ten minutes later, the telephone chirped. I was hardly startled at all, picked up the receiver fairly calmly and said hello.

'This is Fred. Just now, as I was driving along Willem de Zwijgerlaan, I saw Rose walking near the pedestrian crossing. Dammit, I couldn't stop, I couldn't do a thing, but what's going on here? Were you making up a story? If that wasn't Rose, it looked an awful lot like her. I can hardly believe you lied to me. What good would that do you? People don't lie about somebody being dead who's still alive, right? But then who was that marching around? Who?'

I wanted to say something, but he growled: 'It was her red leather jacket, I'd be willing to bet on it. Okay, I saw her for just a moment, maybe it wasn't her…maybe it was a fantasy. I remember when I was still young, and the hormones used to pump through my body like mad, late one night once, when I was smashed, I even mistook a traffic sign for a sexy broad…but this…it's enough to drive me crazy. I saw her from the corner of my eye, walking so briskly, so beautiful and bolt upright. God, what a piss-off that I couldn't stop right there. Rose dead of sunstroke? Give me a break! Rose dead, but I saw her walking there… I smell a rat. I smell two rats… I've got to find out more, at the beginning of next week I'm going to city hall to see if she's really dead, they bloody well ought to know that; I'm going to suss that out first.'

Without waiting for an answer, he hung up.

10.

At the end of a Sunday afternoon more than a week later, the doorbell sounded. This time I wasn't startled. In the week that had just ended, I had met a surly meter-reader at the door, two very sweet young Mormons and a gentleman who was collecting for the Kidney Foundation. Calmly I walked to the front door. This caller must also have slipped in downstairs with a resident. Through the peephole I saw a scrawny man. Casually I opened the door. The man looked at me and turned pale, while his pupils dilated. He wanted to say something but could hardly get a word out, got stuck in incomprehensible phrases.

There he stood and stared at me, and I stared back. Then the man shook his head the way a dog shakes its wet fur. He thrust out a weathered paw.

'I'm Fred,' he said, 'Fred Volbeda.'

'Fred?' I stammered, totally dumbfounded.

'Yes, I'm Fred.'

'I had pictured you quite differently, Mr Volbeda,' I said. Did the flat harsh voice I had heard on the phone belong to this skinny person? Now that I saw him his voice, although unmistakably the same one as on the phone, sounded lighter, less sinister.

'I'm baffled,' said Fred.

Then he stepped past me into the hall, apparently sure of himself. He even shoved me aside. 'We've got to talk, Mrs Kuyper,' he growled and headed towards the living room. What could I do other than close the front door? He wouldn't have stepped past Rose so rudely; I wasn't there yet, not by a long chalk.

'Well,' Fred said when I also entered the living room, '*one* riddle has been solved. So it was *you* I saw hoofing it along Willem de Zwijgerlaan the other day. Why didn't you tell me that when I phoned?'

'I didn't get the chance,' I said.

'Are you maybe that sister she was always talking about?'

'She always called me her sister,' I said, 'but I'm…'

He interrupted me. 'Couldn't easily be anything else. What really bugs me something terrible – I'll say it right off the bat – is that Rose died out of the blue. Out of the blue. She was healthy as all get-out the weekend before, I can vouch for that, at that time she was…we had a real fun time with her…three days later she dies, she's dead just like that, dead as a doornail, how can that be?'

'Sunstroke,' I said.

'Come off it, someone in perfect health doesn't die of sunstroke. Whenever there was the slightest hint of sun, she was lying on her towel at the beach, drenched in suntan oil. Never had complaints or problems or anything like that. And even though the sparrows weren't exactly falling off the roofs that day because of the heat, she is supposed to…well, there's hardly any sparrows left, I read in the paper the other day, but okay. So even though the *crows* weren't exactly falling off the roofs because of the heat…funny expression, come to think of it. As if those bloody animals can't fly, never mind, what was I saying? Oh, yeah, there was heavy cloud that morning…I should know. We were driving the first pile at a job site, then you have to keep looking up…so she is supposed to have died of sunstroke, just like that…? I don't believe a single damned word of it, zip, zilch, zero.'

'She died in the hospital, where they did…'

'I was there last week, after I first went to city hall… So after a lot of hassle I got to talk to a youngster, a rookie, some kid in a white coat who had done the autopsy. Yes, sir, believe me, sir, it was sunstroke, there's not a shadow of a doubt.'

He looked at me as though he wanted to kill me with sunstroke too.

'If you don't mind, I'll sit down.'

'Go ahead.'

'Thanks.' And he fell down on the couch. He shut his eyes tight, opened them again and looked at me with the kind of look that comes from the bottom of the heart.

'A rookie like that…yes, sir, really, she is…we have…she had a donor card, so we checked her out thoroughly, he said that too. That's all I needed to know, the vultures laid her out right away and dug out everything they could use, her kidneys, her heart, and who knows what else. They took her corneas…what did *they* care what she died of? They were much too happy they had got hold of somebody else they could mine for parts, that was job one, the cause of death, what did that matter, for God's sake?'

'That's what *you* say, Mr Volbeda, but let's assume she was poisoned…then they would want to sort that out before taking the kidneys…'

'You said it: poisoned. So that occurred to you too, or did it occur to you just now?'

'Something like that did go through my head,' I said. 'I don't see either how she could have had sunstroke, she was pretty well seasoned.'

'You said it.'

'And yet, the funeral director told me he had come across cases like this before, and he said it really wasn't all that exceptional, doctors had told him often enough…'

'Doctors, those guys, they're such turkeys. Not that I'm not a turkey, God help me… Ober, little guy, there you are, what's up, is your mistress dead?'

Ober jumped in Fred's lap, settled himself, started purring. Fred stroked the white triangle under his chin.

'My old man…they cut him open, they sew him shut again. One of those white coats says to me: he's got cancer of the pancreas, six months max. We launder the flag so we can fly it all nice and clean when he kicks the bucket, and we inherit big time from that miserable…yeah, right, that's fifteen years ago now, and you should see my old man, still alive and well and exactly the same old bastard he always was, and we keep thinking we would get that cash…no, those white coats.'

He stroked Ober, who was purring like a Singer sewing machine.

Tiger came walking up, jumped onto the couch, nestled himself up against Fred.

'Start petting one, and in no time at all you'll get to see all three,' said Fred.

'I do believe you're the only one who can manage that,' I said.

'So you're looking after them now, Mrs Kuyper, you've inherited the lot?'

'That's what it looks like,' I said, 'but it hasn't all been sorted out yet…'

'No, that figures, a notary…he's got to have his cut, can't just do the whole thing at the end of the afternoon…well, sure, he probably could but then try sending a big fat bill.'

'Rose never talked about you, never, I didn't know of your existence.'

'That's really not so strange. We…our little club…quite probably she never talked with others about it, and I don't have the slightest wish to explain why. She always spoke very highly of you, and then we'd say: bring that fantastic sister along some time, and then she said: "No, she is so pure and innocent and unspoiled and unsullied, no, forget it," and that's probably how come she never talked to you about our club, she didn't want to sully you.'

'I've always admired her enormously,' I said. 'She had such flair, such daring, such...'

'You said it! No flies of any kind on her...a wonderful woman, it's a terrible crying shame she is dead. But sunstroke? You can't make even her cats believe that.'

'I have a videotape of that last afternoon,' I said. 'You can see for yourself that she's lying there, sunbathing peacefully, that nothing suspicious happens before she gets taken away by an ambulance.'

'A videotape? Of that last afternoon? Who made it?'

'A man from Katwijk. He used to tape her regularly.'

'Used to tape her regularly? Some clown from Katwijk? How?'

'He always taped her.'

'Did she know about it?'

'I doubt it. He gave me some cassettes. Every year he taped about ten minutes' worth...'

'God almighty, do you know the name of this weirdo, this bikini-spotter, this camcording peeping tom?'

'Piet Mastenbroek.'

'Means nothing to me. But okay...right away we've got ourselves a suspect, a guy who several years running secretly puts Rose on tape, oh boy, the things that happen on this planet of ours! Could I see that tape of the last afternoon?'

'If I manage to get things working.'

'Oh, let me do it, no trick at all, I own the same piece of junk as her, I was able to buy a couple of them for next to nothing, kept one for myself and gave the other to her, well, gave...'

A moment later we were looking at the white bikini and Rose's immobile back. We saw that shadow brush over her twice, we saw how the ambulance took her away, quick as a wink.

'God almighty,' Fred said hoarsely as he stopped the tape. He sighed deeply, stroked Ober's back fiercely, which the cat put up with manfully, then said: 'Sorry.'

He placed Ober on the couch and, taking big steps, headed for the kitchen. I heard the tap run, heard him drink. Big gulps. He returned, sat down again, put Ober back on his lap.

'Rose...a great broad like that, the greatest, it really got to me, seeing her again... God, Rose, how is it possible, what son of a bitch has got this on his conscience?'

'How come you're so firmly convinced that...do you think...? By the way, my name is Leonie.'

'Mine is Fred, as you know, yeah, we might as well use first names.'

'Why do you keep on thinking she was p...poi...?'

'You can't even get it out properly,' he said. 'I can relate to that, but you're right. I think...what am I saying? I am *sure* she was murdered, no doubt about it.'

'But that tape? Nothing happens.'

'Yeah, come on, that's just a bit of the afternoon. All kinds of things could have happened before or after the part we saw. Between that first ten minutes and the arrival of the ambulance there's a big gap. It could have happened then.'

'But *what* could have happened.'

'Yeah, if I knew that, but, well, that's not my job, I'm in construction. I'm a contractor. What's your line?'

'I translate, and I'm a supply teacher.'

'Supply teacher? What subject?'

'I have a teaching qualification in French. If a French teacher somewhere in the area is on leave for a longer period, they phone me, and I step in for a couple of months or so.'

'Don't they want you full time in those schools?'

'Sure, *they* would like that, but I find it too tough. In front of the classroom...that's terribly demanding. As a supply teacher you may be in front of a classroom for two or three months, and then you're off for quite a while.'

'And what do you do with that time?'

'Translation.'

'What does that involve?'

'A publisher sends me a book, in my case always one in French, and I have to turn it into one in Dutch.'

'Do you have to read that book too?' he asked, deeply horrified.

'That happens automatically,' I said mockingly, 'but not long ago I translated the philosopher Michel Onfray. He quotes from Schopenhauer. To find the quotation I had to read through Schopenhauer's *The World as Will and Representation*, sixteen hundred pages! Of course you can't translate a quotation like that out of French, you have to translate it directly out of the original German.'

'Christ almighty, what a calamity. Reading a book of sixteen hundred pages! That's about the worst thing I can imagine. So translation must pay a bundle.'

'No, not really. It's an incredible amount of work for incredibly little money. But if the book you have to translate is good, it's enormously rewarding. It's a task, a project, and I've found there's just one way to be really happy: to perform a difficult task with the greatest possible dedication. And a translation like that brings any number of things with it: you have to go to the public library to look up things, though nowadays you can find just about everything you want on the Internet, and you have to consult all kinds of people. A translation takes you many different places, lets you learn a lot, fills your life. But sometimes there's nothing to translate, and then I do volunteer work.'

'That doesn't pay either. Yeah, we've got one in the office...we're allowed to give her forty-two guilders a week. With a ceiling of fourteen hundred annually, not enough to keep a church mouse alive. Beyond that, what do you live off? Welfare?'

'From teaching and translation I earn just enough to make ends meet, more or less. I've never wanted to accept alimony.'

'Jesus, so you're divorced. I've got two exes I have to pay, two of those pains...both with kids...you're stuck with that for twelve years, they clean you out, all your money goes down that particular drain. You've got just enough left over to buy a bag of fries...but without sauce, because you can't afford fries *with* sauce. Alimony, lucky you, you're on the right side of it...and now you get a small inheritance...your very own sister dead...women, it's unbelievable.'

'Sister? Before there's a misunderstanding...'

But he kept on ranting: 'Liberation...they talk about women's liberation. What the hell does that mean in practice? That they clean you out for years, while they sit around on their fat asses?'

'She was an only child,' I said, but he was a real man all right: he simply wouldn't listen.

'Did you know she had left you everything?'

'No, I didn't. She only asked me whether I would care for her cats if something ever happened to her.'

'Don't I know it, so you...well, then you are quite simply prime suspect number one, Leonie, you had every interest in her death.'

'Come off it,' I said, 'prime suspect, you've been watching too many of those American police dramas.'

'What else is there to do, if you're home alone at night? You can't go to a bar every evening, can you?'

'So *that* is why you think...? In those shows people who seem to have died a natural death often turn out later to have been murdered.'

'No,' he said, 'no, that's not it. I'll tell you what it is. Our little club had one hell of a weekend before the Wednesday she died of sunstroke...get out of here: sunstroke...well, okay, Saturday night we all went out to dinner together, and we really got into the sauce. I took her home because she was way too wasted to drive. To tell the truth, I was fairly well oiled myself when I got behind the wheel... I went in with her when we got here, I even put her to bed, I don't mind telling you that... And when she was in the sack, and I sat on the edge of her bed for a moment, she said: "There's someone who wants me dead." "Someone wants you dead?" I asked. "Yes," she said, "you won't believe it, but I am...there is...promise that if I die all of a sudden you won't just let it pass.". "It's a promise," I said, "but who wants you dead?" But by then she was out like a light, she'd already fallen asleep, and I tiptoed out of the place. I phoned her Monday bright and early, I asked her: so who wants you dead? She started to waffle, said she'd been drunk and had just been babbling when she got to bed. Could be true, of course, but if you'd seen her when she said that to me...it didn't sound at all like silly drunken babbling, no way: there was more to it than that.'

He swallowed. 'You got nothing to drink in this place? A pick-me-up would really hit the spot.'

'I'll go have a look.'

When I returned with a bottle of Dutch gin, he said: 'What an old-fashioned girl she was! Had Dutch gin in the place! Where do you still find that nowadays? These days it's all Scotch and vodka and South American concoctions with scary animals in them... Dutch gin, that Rose...promise me, she says, that if I die all of a sudden you won't just let it pass. So what happens? She dies right out of the blue. If somebody, no matter how drunk, had said that to you, wouldn't you think there was something fishy when people keep going on about sunstroke? But how in God's name do we figure out who did her in and why? You tell me. At first glance you're the only one who benefits because she is no longer around, you are...'

'Lay off, Fred,' I said.

'Shall we go get a bite to eat somewhere or did you already have other plans?'

'A bite to eat?' I said, astonished.

'Sure, why not? Rose and I often went out on Sundays to get a bite to eat. We could go to De Avonden, she liked it there.'

'Where is that?'

'In Choorlammersteeg. They've got a small menu there. The less choice you've got, the easier it is to choose.'

11.

'I often came here with Rose,' said Fred.

'I never eat out,' I said. 'You can make a meal at home for a fraction of the cost, and it'll have less fat.'

'If you've got time for that,' said Fred, 'but I haven't got time. When I get home from work I don't feel like working in the kitchen. So I often eat out. Or I get takeout, there's so many places these days, Chinese, Thai, Indonesian, Italian, Greek, Turkish, you name it.'

'Home cooking is much healthier. In restaurants they improve the taste of everything with overuse of the holy trinity of butter, eggs and cream. And here and there they add a dash of sugar. People's tastes are mostly focused on sweet and fat. So what do you end up gorging yourself on? Cholesterol.'

'Cholesterol? Are you the same kind of scaredy-cat Rose was? She was constantly worked up about cholesterol too, about her health...maybe she got that from you...? And yet, think for a moment, she paid close attention to what she ate, just like you, and did it do her any good? No, because some dirty bastard did her in.'

'You really think so?'

'I'm sure of it,' he said grimly.

'I can't believe it; everybody loved her. Take it from me: she had no enemies.'

'Friends commit murder too,' he said.

'She is...'

'We're dealing with a damned cunning murderer here.'

'What nonsense.'

Lobster bisque, to which an ample shot of cream had evidently been added, appeared.

'Enjoy,' said Fred.

'Thanks, you too.'

'I'm sticking to the idea she was poisoned,' Fred said after swallowing a mouthful of cholesterol soup.

'Poisoned? What makes you think that?'

'Yes, she was poisoned all right. She worked in a lab. She told me about it sometimes. Everything that happened there. Drugs, powders, pills, ointments, tranquillizers, sedatives. Nifty medications that ordinary mortals know zilch about. Tricky tablets with some clever little thing built in whereby a drop leaks out every once in a while so that you don't get the whole load in your body all at once but on the instalment plan as it were; it has a name too, but even if you were to drink my wine I can't remember what it's called.'

'A time-release mechanism,' I said, 'but drops from a tablet...how do you picture that?'

'Well, okay, it's only a manner of speaking, what do I know? You seem to know more about it than me. All I want to say is this: if they know how to make smart pills like that over there, some clever son of a bitch can also figure out a little tablet or pill that only starts to work after a few hours. He secretly drops it in her coffee in the morning, and at the end of the afternoon: bingo!'

He said it with such comic-sounding emphasis that I began to laugh.

'What's so funny?' he snarled.

'Sorry...it sounded funny.'

'She's dead,' he said, deeply offended.

'I know,' I said, 'I'm ashamed, really I am...but...'

'I still think it's a nifty little pill like that, really, just you wait and see, there's so many smart cookies in that lab, so many smooth operators.'

'But a while ago you said doctors were all such dimwits.'

'Yeah, but now we're not talking about ordinary white coats in unpainted offices, we've got a totally different kind of scum here, these guys are razor-sharp wheeler-dealers who are out to charge you an arm and a leg for tiny little pills you need a magnifying glass and pincers to prise out of strip packages. Then half the pills promptly slip through your fingers and get lost in the carpet, they're so small. It takes the rest of your life for them to make you better, so you've got to keep popping them and paying up until you croak.'

I couldn't help myself; I began to laugh again.

'I can't for the life of me see what's so funny,' he said angrily. 'I'm trying to explain something to you...'

'Yes, sorry, but you do keep contradicting yourself so oddly: you see medical doctors as incompetents, and yet these people, who mostly also studied medicine, you see as a species of super magicians who turn out smart pills.'

'Don't give me a hard time, woman, what I wanted to say is: they've got the know-how to make pills. Ten gets you one some son of a bitch or other...'

'But who? I know everybody there, because Thomas...because my ex used to work there... Who would have wanted to...? No, out of the question, everybody there worshipped her. She was by far and away the best research assistant in the place. All the pharmacologists and physicians were eager to work with her. All of them knew this much: do research with her, and it's bound to lead to a publication that will get you noticed. Both the retired Department Head as well as his successor owed their promotion in large part to their outstanding collaboration with Rose. A lab like that...if you only knew what goes on there...properly considered it is scandalous... The professors and associate professors get all the glory, but the real work, the precision work, gets done by the research assistants and the lab technicians. They get stuck with all the horribly tedious routine work that gets the dignified name of scientific research.'

'That's the way it goes all over the place,' Fred said, 'behind every cabinet minister you'll find some bigwig who does the real work. And a good thing too, because when the shit hits the fan the minister can be dumped while the bigwig stays high and dry.'

'I think it's just the same in the fashion world,' I said. 'Wherever you have a top designer, there's a tailor with brilliant ideas in his design shop.'

'So how do you think it is in *my* line of work, Leonie? There's architects, okay, but we do the actual construction.'

'But that's different, isn't it?'

'Oh yeah? Did you think we just slavishly carry out what some architect puts on paper at his drafting table?'

'You can't deviate too much from the drawings, I imagine.'

'You really think so? Mostly you've got to fix them up and put in an extra support here and there. Otherwise the whole damned thing would collapse about the time the construction crew get their bonus for finishing.'

'And yet I simply can't believe that even *if* Rose were murdered, it was someone from the lab...'

'Who else?'

'How should I know? One of the members of that secret little club of yours?'

71

'You…you…'

He stared at me over his empty soup bowl, deeply outraged.

'Don't look so furious, Fred,' I said.

'Well, okay, but…oh, forget it, God almighty, we won't get any farther *this* way, dammit. We've got to consult someone.'

'Consult someone?'

'Yeah, someone who's got experience with this kind of thing, we can't just muddle along on our own, we've got… I think we should…'

'Go to the police? You want to go to the police?'

'The cops? The fuzz? No, absolutely no way, they won't do anything for us. They're up to their necks in shit, they're drowning in cases, they're completely overworked, and they're jerked around by crazy rules and regulations coming at them constantly from Den Haag. And what the hell would you tell them? There's no corpse you can do an autopsy on. If she was poisoned, and that crap settled in her kidneys, because that's where it mostly heads for, I believe, maybe there's a small chance you can prove it by examining somebody who's happily walking around after a successful transplant…you'd have to find out who…no, I doubt you can do that, I've never heard of such a thing. So, no…autopsy is a non-starter. And another thing. Why did she have to be cremated? Was that by her own choice, or did the murderer manage to arrange it? So that all traces are gone. Can you remember? A while ago, some quack in England who used poison to bump off almost all the widows in his care, altogether about a hundred, always advised the next of kin: have your mother cremated.'

'As I recall, Rose belonged to some cremation society.'

'Are you sure? I can have that checked out. I belong to a Rotary breakfast club, we meet every Wednesday morning at 7:30 in the Off Limits; one of…'

'Off Limits?'

'Yes, can I help it if the crummy joint has a name like that?' he said grumpily. 'Can I help it…what was I saying, oh yeah, one of our members specializes in investigating this kind of business.'

'A private detective?'

'He doesn't want to be called that, and he doesn't care to say what he does want to be called; anyway, I don't care, but he could… I'd like to consult him.'

'You could do that,' I said.

'Yeah, I'll do that; myself, I really don't have the time or know-how… No, these kinds of jobs, you've got to farm them out.'

Feeling irritated, I wanted to burst out, but at that moment the girl who was serving us asked timidly 'How was the soup?' while she discreetly removed the soup bowls.

'Good as ever,' said Fred.

The interruption enabled me to avoid showing my annoyance, which in any case ebbed quickly. Fred said: 'Please don't make us wait too long for the main course.'

'It'll be here in a moment,' the girl said.

'That's good.'

A shape brushed by our table. From high above my head a man's voice said: 'God, Rose, you're here... I thought...how can this be, I heard that you...sunstroke...'

I looked up. A man who smelled strongly of aftershave looked at me as though he was watching me walk on water.

'I'm very sorry,' I said. 'I'm afraid we haven't met.'

'You're barking up the wrong tree, pal,' said Fred. 'This isn't Rose.'

'No, I can hear that now, but...but...'

The man walked away between the tables in the badly lit space. He looked around twice before he stepped out into Choorlammersteeg. And when he was out in the alley, he peered at our table once more through one of the small windows of the restaurant.

'That fellow crapped his pants in Technicolor, he was so upset,' Fred said matter-of-factly. 'I had been noticing him, he didn't seem to me like a guy who's easily shaken.' He took a big gulp of his wine and added: 'He was sitting with his back towards you, so he saw you for the first time just now...well, it is pretty dark in here. So that's why he thought you were Rose...but I wouldn't mind knowing why he was so startled. Who was it? Did you know that guy?'

'No,' I said.

'Suppose you murdered somebody. You're in a restaurant, get up, walk out and unexpectedly see the very person you thought you had dispatched to the grave. How would *you* react?'

'I'd be frightened to death.'

'Exactly, that fellow was scared shitless. Must ask later who it was. If he's been here before they're bound to know, even though maybe now he'll never come back. If he paid with plastic they'll know his name too; later...why later, why not right now?'

Fred got up, went over to the timid girl, spoke with her for a moment and returned to our table. He shook his head.

'They don't know who he is. And he paid cash. See, that's what I was saying just now…we haven't got the means or the know-how to find out something like that for ourselves; we've got to consult somebody… I'll have a confab with Peter.'

He sat down again, smiled grimly.

'Actually it's a good thing you look so much like her, it's almost like a DNA test. Whoever gets scared shitless we immediately put on the top-ten list of suspects. Has it happened before that somebody was frightened out of his skull?'

'No,' I said. 'No…uh, yes. Bas, he was quite startled, he even fainted.'

'Bas? Who's Bas?'

'Bas is Department Head and Director of the lab. But he has…no, out of the question, he almost broke up when he gave a eulogy at the funeral service.'

'Good actor, Bas, I'd keep an eye on him. How about that? Fainted, did he?'

'Yes, but he came into her apartment, didn't know I was there too, saw only my hand at first, but then with her nails…'

'What business did he have being in her apartment after she was dead?'

'He was worried about the cats.'

'How did he get in?'

'He had a key.'

'How come he had a key?'

'He must have got it from her sometime, they worked closely together almost every day.'

'How come he was so intimate with her that he had a key? I don't have a key. Am I less important than this Bas? Or did he swipe the key from her bag at some point and have it copied before returning it on the same day? You see, here's something else we can put Peter to work on.'

He folded his hands as if to pray, said: 'Actually it's bloody dangerous.'

'Dangerous? What's dangerous?'

'That you look so much like Rose. Our man might think: Hey, Rose is still alive, got to do it again, finish the job.'

The girl silently served the main course.

'Yes, very good, what a tasty-looking hare this is,' Fred said. 'And what's yours, mackerel fillet with mushrooms? Can you live on that? Fish…I don't understand why people eat fish.' He looked at me mischievously then frowned. 'Pay no attention, I'm just kidding, fish is perfectly okay if you pour a nice little sauce over it. But mushrooms, ugh…'

'So you think I'm at risk?'

'Oh, is that it? You looked so washed-out all of a sudden. Are you afraid that you...? First of all, you've been warned, and secondly, our man is bound to be aware that Rose is gone. You can bet he's bright enough to know that, so...no, it was just a chance thought of mine. Even if somebody was to think: that's Rose, your voice would immediately give you away. It's a crying shame, really. If you had her voice, you could pass for Rose whenever the light was a bit dim. It would really be a fantastic DNA test. Do you think you could imitate her voice?'

'Ober,' I said. 'Ober, little guy, won't you come here?'

'God almighty, how did you manage that?'

'I don't know. I can only do it when I copy the way she always called Ober.'

'Just Ober? Not Tiger?'

'Tiger, big guy, you rascal, would you like some whiting?'

'You see, you can call Tiger too. And Lellebel?'

'Lellebel, Lellebel, where are you, girl, where are you hiding?'

'Well, if you can do this, then you should easily be able to...'

'Yes, but I've heard these things hundreds of times, so I can imitate them without trouble; other things would be harder.'

'Are you sure? She could say so imperiously...'

'Give me my handbag.'

'Yes, that's it. You see you can do it, but you'll have to practise a lot. A voice, that goes right to the core, it's the person himself... Even if you couldn't see a thing, but you heard someone's voice, you'd still know: that's Joe the barber... I mean: over the phone the voice is what matters, the rest is a minor detail. So you're going to have to prepare thoroughly if you want to apply the DNA test...oh, I've got an audiotape with her voice on it. A birthday party, nothing special, a lot of people chattering at the same time... I'd like to hold on to it... I'll copy it onto another tape so you can practise...after all, it's a bit like learning a foreign language, you'll have to give your mouth a workout, you'll have to get the pronunciation down cold. And that reminds me: I'd love to copy those tapes of Mastenbroek's. I'd always be able to see her again. And at the same time we'd have evidence.'

'Come on, evidence?'

'You never know.'

'I'd much rather return those tapes to Mastenbroek as soon as possible. As long as I have them, he's got an excuse to come and fetch them. Best of all, I'd like to put them in the mail tomorrow.'

'Fine by me. When we're finished here we'll go get them, drive over to my place, and I'll copy them…it'll take no time at all, then you can take them back home.'

Small packages of creamer were served with the coffee. I picked up one of the packages and said to Fred: 'Have you ever heard how flammable this creamer is?'

'Creamer flammable? No, I've never heard anything about that.'

'Rose's notary showed it to me, he opened a package, tossed the contents in the air and flicked his lighter. You should have seen the flame!'

Fred immediately ripped open a package of creamer, tossed the contents in the air with his right hand and at the same time picked up one of the candles that were on the table. For one brief moment a huge flame lit up the interior of De Avonden. There were startled reactions at the other tables. The timid girl came running up and said: 'Would you mind not doing that, please?'

'I've already done it,' said Fred, 'and I don't need to do it again. I've seen enough.'

Much later that evening, after he had copied the tapes and made a composite tape for me, as we drove into Grimburchstraat, I thought nervously: if only he doesn't want to come in with me to tuck me in, the way he did with Rose.

He stopped in front of the main entrance and asked: 'Say it once more, please.'

'Say what?'

'Ober, little guy, come…'

'Ober, Ober, little guy, won't you come here?'

'Hard to believe,' he said. 'It's just like I'm hearing her. She always called Ober "little guy" and Tiger "big guy", even though Ober was at least twice as old. Rose, my little Rose…gone just like that, and in a while we'll be gone too, and that pile of garbage all around us, it's hard to believe, we're allowed to fart around for sixty, seventy, if we're lucky eighty years, and we don't have a clue why, even though there's guys who claim we're in this place for the honour of God, like it does *Him* one bit of good that we're freezing our butts off here in the cold, no, God can kiss my ass. Oh well, what does it matter? When Ober and Tiger and the handbag are fixed in your brain the rest will be there too, so keep on practising.'

'All the same, it might be risky.'

'No, it isn't, that murderer was just a fantasy of mine. *If* there's anybody like that around…honest, he won't think: "there goes Rose."'

'Fine, but maybe…well, I want … I can't believe she was murdered, and you're apparently not so sure yourself if you say *if* there's anybody like that around. All right, it's possible that someone loathed her and then murdered her. Someone like that is going to loathe me too, certainly if I start using a deep alto voice like hers.'

'Sure, anything is possible, but it strikes me as farfetched. Good night… Hey, one more thing, she had a safety deposit box at the Rabobank branch near here, did you know that?'

'No.'

'She was keeping some undeclared cash in it. It might be better to get it out and spend it before the taxman…spending it would be a good idea in any case. Soon they'll be forcing that crummy euro down our throats, and our Dutch money will be worth squat. Maybe it would be an idea to use it to pay my Rotary friend, though I sense you're not overly enthusiastic about consulting anyone. She'll be paying from beyond the grave for the investigation into her own death. That would have appealed to her, I'm one hundred percent sure of that.'

Before I turned off the lights later that evening I listened to his tape. It had clearly been recorded at a birthday party. Much laughter, much talk, now and then Rose's beautiful voice cutting straight across the booming men's voices. She was saying something about her work, she asked for a glass of wine, it was nothing special, but it might help me if I wanted to try imitating her voice. Then, as glasses were tinkling, I heard her say something that made me sit up and take notice. It was almost incomprehensible and was immediately drowned out by the roaring laughter of the celebrating men. Had I heard it right? I reversed the tape. There it was again. Tinkling glass, and then, weakly, her voice: 'I peed on Fred.' Was this merely a crude remark, uttered while she was tipsy? That's what I would have to assume. After all, she wouldn't have indulged in kinky sex with that scrawny contractor, would she?

12.

To tell the truth, I didn't really approve of a safety deposit box like that. Nevertheless, every so often I looked for the key. Or had she not kept it at home, did I have to pick it up at a counter in the bank on showing proof of identity? I couldn't find the key anywhere in her apartment. Maybe I wasn't looking hard enough. But my superficial searches brought an unexpected benefit. As I opened a desk drawer rather impatiently and my right thumb got caught, I heard an odd grinding noise, and one of my artificial nails fell on the carpet. My own nail reappeared, a dull and unpleasant-looking shade of greenish white. One artificial nail gone, what a stroke of luck!

Carefully I tried the other artificial nails. I was able to pry off the claws on the index and little fingers on my left hand. Had the glue become brittle? Maybe the growth of my own nails had loosened the artificial ones.

This much is certain: after a persistent and protracted struggle, in which I used acetone and heated soda water as my weapons, I finally got to see all my own nails again. Damaged, to be sure, but I hoped time would take care of that.

If I wanted to imitate her, I couldn't really escape using those awful things, but the dinner in Choorlammersteeg had struck a blow at my secret desire to recreate myself in her image. By saying it was bloody dangerous that I looked like Rose, Fred had succeeded in frightening me. I wasn't *very* frightened, but frightened enough to have it undermine the sparkling tingling excitement that had accompanied the effort to transform myself. Too bad, really, because that excitement had taken me straight back to my childhood, to all the great expectations that had preceded my first day in elementary school, birthdays, outings, staying over at a girlfriend's place, St Nicholas Eve and the gifts it promised.

Why, as they get older, do people have to lose the ability to look forward eagerly to events that are ultimately unimportant but cast enormous shadows before them all the same? Perhaps if I had a child, or a grandchild…no, for God's sake, don't go there. I could console myself with the knowledge that I had been able to experience a sort of aftertaste of that childish excitement, even if the words 'bloody dangerous' had cast a pall over it.

All the same: how marvellous that my fingertips had been liberated! And the artificial nails were not essential, less essential in any event than her hairstyle. But the feeling lingered that I should not make compromises. I had vowed to walk in her footsteps, however perilous that might be. If you renege on a task that you have imposed on yourself, life becomes a bit drabber.

Still, I couldn't go to the notary with claws like that, could I? I had a proper appointment with him, in fact: wonderful to relate we had managed to agree on a time. In the golden light of the September sun I cycled to Galigaangracht.

The first thing he said when he saw me was: 'Well, Mrs Kuyper. Have you thought about working here part-time?'

'I don't have the necessary qualifications for the job,' I said.

'You don't need any, I'm not asking for any, you seem to me to be g…g…fine for the job, *ach*, look me squarely in the face, please, tell me straight out that I stutter.'

'You have a terrible stutter, Mr Graafland, you get hung up in every word that starts with a "g".'

'Great, just great. You see? It's working again, excellent. Oh, please do come and work here, Mrs Kuyper, even if it's only for an hour a day, you're worth your weight in gold, I press you to my heart… Never mind, I won't insist, you'll notice in your own good time that a little job wouldn't be a bad thing. You could make the payments on that mortgage you may need. Now if you'd be so good as to sign a few documents, we can make real headway, we can wind up this rather complicated inheritance business, not from one day to the next maybe, but within the foreseeable future. Are the pussycats doing well? They're still alive?'

'They're all three healthy as can be.'

'Perhaps a visit to a vet…for checkups. It could be that, in line with the will, I should ever so gently insist on that.'

'Then I'll do it,' I said, 'no problem. It'll take at most two hours to catch the three of them and put them in cat carriers. They'll all be meowing heart-rendingly as we take a taxi to the vet, where they'll be sitting between barking dogs and will get thoroughly upset. And when they get back home they'll be shaking with fright and will be hiding under the beds for three days.'

'Yes, a taxi...you're quite right, it's incredible, there's no trace of the Saab. I've been in touch with the Katwijk police, but to be frank, I've given up all hope. Never mind, I don't think you're all that worried about it, and it makes a substantial difference to the death duties, an expensive car like that gone. That is, if we can convince the tax department the car has really been stolen. Another thing I've never had to deal with before. As a result, I don't know exactly what to expect.'

'In the first place her car wasn't all that expensive, she bought it used, and in the second place...we've reported it stolen, right? The police sent me some kind of form. We can show that to the tax people, can't we?'

'Yes, but the tax people are not retarded, they know that heirs, hoping to reduce the death duties, often spirit away an expensive car and then report it stolen. That way they're able to remove it from the list of possessions. When everything has been wound up, they retrieve it from the chicken coop with the false roof where it's been squirreled away. I mean, a Saab, the tax people need only to see the name, and they'll go straight up the wall.'

'It was a used car.'

'Are you sure?'

'I do believe she said that.'

'As *I* understand it, she bought it new.'

'What with? She was a research assistant. After deductions, three thousand guilders a month tops.'

'You're quite right. It's a mystery. Perhaps she had inherited something? She was well-to-do, she presented herself as a gr...gr...help, it's back, look at me sternly, Mrs Kuyper, tell me that I'm stuttering.'

'You're stuttering, Mr Graafland,' I said, while I thought: either he's off his rocker, or he's coming on to me in an unusually elaborate way.

'Good grocers in green graves...yes, thank God I'm on track again. She presented herself as a *grande dame*. She lived in a luxurious apartment. All right, she bought the place when they were still going for a song, with the blinds thrown in free of charge, but she paid off the mortgage quickly. She had saved a pretty penny, owned a fair number of common shares, showed up in winter in a mink coat worth at least fifteen grand, she drove a Saab. And yet she earned a modest salary.... The university is anything but rolling in it...what she got *there* was just enough to pamper her cats, no more. So...so...'

'Well, so what? I didn't know her *that* well. Maybe her parents left her something, she was an only child, she didn't have to share anything with anyone.'

'Could be, we should be able to find out, but *ach*, why bother? Nevertheless, when I lie in bed the little grey cells keep working overtime. So wealthy and then…sunstroke…*ach*, sure, it's altogether possible that some person found her sunstroke very convenient, it could well be that somebody gave the sun a little push.'

'But why, for Heaven's sake?'

'I don't know. I'm not the one you should ask. I'm only a simple village notary. Just starting out, a greenhorn. Incorporations, conveyances, legacies, that kind of thing.'

'Those shares. Am I allowed to I sell them?'

'You want to sell her shares? What for?'

'They scare me, shares. From one day to the next they can suddenly be worthless. I also think…no, making money with money, ugh, it's obscene, it's immoral, shares don't share and share alike, my father used to say.'

'That's how business works,' he said. 'It would be silly to sell them now, they're going up like rockets.'

'Just for that alone,' I said, 'it's an idiotic swindle; what goes up will come down.'

'You can sell them just as soon as everything has been wound up.'

'That might take years.'

'No, no, it'll take a year at most, and maybe you can sell them even now, *ach*, why not? The heirs are allowed to… See, that's what happens when you're just starting out and haven't had to deal with anything like this before… I don't know everything yet…if you absolutely want to sell them, I'll look after it…people are lining up to buy, you'll be rid of them in a flash.'

'That'll suit me just fine, please get rid of them.'

'And then, after that, you'll take a small job. You'll come and work here.'

'How come you're so keen for me to come and work here?'

'You liberate me from my disability: goats graze on green grass.'

I burst into laughter.

'Sure, keep on laughing,' he said, 'you can make fun of me. Go ahead, it doesn't matter. I'm already married, otherwise I'd get on my knees before you, live with you forever, never stutter again.'

'Mr Graafland, do you really think I would want to work here if you…behave like that, so oddly …if you come…?'

'Say it, please, finish your sentence.'

'*You* finish it, there's no "g" in it.'

'No, Mrs Kuyper, that's not it, I don't have eyes for you, but you... I'll be frank, you have something special, something that's given to very few others, and for that reason I'd really like to have you in the office now and then.'

'So what *have* I got?'

'You have the ability to put people at their ease, you're like a mother to them, and in addition you look very presentable, you make a good impression; and what's also important, I've seen the documents, so I know when you were born, you're a fair bit older even though you still look like a teenager. I've had so many bad experiences with very young girls...these kids, they're so astonishingly demanding, they've been spoiled ever since they were in diapers.'

'I've got three cats to look after. That's a job in itself. Especially if I've got to drag them over to the vet for checkups every now and then.'

'You're bound to have a little bit of time to fill, just enough for a part-time job. It can't be good to be at home all day with the cats, you have to get out...it's a safe bet you'd feel right at home here...'

'If I showed up here in her fur coat.'

'*Ach*, it would look good on you.'

'I don't see how I can wear a coat like that.'

'You can't very well throw it out. And if you were to sell it, you would just be shifting the dilemma, saddling someone else with the problem. Follow the example of your testator. *She* wasn't troubled by it.'

'But she *was* troubled by it. In fact, she belonged to Respect for Animals.'

'You can join too, can't you?'

'A hypocritical way to salve my conscience.'

'That's what we all do, that's what our government does. All that development aid.'

'Back to that job for a moment, Mr Graafland,' I said. 'A question that may embarrass you: would you have offered it to Rose?'

'She already had a job.'

'Well, sure, but if she hadn't had one.'

'It wouldn't have occurred to me right off. I need someone who can put people at their ease, who can be like a mother to them. Maybe she was not that kind of person, and besides...she looked so fabulous...expensive suits, heavily made up, spectacular earrings, scary long fingernails.'

As I cycled back in the golden sunlight, I kept thinking: big mistake. I should have gone there in full ceremonial getup as her look-alike. Maybe then he wouldn't have bothered me. What did I need that crummy job for, anyway? Why on earth did that fellow want me so badly for a part-time position? Was he infatuated? Of course he had denied it, that idiot with his ridiculous moustache and his roving eye. And just think: he was maybe thirty-five, I was more than ten years older; surely it was out of the question. Or was he a gerontophile? And to think he actually had a photo of a gorgeous woman and three darling children on his desk!

I cycled along in that generous late-summer sun, and time and again I felt my eyes becoming moist. 'You're like a mother to them,' he had said.

When I was back home, Tiger, who was snoozing on the windowsill, looked up in surprise when I suddenly started to giggle. What a strange little man he was. Even as I was going through her cheque stubs for the last few months, hoping in this way to lift the vague feeling of dismay the notary had caused me with his mysterious remarks about her wealth, I kept bursting out laughing. I had to admit the cheque stubs told me nothing. The only thing that struck me as unusual was that she was never overdrawn. Perhaps I noticed this because I was regularly overdrawn myself. 'She just happened to be good with money,' I said to Tiger. 'In fact, she was frugal, and that's why she could afford the occasional splurge.'

Tiger looked at me as though he didn't believe me.

'It's absolutely true, Tiger,' I said. 'She wasn't rich: you know that full well. The Saab was used, and she picked up that gorgeous fur coat second-hand as well, and those expensive clothes…one or two outfits a year at most, so what are we talking about, really? Other women have their nails done at Art Nail for a hundred guilders, but she did her own. No, he's completely out to lunch, that nutty notary.'

13.

'Just over a month ago she was standing right here,' Riet Goudsblom said. 'She was the very picture of good health.'

She sat with her legs dangling down on the long wooden table that stretched along the tall arched windows of the Pharmacological Laboratory. On either side of her sat, slouched or stood several students, the two handymen from the workshop, three lab technicians and the animal caretaker. The secretary and the sole remaining research assistant were a bit farther along the table.

Was it coincidence that I had shown up precisely at the ultimate, most exalted moment of the day – the start of the morning coffee break! – in order, as Bas had requested in a brief note, 'to look through Rose's stuff that was still lying around to see if any of it needed to be saved'?

Even though there's no such thing as coincidence, I was a bit surprised to have unconsciously chosen just that moment to walk in.

'You want a mug of coffee too?' asked the aged coffee lady who had already been there when Wehnagel was still a student.

'Yes please,' I said. 'At least if you have latté the way you used to, because the coffee here is always so horribly strong.'

'Of course I can make latté. John from the workshop always wants a mug of milk with a splash of coffee in it.'

When Thomas still worked here, and I dropped by during the coffee break, it had always amazed me that everyone turned their backs on the outside world almost demonstratively as they sipped their large mugs of piping hot, ridiculously strong coffee. They rarely looked at the elegant quadrangle around which the lab had been built. In the exact centre of the lawn, whose grass was kept almost preternaturally short by the handymen, stood a majestic sundial. The names of the heads of the Department of Pharmacology since its foundation in the early nineteenth century were chiselled into the pedestal in small gold letters. White markers had been placed in the grass around the sundial. Provided it wasn't overcast, you could tell what time it was by looking at the markers in the lawn.

I stood facing the coffee drinkers. I wanted to see that magnificent sundial. It reminded me of the summer Sundays of my childhood. The strange little fellow who conducted the weekly services in the tiny Christian Reformed church where we went twice each Sunday, 'to give thanks unto the name of the Lord' as it says in Psalm 122, had often preached about King Hezekiah. That was, I later realized, his great example. He hardly ever mentioned Jesus; Hezekiah was his Saviour. Invariably he became emotional when he preached about II *Kings* 20, or II *Chronicles* 32, or *Isaiah* 38.

I could recall those sermons almost word for word. 'Dearly beloved, speaking in the Scriptures, the Holy Ghost tells us three times of the wondrous sign that the Lord of Hosts wrought at Hezekiah's sickbed. In II *Chronicles* 32, it is indicated summarily: "In those days Hezekiah was sick to the death, and prayed unto the Lord: and He spake unto him, and He gave him a sign." And what, then, was that wondrous sign about which the book of *Chronicles* so succinctly informs us? What illustrious act of salvation flowed from the hand of our Lord Jehovah of the Covenant? We read about this in II *Kings* 20. Hezekiah is sick unto death. Isaiah comes to him and says: "Thus saith the Lord: behold, I will heal thee: on the third day thou shalt go up unto the house of the Lord." And then, brothers and sisters, Isaiah says: "Take a lump of figs. And they took and laid it on the boil, and he recovered." But before that happens, Hezekiah receives a sign. As a king after God's heart, he gets to choose it himself! Isaiah asks him: "Shall the shadow go forward ten degrees, or go back ten degrees?" Then Hezekiah says: "It is a light thing for the shadow to go forward ten degrees: nay, but let the shadow return backward ten degrees. And Isaiah the prophet cried unto the Lord: and He brought the shadow ten degrees backward, by which it had gone forward in the dial of Ahaz."'

Whereupon it was made clear to us churchgoers that, in order to return the shadow ten degrees backwards, God had interrupted the progress of the entire universe with all its billions of constellations of stars for 'ten degrees' and therefore made time itself run backward. Simply to show just one insignificant human, King Hezekiah: I, the Lord God, hold the entire universe in the palm of my hand, I can play with it the way a toddler plays with grains of sand or drops of water.

I stood there, facing Riet ('one of those ancient, unmarried, bespectacled old maids you'll find on the staff of every lab' as Thomas had often said scornfully), a researcher known to almost everybody as Miss Goudsblom, who since time immemorial had been trying to find a drug that could influence temperature regulation in rats' tails, and I looked at the shining sundial. Evidently one of the handymen had polished it recently. The shadow of the horizontal bar fell across the clock face that lay in the exact centre of the lawn. Behind the sundial, a huge thorn apple bush rose up like a sort of forked screen. Its disagreeable smell entered in waves through the open windows.

'Too bad that thorn apple is there,' I said to Riet, 'because its shadow falls across the dial. In the afternoon you can't quite see what time it is.'

'Yes, child, the Datura has got a bit out of hand.' (She had always called me child.)

'I don't understand,' I said, 'how you people can allow that beautiful lawn and sundial...'

'We didn't mean for it to grow that big,' she said. 'It just got out of hand a bit, it grew faster than a weed, and to be honest, we liked the look of it. It flowered so beautifully.'

'It's still flowering,' I said.

'Yes, but it's no longer what it was,' she said. 'You should have seen it this summer. One huge riot of flowers, and before one o'clock there was no problem, am I right or wrong, Mijna?'

'You're right,' the coffee lady said proudly. 'Out there we have the most beautiful clock there is. One glance out the window, and you know exactly what time it is.'

'But only when the sun shines,' I said.

'Oh, but the sun almost always shines,' Mijna said.

'Here in Holland?' I said in surprise. 'It can be heavily overcast for days on end. When that happens a sundial is no use at all.'

'The sun doesn't often shine all day long,' said Mijna, 'but it does show itself a couple of times a day at least. There's no Saturday so bad that the sun doesn't show itself, my father always used to say. He was right, and it applies not just to Saturday, it applies to every day. You don't need to know what time it is all day long, do you? You only need to know it when the sun is shining.'

I couldn't beat that logic, so I changed the subject and asked Riet: 'Is it an ordinary thorn apple bush?'

'No, child, it's not a *Datura stramonium* but a *Datura fastuosa.*'

'Seed from India,' Bas, who had come sidling up, said proudly
'The unbelievable colour of the flowers...' a lab technician said.

'A shade of purple you almost never see,' said Riet. 'When the first flowers appeared, Rose took one of the petals to Ici Paris and said: I want nail polish in this colour.'

'And? Was she able to get it?' I asked, although as soon as I had asked I realized how that bottle of reddish purple polish with the blue glow had come to be on her dressing table.

'What she was wearing the day after came close,' the secretary said.

'*Ach*, yes, those astonishing nails of Rose's, just thinking of those nails is enough to make me miss her,' said one of the handymen longingly.

'I didn't care for them,' Riet said with disapproval, 'I never did understand how she could weigh and titrate accurately with those claws. If I had nails like that I might as well be without hands.'

'I wouldn't be able to type with them,' the secretary said, 'but they were part of her. No Rose without thorns.'

'Maybe,' said Riet, 'but why thorns like that? When she came to work here she had long nails too, but nothing like the frightening spurs she was sporting the last few times.'

'She bought them in Den Haag,' the research assistant said. 'She said they stayed on better.'

'I always asked myself: Rose, child, who's threatening you, why do you have to arm yourself like that?' Riet said

'You think she felt threatened?' I asked.

'Why else do people arm themselves?'

'I don't think she was arming herself,' the secretary said. 'She did it because she thought it looked beautiful.'

'Beautiful,' said Riet, full of contempt, 'beautiful, no. That wasn't it, that didn't matter to her, in my opinion. When she had just begun working here she often stayed over the lunch hour. Often she was here all alone. Once there was a trespasser. He had designs on our supply closet, wanted to graze on some drugs. She attacked him with her nails. Later she said she had read once how you can put someone out of action by opening the skin above his eyebrows. Then the blood runs into his eyes. When that happens, he can't pay attention to anything else: he's fully occupied with himself. Whether it's true, I don't know, but I tend to think it is.'

'It's true,' said Bas. 'She even made the papers. When the blood ran through his eyebrows into both eyes, that guy was completely out of commission.'

'So take it from me,' said Riet, 'those claws were primarily meant as weapons.'

'Even though they were so curved? Long and pointed is much more effective, isn't it? You only have to use them as razor blades just above the eyebrows…' And with pointed fingers the secretary drew imaginary nails over her own forehead.

'Not at all, claws are more effective. Look at birds of prey, they've got curved claws too,' said the research assistant.

'To seize prey,' said the secretary, 'not to scratch with.'

'The way I see it, you can scratch better with curved nails. You don't need to hold your hands out straight, you can attack someone with your hands curved,' said the research assistant.

Riet bent her fingers as though she was going to play piano, looked at them and said: 'Yes, I do believe you're right.'

'And besides,' the research assistant said, 'those curved nails were stuck on really firmly. "This model stays on by far the best," Rose used to say. After all, you don't want your nails to come off when you attack someone.'

'It is true that at one point she used to complain about her artificial nails coming off, but she had stopped saying that recently,' said the secretary.

'Yeah, but that's because the glue they use now is better. That stuff with cyanoacrylic in it, it works like instant glue,' said the research assistant.

'They're murder on your own nails,' I said.

'Yes,' the research assistant said, 'but if you use those tiny bits of paper or whatever, those Tip Stickers you can buy at Etos, you damage your nails much less.'

'With those Tip Stickers the artificial nails aren't properly attached,' the secretary said.

'That's true, they're just meant for an evening on the town, but if you put a tip sticker on your own nail first and then a drop of glue on the artificial nail, it works really well. Still, it's better to have it done professionally. There's any number of places these days. I used to say to Rose: "Why not go to Art Nail?" but she always said: "They don't have this curved model there."'

'She wanted weapons,' Riet said stubbornly.

'All this nail talk,' Bas said grumpily, 'it's time to get back to work.'

Except for Riet Goudsblom, who demonstratively remained seated to show she had known Bas when he was still a student and therefore didn't need to pay any attention to him, everyone immediately scurried off to their workstations. Bas himself lingered for a moment and said to me: 'You live and learn! Too bad it's no use to me as a male.'

'You shouldn't say that,' I said teasingly. 'Now you know you've got to watch out for women with claws.'

'That I knew already,' he snapped. 'As far as Rose's things are concerned, Riet has taken charge of them, so if you'll go to her office with her you can have a look at them. You'll have to decide. Legally it's all yours now.'

Riet waited until Bas had disappeared, slid off the table and said: 'Let's go too, then.'

I followed her along a chilly corridor and up a creaking stairway. I thought of what Thomas used to say: 'These old maids seem sour and bitter, and they're always a bit tart. They often have moustaches and warts with a few stray hairs on them. And yet they're more helpful than you'd think. You can always make an appeal to them, in fact they're the nicest people around.'

We entered her office, and she closed the door carefully. She pointed to a small table.

'There it is,' she said sadly. 'So that's how it ends.'

As I walked over to the table, I asked: 'You really think she felt under threat, Riet?'

'I certainly do.'

'But from whom?'

'I wouldn't know. There were always hordes of men in pursuit of her. From time to time she would have needed to get rid of some of them who, on closer examination, had turned out badly. As you yourself must have experienced, that is not always gracefully accepted.'

'But that seldom leads to murder.'

'There only has to be one bad apple in the barrel. Really, men, they're pretty strange creatures, you can't be too careful in dealing with them. If we could just store them all away, like sodium hydroxide, and only get them out when we really needed them.'

'*One* bad apple...sure, but would a bastard like that have been able to murder her so cunningly that it seemed like she had sunstroke?'

'How would *you* know?'

'It seems more likely...you people have all kinds of things here that you can...'

'Here? Are you suggesting that one of us...? Where did you get that idea? She had worked here for twenty years, we were devoted to her...ridiculous.'

'Sorry, I was just thinking out loud.'

I bent over the items displayed on the table. I picked up a small handbag. In it were a small mirror, a comb and a lipstick. They made me feel immensely sad, and I put the bag down again. Behind me Riet said: 'She felt threatened, all right.'

'You've said that a couple of times now,' I said.

'I'll tell you this: you know just as well as I do that she was always cheerful, full of energy, very much the optimist.'

'That's why it was such a pleasure to be around her,' I said, tears coming into my eyes.

'You're telling me,' said Riet, 'but hear me out: so she was always cheerful. But here's what happened sometimes: she'd get a phone call. She'd say nothing, just listen then put down the receiver. After that she was unrecognizable. She was like someone who has just heard from the doctor that she has only a year to live. And if she walked past you, over her perfume you smelled a peculiar odour. A cold sweat, I think. There you are. More I can't say.'

'Can these things stay here a while longer?' I asked.

'Of course,' she said. 'It's fine by me; they can serve as a memento.'

'I always thought you didn't have much use for her, like Thomas.'

'You weren't the only one to think that. It's true she was not my type. My mother wasn't my type either. She was frivolous and shallow, she flirted with every man who crossed her path; my father suffered terribly under it, and oh, how I hated my mother just for that alone. But after her death I started thinking differently about her. When she died my hate melted away. That was such a relief. It was similar with Rose, although I didn't hate her the way I hated my mother, rather, I envied her... What do you expect? What I didn't get any of she got twice over. Where favours are unevenly divided there's bound to be envy. Someone like me isn't born to be lucky. I don't know why. That used to bother me more than it does now. Good luck turns so easily into grief. If you're never lucky, you save on sorrow. When you win, losing becomes a threat. If you've never won, you can't lose anything either. Well, I should get back to work.'

On the way out, the heels of my boots echoed under the high, vaulted corridor ceiling. Bas opened his office door.

'Have you got a moment?'

'I do,' I said.

I entered; he closed the door behind me. I walked over to the tall window and gazed at the sundial, the shadow of the Datura bush falling over it.

Bas joined me at the window and cast a sidelong glance at my boots.

'Same size?'

'Yes,' I said.

'You've had your hair cut.'

'Right.'

He inhaled deeply, balled his hands into fists.

'Marjolein saw you in Choorlammersteeg on Sunday evening. You were so much taken up by your companion that you didn't notice her. She said you were decked out like Rose from head to foot. Why are you doing this?'

I didn't answer, shrugged my shoulders.

'You know what Marjolein said when she got home?'

'Nothing very agreeable, I expect.'

'She said: what a grave robber.'

Silence seemed the only suitable response, so I said nothing.

'I can accept that you're using her things, Leonie, but that you're walking around as if you are Rose, we think it's scandalous, Marjolein and I.'

'Rose always said we were like sisters, Rose herself wanted me to put on her clothes, to use her makeup, her...'

'That doesn't give you the right, now that she's dead...you're besmirching her memory, I forbid you to walk around like that.'

'By virtue of what authority?'

'I forbid it.'

'I repeat: by virtue of what authority?'

'We were very close to Rose, Marjolein and I, she often babysat our four little fellows, we were constantly at each other's place. I just don't get it...I, you...she left everything to you. How come?'

'Because of her cats. She wanted her cats to be well looked after, wanted them to be able to stay where they had always lived.'

'As if we didn't... After all, we looked after the cats often enough when she was away on vacation. We just don't understand.'

'You feel you've been short-changed?'

'She could have left us...something...a keepsake.'

'I feel sure I'm speaking on her behalf when I say: come to Grimburchstraat and take whatever you want. She was drowning in clocks. Maybe you'd like one? That big old Friesian wall clock? Will that make you happy, Bas?'

I saw the greed glistening in his eyes.

'I've got to stop by Digros on the way home to get Sheba for the cats. Then I'll go on to Grimburchstraat; I should be there in half an hour. You can send the handymen with the lab van in forty-five minutes. It's a gorgeous clock, a jewel, Rose would love you to have it.'

'You don't have the right to speak in Rose's name,' he said, 'but I…we accept your offer with pleasure.'

'I'll keep an eye out for the van; bye now.'

'Goodbye, and I must say: although I really do appreciate your willingness to give that clock away, I nevertheless forbid you…'

Before he could finish the sentence, I had closed his office door behind me. In the empty corridors I was able to give free rein to my fury, pounding the heels of Rose's boots down on the marble-and-cement composite floor. Four little fellows, they had four little fellows, and Rose had often babysat them, and I…what did I have? Four in-vitro fertilizations, all four of which had succeeded, glory be, thereby raising my hopes, only to be dashed.

14.

More than an hour later, after the handymen had unscrewed the Friesian clock from the wall to which it had been firmly bolted and had carried the heavy thing off, cursing and groaning, I walked around her apartment, still quivering with rage. I could hardly believe how furious I felt. 'Grave robber': the gall of that woman!

At times, though, it passed through my mind that she might have a point; maybe it *is* dismaying to encounter somebody who has decked herself out from top to bottom like a dead friend. All the same: 'I forbid it.' I didn't take that from anybody: that was ridiculous.

When I had regained my composure I settled down at the dressing table and looked through the drawers. Maybe she had some of those Tip Stickers somewhere. If not, then it would have to be rock-solid claws once again, if only to be able to claw out Bas's eyes at our next meeting. Thank God, one of the many drawers turned out to contain Tip Stickers. It figured: was there anything of this kind she did *not* have?

She also had money, but I couldn't touch it. For the time being all her accounts were blocked. The cats' culinary treats I had been paying for out my own pocket. At the notary's instructions I had paid fifteen hundred guilders rent to the Berczy estate on September 1, and over and above that I had paid two hundred and thirty guilders service charges to the Grimburch Estates Owners' Association. I was now so far in the red that I could make no more withdrawals.

I kept thinking about that mysterious safety deposit box. Who could I ask for advice about this well-guarded nest egg? Would my sister-in-law know anything? Normally I saw her once or twice a year. I hadn't told her yet about the amazing changes in my life, I hadn't even sent her a change-of-address card. I phoned her at work, said that I had moved, gave her my new address and phone number then said: 'Your safety deposit box was once emptied in a bank robbery, so you ought to know something about safety deposit boxes. Do people keep the key at home?'

'If things are where they're supposed to be, yes,' she said.

'So you take your key along to the bank. Then what?'

'You have to give proof of identity, your name and the date and time are entered in a register, you have to sign, and then some bank employee goes with you into the safe where the boxes are. He has a key too, because two keys are needed to open the door to the box. The employee uses his key first, and then you open the door with your own key. Then you take out the box with your valuables and sit down at a table, and you put something in or take out whatever you came for.'

'Does the bank employee look over your shoulder?'

'Not normally. He withdraws discreetly and does no more than shepherd you out of the safe after you've returned the box and closed the little door.'

We carried on talking for a while, but my thoughts were elsewhere. I kept thinking: Rose's death must already have been noted in the safety deposit box register. Or their computer will give them that information with one keystroke. The safety deposit box will be inaccessible. But suppose it isn't...just suppose... I can give it a try, can't I? What's the worst that can happen, if they discover I'm not Rose? Will they call for the police? In a pinch I can explain my problem tearfully. Blocked accounts, expensive cat food, high rent, service charges, financial embarrassment. Why not be bold and try it? I needed money very badly. Today.

My curious desire to crawl into her skin was no longer a game now but bitter necessity. While I was touching up my lips with one of her thin Lancôme lipsticks and looked at myself attentively, my mirror image seemed to ask: all well and good, but *where* is the key to the safety deposit box?

'There's one good thing,' I said to Tiger, who was intently observing my activities from the vantage point of Rose's bed, 'I can look for it without being hindered by Curve Oval. Maybe you know where the key is?'

I looked at him questioningly, and he returned my gaze, sat up and began to wash his right front paw. Where do people keep important keys? In drawers, in chests, in handbag compartments, sometimes even in coat pockets. I had already looked in all these places. Where would *I* keep the key of a safety deposit box with money in it? Then suddenly I knew.

I walked over to the fridge, opened the freezer compartment, and after groping around in it for a while with a hand that was very quickly getting very cold, I found the key under some frozen fish for the cats.

After that my nails – like Nebuchadnezzar's as related in *Daniel* 4, verse 33 – grew 'like birds' claws.' It took me an enormously long time, but I realized only when I was finished that I had worked as slowly and patiently as I did because I had wanted to postpone, for as long as I possibly could, the moment when I would have to set out for the bank. Thanks to my fear-induced patience the nails looked noticeably better than they had the first time. Perhaps some day I would get used to them. As a means of gradually adopting someone else's identity they were definitely a godsend.

On the way to the bank I lost my nerve. I was so nervous! My hands were shaking as I handed her passport to the attendant. Back home I had spent a good deal of time practising her signature. I could fake it almost perfectly, but what I made of it when I had to sign the bank's register looked like nothing on earth. Thank God the bank employee came to my assistance without knowing it, being fascinated by my Nebuchadnezzar nails. 'Nice to see you again,' he said, 'gorgeous colour nail polish, almost even more beautiful than that crimson last time.'

'You still remember that,' I said. 'As I recall, that's quite a long time ago.'

'At least six months, if not longer. As far as I'm concerned, you're welcome every day, oh, if only I could get my wife to...'

He sighed heartrendingly, walked ahead of me, used his key and did not, as I was using mine to open the door to the box, miss a single movement of my fingertips. Men, I thought, strange creatures indeed, but sometimes that is really useful. If it had been noted down somewhere or registered in a computer that the safety deposit box was inaccessible because of its owner's death, he had overlooked it, merely because the sight of ten small pieces of plastic had caused him to lose his cool.

And then I lost my own cool, because I found ten envelopes in the box, each filled with a big wad of banknotes. First I put just one envelope in my bag then I thought: here I've got the opportunity to take the lot, perhaps I'll never have that opportunity again, so I took every envelope, meanwhile praising God that He had sent me to the bank carrying a large shopping bag.

Like so many other activities, counting the money after I got back home turned out to be a difficult task with Curve Oval. And of course I didn't really need to do it at all. Why was I so keen to know exactly how much cash I had brought home with me? I kept on counting, although it was clear to me after the first envelope – which contained five thousand guilders – that the total would come to fifty thousand guilders.

Fifty thousand guilders! What on earth would I do with it all? It was just over fifteen months until the introduction of the euro, sixteen months, rather less than five hundred days, before the guilder disappeared from use. I would have to spend over a hundred a day! For Heaven's sake, what on? Sheba didn't cost *that* much.

Meanwhile, I was faced with the problem of where to tuck away fifty grand safely, as well as the question of how Rose had got hold of so much money. My temporary solution to the first problem made the second even more pressing. When I took one book after another from the shelves to put two bills in each, it turned out that many, especially the larger reference works, already sheltered bank notes between their pages. I actually shook a fortune loose from the Bible I had once given her on learning that she didn't own one. This made me catch my breath: the Word of the Lord used as a safe! Well, I could have spared my nerves the ordeal of the safety deposit box. Nevertheless, it gave me enormous satisfaction that I had dared to face it. Oh well, the operation had succeeded only because of a bank employee's nail fetish.

After I had hidden the money in her books I took a paperback off her shelves: *Les Thibault*, by Roger Martin du Gard. I had money, lots of money, now I could do what I had always wanted: translate that masterpiece into Dutch. The question remained whether I would be able to find a publisher for the completed work, but what did that matter? There simply had to be a Dutch version of this book, one of the most beautiful novels in French literature. Constant van Wessum had once done an outstanding job of translating Parts One and Two; Part Seven had been ably translated by Bernard Bekman and published in the Pantheon Series of Nobel Prize-winners for Literature. So I needed to translate only Parts Three through Six and Part Eight. I dug up an exercise book out of a still-unpacked box of my own possessions, opened Part Three of *Les Thibault*, picked up a pen and contemplated the first sentence of the many thousands I planned to translate: '*Les deux frères longeaient la grille du Luxembourg.*' I wrote: 'The two brothers ran along the iron fence of the Luxembourg Gardens,' and as I wrote, the entire book and the summer vacation in which I had read it came back to me. That had been perhaps the best summer of my life, the summer of *Les Thibault*, the summer when I still thought I would some day bear a child.

After nine that evening, as I continued translating while racking my brains over where all that money could have come from, I became ever more afraid. I became aware of my fear very gradually. First I thought I heard someone mumbling in the kitchen. After the stab of fright had ebbed away I thought: it's the fridge humming. When I got up and went to the kitchen to verify that hypothesis an elongated, grey little thing flashed along the counter from range to sink with the speed of a Formula One racing car. Probably a silverfish or some similar insect. No big deal, nothing to be scared of. But I'm really turned off by ultra-fast little creatures like that. It's as if they can go in all directions at once. They seem to consist of segments connected to each other with supple hinges. Where their heads should be they have two long antennas. That would be fine, except that they wave them around like spider legs.

'Get lost,' I yelled at the insect. At once Ober and Tiger came running up. They jumped on the counter and hissed mightily. Ober actually tapped the silverfish with his paw, making it scurry around even more wildly.

To be honest, I miss Thomas less than I had once thought possible, but on that September evening I would gladly have taken him out of storage. He would have said reassuringly: 'Silverfish are arthropods and really quite harmless.' He would have put me at my ease with exaggeratedly scary stories. He would have told me about one kind that secreted hydrocyanic acid and about a zoologist who had collected a number of specimens in a plastic bag. When he opened it, he inhaled some molecules of hydrocyanic acid. 'What an original way to die; too bad the person who died couldn't appreciate the originality of it,' Thomas would have said then would have added reassuringly: 'You don't find these scary kinds in the Netherlands.' Once he had told me over breakfast: 'There's a species of millipede in which the males shed their skins in reverse, as it were. Organisms shed their skins as they become older, but with this species it's the other way around. As the males shed their skins they become younger. And they shed their skins only after they mate. As they mate they return to their childhood.'

Back to my childhood: I wouldn't mind that:

To have only a child's book for reading
And only a child's thoughts to nurse,
To let all grown up things disperse,
To rise out of deep grieving.

Using a front paw, Ober deftly knocked the silverfish off the counter. But that didn't exorcise my fear. I turned the TV on. Commercials on every channel. Happy families with exemplary children everywhere. Shovelling food back happily. Chatting in the kitchen. Rocketing along in a roller-coaster car. I turned the TV off, said in her voice: 'Ober, I'm off to bed.'

Once I was in bed Ober stretched himself discreetly behind the pillow. He was purring so loudly you'd think he was rewarded with a bowl of Sheba for each decibel. At the beginning I had chased him away, but when I woke up he was always there anyway. So now I let him stay. It was pleasant going to sleep to the accompaniment of that peaceful purring.

Just after two I awoke with a start. The alarm clock's fiery numbers said 2:01. K 201, the most beautiful symphony ever composed by a youth of eighteen, was my first thought. Then I lay there, my heart pounding, listening to the curious scratching noise that had apparently woken me up. It took me a while to realize what was making it. Somebody was trying to open the front door with a key. Over and again the key scratched around the lock.

'Surely by now the intruder must have noticed that the lock has been changed?' I whispered to Ober.

I threw the duvet off, got out of bed and crept to the front door. Their tails swaying, the three cats crept along with me.

I peered through the peephole. There was a little more light on the other side of the door than there was on mine. I saw practically nothing. I remained there, stock-still. The key kept on scratching. How odd! Didn't this person realize that the key didn't fit any longer?

Slowly my eyes accustomed themselves to the gloom. Now I could discern something. The intruder was amazingly slender. I saw long hair. A woman, I thought in astonishment, it's a woman. What a relief. And I slipped back into bed.

Funny that I didn't realize who was standing out there. It occurred to me only after I woke up early in the morning that it must have been the alabaster-skinned girl I had met at the funeral service. Then I regretted not having opened the door. Her I might have let in, even at 2:01 a.m.

So she too had belonged to the circle of Rose's intimate associates, she too, like that oddball Bas, had enjoyed the use of a key.

15.

Even though I was still cursing him, I decided to phone Bas.

'Do you have any idea who that slender girl was, the one who expressed her condolences to us right at the end?'

'I don't recall any slender girl,' he said.

'She looked fragile and had a narrow white face. Long red hair. Little freckles.'

'Are you sure she shook my hand?'

'I don't recall. In any case she shook mine.'

'Why are you interested in her?'

'She was at the door at two a.m. last night. Tried to get inside with a key.'

'Last night? Where?'

'Rose's apartment.'

'So you've moved in? Are you sleeping there now?'

'I've been for a couple of weeks.'

He said nothing; I heard him breathing heavily.

'She couldn't get in; I had the lock changed.'

Now he knew that too. Could throw his key away on the spot.

'So you've got no idea who that girl could have been?' I asked.

'No.'

'Apparently you didn't know Rose all *that* well,' I sneered.

Immediately he gave as good as he got.

'You're not very bright, are you? If you want to know who that girl was, you only need to look in the condolence register. The funeral director gave it to you.'

From the tone of his voice it was clear that this was yet another source of grievance for him.

'You're quite right,' I said in a conciliatory tone, 'stupid of me not to have thought of that. As long as she did sign it.'

'Why wouldn't she have signed it?'

'She seemed to be rather confused.'

'Confused? Then she is not the only one. Perhaps I expressed myself too bluntly yesterday, but don't you yourself think this is going too far?'

'What's going too far?' I asked, feigning surprise, although I knew very well what he was driving at.

'That you're walking around pretending to be Rose. I worry about you. Yesterday I phoned an old college friend. He's a psychiatrist now. He said he recognized the symptoms. It seems to be not uncommon. Wouldn't it be a good idea to go talk to my friend? I don't have his phone number here, but he's in the directory, Patrick Hoppenzak, you can't miss him, he's the only one in the book.'

'Thanks for the suggestion,' I said. 'I'll see you around.'

I had put the condolence register on a bookshelf beside her photo albums. Now I took it off the shelf and walked over to the big living-room window. As I was leafing through it, I looked up for a moment and saw Piet Mastenbroek below. He was holding onto the bars of the fence on the other side of the street. I put the register in my bag and picked up the cassettes I should have sent back long ago. Why was I always so slack in these matters?

When I left the building he had just let go of the fence. Quickly I crossed the street.

'Here are your tapes back,' I said, 'with my grateful thanks; unfortunately I've got to run.'

'Too bad,' he said. 'And? See anything else unusual?'

'No,' I said, 'she just lies there sunbathing, always by herself. But there are only a few minutes of tape each time, and she spent whole afternoons lying there. Ever see a red-haired girl?'

'Quite pale? Yeah, she dropped by once in a while, but she never lay down.'

'Makes sense, she'd have been sunburned.'

'That doesn't have to happen, with a good sun-block…'

'Did the girl maybe come by that last afternoon?'

'I don't remember, but she could have.'

'I must be going,' I said.

'We'll keep in touch,' he said.

As I started to walk off slowly, and he followed me for a few steps, I said, half over my shoulder: 'Strange, that hobby of yours.'

'You think so? Nothing more restful than playing those tapes in wintertime. Sea, summer, a beautiful woman sunbathing. Really calms me down. It's so peaceful to look at. Definitely a change from what you see on TV – all that misery. I pick up what others ignore.'

'There's something in that,' I said, thinking that delusions can seem completely logical.

'Can I drop you off somewhere?' he asked.

'No, thanks, that won't be necessary, I have to go to the laboratory. It's pretty well impossible to reach by car.'

'The laboratory? Where she worked?'

I picked up the pace, heard my high heels clicking on the sidewalk. If only he didn't follow me.

As I walked along, I took the condolence register from my bag and leafed through it. There it was, on the last page: Fiona Sterkenburg, Houseboat *Poseidon*, Zevenhuizen.

'That's got to be her,' I said to myself in a low voice. Once upon a time people would look at you strangely if you talked to yourself in public. Now they think you're on your mobile. Who says there's no such thing as progress?

Pity there was no address. No matter: it should be possible to locate a houseboat in the village of Zevenhuizen. I walked to the railway station, looking apprehensively over my shoulder now and then to see if Mastenbroek was following me. At the taxi stand I got into the Mercedes at the head of the line. I had to spend well over a hundred guilders a day, so I could afford a taxi. Besides, a *grande dame* like me wouldn't go by bicycle.

'To Zevenhuizen,' I said.

'Where exactly?' said the driver.

'I'm not sure,' I said. 'Houseboat *Poseidon*.'

'Could be moored anywhere, tricky business finding it; could also be on the other side of the lake. No address?'

'No, Houseboat *Poseidon*, that's all I've got.'

'Creeks and ditches and inlets all over the place where it might be moored. Or behind some damned dike. Impossible to find if you haven't got an address.'

'So you'd rather not take me there?'

'Lady, you didn't hear me say that. We could drive to Zevenhuizen postal station. Maybe they'll know over there.'

For a while we crawled through the city, but we moved faster once we were in the polders, huge clouds sailing silently eastward above them.

When we had driven through most of Zevenhuizen before realizing that we were actually there we saw a postman walking behind a little pushcart with mailbags. The driver stopped and opened his window. 'Excuse me, do you know where the *Poseidon* is moored?'

'The other side of the lake,' said the postman. 'Ask for directions over there.'

We drove on, along narrow polder roads with occasional parking places you could go into if opposing traffic appeared. But nothing did appear, and a little while later we drove into the village on the other side of the lake. We stopped at the postal station. The driver left the engine running as he dashed inside, returning almost at once. 'They didn't know; said I should ask a postman.' So we drove slowly through the village looking for another lonesome letter carrier.

'Nice place,' the driver said. 'Everybody who can pay the freight seems to be settling down here. But where are the postmen? About the only thing you see around here is expensive women walking their dogs.'

He was right. Only after we had passed numerous bouviers, terriers, and rottweilers with their owners attached did we see another postman pushing his cart.

'The *Poseidon*? Behind Krans Woods near the Heemskerk Brothers' place. Go back the way you came, to the end of the lane, past the ruins, past the Catholic churchyard, then past Krans Woods. When you see a bus stop, go right. Path into the meadow. At the end you'll see a farm. Not the Heemskerk farm, but you can't reach *it* by car. Look for someone who can point you in the right direction, and then the Heemskerks will be able to tell you where the *Poseidon*'s moored. You can't reach it by land, you'll need a boat.'

We followed his instructions and drove into a farmyard. The driver honked his horn, a farmer's wife appeared, chased some cackling chickens away and shouted in response to his question: 'Heemskerk? Yeah, over that way a piece, go down the path, then ask again.'

I paid, got out and walked along a glistening stretch of water. Woundwort was still in bloom right next to the path, ragged robin could be seen everywhere, and in the water I saw bur reed and the pointed leaves of arrowhead. I walked and forgot why I was there. A breeze murmured through the leaves of the pollard willows. I inhaled the summer scents deep into my lungs. It smelled the way it used to at my grandmother's.

'Grandmother': the word that expressed what I would never be; I buried Curve Oval in the palms of my hands and said in Rose's voice: 'Whoever gives birth these days is irresponsible.' I kept softly repeating it until I reached a farmyard. Two men were loading a delivery van, saw me and acted as if I had frightened them witless. How will that van ever get out of here? I asked myself and then asked them: 'Is this the Heemskerk farm?'

'No, it's just beyond here, across the yard, around the back and then along the narrow lane.'

Quickly I got moving again. Whatever illegal things were happening there in the yard with that mysterious van, I wanted no part of them. I walked along another glistening bit of water. There were dirty-brown stinging nettles on the shore. Evidently someone had used herbicide with a very free hand.

At the end of the lane I came to a sort of settlement where greenhouses and sheds and houses had been built cheek by jowl in a disorderly fashion. In the middle of a grassy quad a dwarf sat in a motorized wheelchair.

'Do the Heemskerk Brothers live here?'

'No, that's a bit farther on.'

Would that be the answer every time? I kept on walking and reached a path at the top of a dike, with stagnant smelly ditches on either side. Then I met up with an enormous, canary-yellow tractor on which someone had written the name Heemskerk in huge letters. After that I passed a strange-looking iron dinosaur with tubes and rods and blades whose cabin carried the same name. Somewhat farther along I saw a fire engine-red crane on which the name appeared twice.

And after that – nothing. No farm, no lane, no ditches, a few alders and ash. As I ventured on I thought I saw a path. When I followed it I found myself zigzagging between the trees. Anyway, behind them – how about that? – lay a farm with stables and barns and haystacks.

I heard a church bell ring. Half past twelve. Maybe the Heemskerks were having lunch. Seeing me, a red tomcat ran away. 'Please stay,' I shouted. 'Next time I'll bring you some Sheba.' Other cats appeared and also sped off hastily, all of them running towards a Dutch door. They jumped up to the top of the closed lower half and gained safety by way of the open upper half. I walked over to the door and looked inside. With a loud clanking of chains some forty cows turned their heads languidly in my direction.

'Visitor,' I shouted, and when that didn't produce a response: 'Hello!'

I walked up to another door, moved the latch. It opened. Behind it was a barn-like space with a wood floor. Again I shouted: 'Hello!'

There was no response. A kettle began to hiss and then whistle, softly at first, then much louder. 'Now someone's bound to show up,' I muttered, but no one seemed to pay any attention to the shrill shrieking of the kettle.

Soon the kettle would boil dry. I walked boldly over to the stove and turned the heat to low. I returned to the door, waited patiently, called out once more. The kettle moaned a kind of nasal one-note tune.

I walked around the house; saw no one in the rooms. Perhaps they were busy in one of the barns. I walked back, cautiously opened a shutter, and once again heard the heavy clanking of chains. Forty cows, all of them still staring at the spot where my upper body had appeared a couple of minutes earlier, again turned their heads slowly and disapprovingly in my direction. They looked as though they mistrusted me. Huge, black-tarred beams seemed to be floating high above their heads. The beams were obviously attached somewhere, but I could not make out exactly where.

'Is absolutely no one home?' I asked the cows despairingly. By way of an answer they all began to sway their heads, whereby the clanking and rattling gained symphonic proportions. I went back to where the kettle was. In the short time that I had been gone, the decor had changed. The upper door to the barn had been closed, the kettle had been taken off the stove, and through an open door I saw three curly-haired men wearing orange overalls sitting around a table. I walked to the door, knocked on it and asked: 'The Heemskerk Brothers?'

The three men grinned as they turned to look at me but didn't answer.

'May I ask a question? Is the *Poseidon* moored somewhere around here?'

'It certainly is.'

'But where, in that case?'

'You want to go there? It's a pain. You'd like a boat? You want to borrow ours? Henk will go with you, right, Henk?'

There was a growling sound, like a pig trying to say yes.

'What do you want to do there, lady?'

'To speak with Fiona Sterkenburg.'

'Nobody's going to be there right now. This morning everything was closed up tight. Mostly they're only there on the weekend. During the week you hardly ever see them. In the evening sometimes. But they always come from the other side, so from here it's kind of hard to keep track.'

'Should I have come from the other side too?'

'Makes no difference. From this side you can't use a motor boat, rowing's the only way, and maybe they don't care for that.'

'Come off it!' said another Heemskerk. 'It's not because of the rowing that they... No, they've always got stuff with them, a rowboat's much too small for that. They carry stuff there, and they take it away.'

A seventy-ish woman entered, put an enormous pot on the table, wiped her right hand on her apron and extended it to me.

'Clara Heemskerk,' she said.

'Rose Berczy,' I said, and that gave me real start. For a moment I debated whether to say: 'Sorry, I mean Leonie Kuyper,' but that would have seemed weird. And what did it matter, after all, that I had appropriated her name. Names are so soon forgotten.

'We were just going to start in on beestings, first milk,' said Clara Heemskerk. 'On the whole, it's not the right time of year for first milk, but Geurtje's mixed up, she calved the day before yesterday, so we've got ourselves a bucketful. Koos, clear a chair.'

Koos simply brushed a small pile of newspapers off a chair.

'There you are,' he said. 'Come and sit down.'

'Yes, but...' I said.

'No buts,' Clara said assertively. 'You're not going to tell me that you get first milk put in front of you wherever you go. Even in the top restaurants they don't serve it.'

I walked over to the empty chair and sat down.

Clara filled four enormous plates, took another one the same size out of a wall cupboard, put it in front of me, and filled that as well.

'Enjoy,' said Henk.

'Likewise,' said Koos.

'Ditto,' said the Heemskerk whose first name I didn't know yet.

'Sugar?' Clara asked me. 'You want sugar in it?'

'First I'll try it without,' I said. I had tasted first milk once, but that was so long ago I couldn't remember what it was like. Cautiously I took a spoonful of the smooth, dark-yellow, creamy substance. The taste was not like that of milk, nor of any other kind of food a person might eat. As I was tasting it, Koos and Henk and Heemskerk Number Three were watching me closely. Clara wasn't watching; she kept on eating steadily.

'It'll give you a bad case of the runs,' said Heemskerk Number Three.

'Klaas!' Clara said reprovingly.

'Just kidding, Ma,' said Heemskerk Number Three, whose name was evidently Klaas.

'And? How is it?' asked Koos.

'It's unbelievably good,' I said.

The three brothers solemnly put their spoons down on the table, picked them up again and drummed on the table top with the handles.

'You heard it,' Clara said tartly. 'You've passed the entrance exam.'

After we had eaten it all, Klaas said: 'So you'd like to be rowed to the *Poseidon* now?'

'If it's possible. I'd like to check whether Fiona might be there.'

'You never know, if she's not there, maybe there's someone else who knows where she is.'

'I'll come along,' said Henk.

'Let me do it,' said Koos.

'If there's no one else who's willing, I'll sacrifice myself,' said Klaas, and he got up, pulled me unceremoniously out of my chair and went outside. I followed him. Beside an overgrown flagstone path, a narrow path worn into the grass led to the shore. Klaas jumped into a rowboat, held out his hand, more or less pulled me on board, untied a rope and used an oar to push the little boat away from shore. When we were in the middle of the creek, he grabbed both oars and began rowing at a remarkably good clip.

'Once upon a time I used to set traps here in the evening,' said Klaas. 'In the morning you'd pull out eels as thick as your arm. They would hiss at you when you grabbed them behind the head, it was enough to scare you. There would be tench as well, big guys they were, and carp, also a tasty fish. But the best thing was eel. If you had one of those whoppers, you'd put it in a bucket of clean water. Then it would spit out everything, the next day the water would be murky. You'd put it in clean water again, and keep on doing it until the water stayed crystal clear. Then all the crud was gone and you could eat it. That could take up to two weeks sometimes.'

'Is there no eel anymore?'

'No, there's nothing left, just silversides as big as a safety pin.'

We reached the lake. Klaas continued rowing quickly.

'There she is,' he said, using an oar to point at an enormous houseboat partly sheltered by tall trees.

'It doesn't look like it's moored by the shore,' I said. 'Can't you reach it overland?'

'Then you've got to go through Krans Wood first. That's okay, but then you end up in a terrible bog. Maybe you could get it through wearing hip boots, but I doubt it.'

As we floated by the *Poseidon*, Klaas said: 'You see, it's dead quiet, there's nobody there, everything's closed up tight. If there was anyone on board right now you'd be able to see light through some crack or other.'

'Are those shutters ever open?'

'No, never, you can't see what's going on inside. If there's anyone there you can see light through the cracks in the shutters.'

'So nobody lives there? Then what do they do there? Could it be a brothel or something like that?'

'No, the cathouse is farther along, you can reach it easy by land, after all, it would be a real pain to have to get the johns over to it by water. If it's busy in the cathouse you can see it swing and sway, even if the water's dead calm.'

I burst out laughing. Klaas grinned, greatly pleased. Men are such simple creatures. Nothing strokes their egos so much as a woman laughing at their jokes. You can get any man to fall in love with you by laughing heartily at his attempts at humour.

'Do you have any idea what's going on in there?' I asked.

'I think they're manufacturing something. They bring stuff there, they take stuff away. More I can't say. They're always very nice, they're okay guys, and the girl is often there, and...'

'And what?'

'What should I say? I've only actually seen them when it's dark. But once they had a woman with them of your age, with...with...fingernails...'

'Just like mine?'

'How did you guess? When I first saw you, I even thought for a moment that you...but that's impossible.'

'But were you so close you could see her hands?'

'How far off was I? Fifty metres?'

'But in the dark you can't see hands at *that* distance, can you?'

'Normally speaking no, but she'd painted her nails. They were a luminous orange, just like our overalls. I'm pretty sure they were fluorescent, it was just like ten tiny little lanterns were hovering over the water.'

16.

The rain clattered so angrily against the big living-room window that it startled Tiger. He jumped off the windowsill and gave me a frightened look. 'Yes, Tiger,' I said, 'it's October once again, it's the season for reciting that wonderful Rilke poem: "Lord, it is time. The summer was very long. Lay your shadows on the sundials..."' At this point the telephone's chirping rudely interrupted me.

'Leonie Kuyper speaking.'

'This is Van Stenis. May I speak to the sister of Rose Berczy?'

'She always referred to me as her sister, but I'm not related to her.'

'Oh, Fred said you're a sister of the deceased.'

'That's because she always talked to Fred about her sister, and in saying that she meant me, but...'

'That's how misunderstandings start. Anyway, it doesn't matter. Fred has asked me to investigate Mrs Berczy's death. I spoke to the man who did the autopsy, and I've visited the lab. As far as I'm concerned, that does it. There's nothing to be gained from pursuing this. I've put out my feelers, and I'm drawing them in again.'

'So you think that...'

'Mrs Kuyper, if anything happened over there, which I doubt, it's impossible to prove it now. But there's nothing to suggest that anything did happen. Things are screwy there in that lab.'

'Things are screwy?' I asked in surprise.

'You don't know what I'm driving at? Then I'll put it another way: it's a shoddy business there in that lab. I mean, they've got the people and the know-how to make all kinds of pills, and what are they doing? They're doing stupid research you couldn't earn a crust of bread from.'

'They certainly *do* make pills there.'

'Pills,' he said, 'but not *pills*.'

He gave the same word two very different emphases. When I didn't reply he said: 'I mean, they could, without any difficulty, make Ecstasy and speed and crack and who knows what else over there, they've got everything they need on the premises, they've even got vaults…have you ever been in the cellars?'

'Yes, when my husband still worked there.'

'Then I need say no more. Those are some dungeons! Even Fred doesn't build them like that! If that lab was a sex-club, a dominatrix could earn her weight in gold working in those catacombs. All she'd need to do is take her customer down into them and he'd get off.'

'Sounds like you've gone down there yourself,' I said.

'Game and set to you,' Van Stenis said appreciatively. 'Yes, I've been down there, and what did I see? Vaulted catacombs. I don't get it, not at all. They could make Ecstasy there, no questions asked. They've got everything they need right there on the premises. Upstairs they could piss around with stupid blood-pressure pills, and downstairs…'

'They're decent people,' I said.

'Exactly, where can you still find people like that nowadays? You're right, and because you *are* right, I'm telling you: nothing happened there. If they were making Ecstasy and speed and crack down below, you can bet your life someone upstairs would sooner or later snuff it under suspicious circumstances, because the easier the money rolls in, the more readily people kill each other, but as things stand…I was unable to discover anything unusual. Fred keeps saying: "They put something in her coffee, a smart pill that worked slow." If that's true, it must have been one hell of a smart pill. No, the coffee…according to the coffee lady, she had exactly *one* mug of coffee before she left. At twelve-thirty. She left the lab right after, the old woman says. And that's confirmed by a couple of other people who were in the lunchroom too…'

'They don't have a lunchroom there.'

'You're quite right, didn't I say the outfit was primitive? They don't even have a proper lunchroom, the coffeemaker is in a grubby workspace with tables along the windows; you can hear the woodworm gnawing away in them.'

'It's a laboratory.'

'I'll take your word for it. The way I see it, it's nineteenth-century. Time has stood still there. You can take it from me: where time stands still, people don't commit murder.'

'If that were only true.'

'*Ach*, Mrs Kuyper, what do *you* know about it? Drugs, everything nowadays turns around drugs, except – strangely enough – in a dark old cave where they've got everything they need to manufacture the most expensive stuff. That's the only mystery I've come across.'

'So you think it was sunstroke?'

'You can take my word for it. I'm going to have to tell Fred: "Old buddy, this is a dead end." I've got just one little problem left, and that's why I'm calling you. Fred said I could send the bill to you. Is that right?'

'That's right,' I said.

'I'll send you a postal bank transfer slip.'

'I'd rather pay cash.'

'Under the table? Oh, that's fine, in fact I prefer it. I won't have to put it in the books. Would it suit you if I drove by shortly? I've got to be in the neighbourhood anyway for another little job.'

'I'll be home all morning.'

'I'll be there in a moment; it's three thousand guilders.'

If you've been raised to be frugal you stay that way, even when you need to spend over a hundred guilders a day. So it pained me to have to pay three thousand all at once to the impeccably dressed fellow who was on my doorstep ten minutes later. Even though I hadn't asked him to, he had been licking his chops while looking at vaulted cellars. Did I have to pay for that?

But when he asked: 'Is that right?' I hadn't protested because, as he was talking about vaulted catacombs and the possibility of manufacturing Ecstasy in them without being detected, he had apparently solved the riddle of the houseboat for me. Had a small laboratory been installed in the *Poseidon* so that Ecstasy and other stuff like that could be produced there? Had Rose been mixed up in it? How else to explain her riches, including fifty thousand guilders in a safety deposit box plus a fair bit of pocket money hidden in various reference books. Fur coats, a black Saab, an expensive mortgage-free apartment. And a wardrobe fit for a queen, with almost as many pairs of shoes as Imelda Marcos.

One of Van Stenis's remarks stuck in my mind: 'The easier the money rolls in, the more readily people kill each other.'

If Rose had earned breathtaking amounts of money by moonlighting in a floating lab, I was suddenly faced with a huge problem. It meant that her money was contaminated, tainted; in that case I would just as soon not have any of it. But then what about her darlings, her pussycats? Should I go back to my dismal rented apartment near Burggravenlaan, taking the cats with me? Hopefully they would stoop to eating Whiskas, because Sheba would be well beyond my means.

It was hard to contemplate leaving this wonderful apartment, parting from that fantastic wardrobe, not doing that translation and, what was probably worst, renouncing what had proved to be something of a fulfilment of my life: to eradicate myself and become Rose's sister.

Did I have to go to Graafland and say: 'Rose made Ecstasy pills in a houseboat, so all her property is tainted. I'm terribly sorry, but I don't want to have anything to do with it; I renounce it all.'? Was I even allowed to do that? I had signed all kinds of documents. Oh my God, what a ghastly mess.

I went over to Rose's sound system: magnificent, like everything else she owned. I put on some of my own music, because I had never met anyone else who knew this piece: Schubert's *Cantata in Honour of Joseph Spendou*. I particularly love the final chorus, so profound, so heartrending, so endearingly beautiful. After the cantata I put on another unknown little marvel by Schubert: the slow introduction to the first part of the Symphony in E major. Schubert never completed this symphony, others finished the job, but the introduction was his, including the stunning instrumentation. As the music sounded from Rose's KEF speakers, subdued and heartbreaking, I hummed along, trying to escape from the dreadful moral dilemma that had come to confront me; but the stream of my thoughts churned on indefatigably.

Van Stenis had told me nothing new: I had already suspected as much. They carried stuff there, they took stuff away, and everything happened at night, in the dark. Yes, I had already realized it, but I hadn't wanted to face it squarely; all that time I had repressed what I knew.

Maybe it hadn't been Rose on the lake that evening. 'Ten little lanterns hovering over the water.' It seemed to be amazingly easy to spot people who walked around with insanely long nails like that. Or could it have been another woman's artificial nails that had glimmered out there on the lake? Yes, that must be it. Stores couldn't keep Curve Oval in stock; practically every woman wore them.

'Oh, Rose, say it isn't so,' I moaned, while Schubert shifted from his amazing opening measures to a cheerful little tune. I went over to the CD player and shifted to the unsurpassed slow movement of the Seventh Symphony, D729.

Next I looked through her dazzling collection of nail polish for fluorescent orange-red, just as I had done after getting home from my boat trip with

Klaas Heemskerk. Of all the things to wear when you were going to make Ecstasy pills: nails that could be seen fifty metres away in the dark! That was Rose for you: she simply didn't give a damn. All you need is nerve.

Just as on that evening after my houseboat mission, I couldn't find what I was looking for. 'So it can't have been her,' I said to Tiger, who scarcely left my side these days. Wherever I was, there was Tiger with his *prunelles pâles* – his pale pupils. And Tiger looked at me with understanding. He seemed to be saying: the little bottle was empty, it went into recycling long ago.

Because I simply *had* to know whether Rose's fingers had been attached to those ten little lanterns, I walked to the shop where she had always bought her makeup. It was still raining. I was under her umbrella, since I had left mine, like almost everything else, in my old apartment. What would I do when I could no longer evade the conclusion that I must part with her property?

At Ici Paris, a sluttish-looking girl regarded me with pity when I asked whether they sold fluorescent orange-red nail polish. 'Another one of those old hags who wants to go discoing,' her chilly eyes said. While she was informing me that they didn't sell so vulgar a shade and that I would do better to try Etos, a saleswoman my age came up, looking intently at me.

'This lady asked about fluorescent orange-red nail polish,' said the slut.

The woman said: 'I seem to recall you asking for it before.' She stared at me, then asked: 'Have you had a facelift?'

'No,' I said.

'Oh,' she said. 'In that case I don't know. You definitely don't look like you did the last time you were here.'

'But not younger, surely,' I said.

'No,' she said, 'but you wouldn't be the first for whom a facelift didn't work out.'

I fled to Etos, where it turned out they didn't sell that shade of nail polish either. 'For a while we carried green fluorescent witch's nails,' the girl said, 'but they hardly moved at all, so we dropped them from our stock. You could try the disco shop.'

In fact my mission had already ended, now that I knew Rose had unsuccessfully looked for fluorescent orange-red nail polish at Ici Paris. In all probability she had kept on looking and had eventually found it. 'Ten little lanterns hovering over the water.' Who besides Rose could it possibly have been?

When I got to the disco shop I hesitated. Did I have to go in? Posters of bats were hanging in the display window. Fortunately I'm not as afraid of them as

I am of spiders. For all I know bats may even be nice, and it's silly to associate them with vampires. Granted, there are species of bats that live entirely off blood, but they don't live in the Netherlands, thank God.

The shop door stood invitingly open. Inside it seemed to be not only pitch black but it was also extremely noisy. The crashing of heavy metal or something equally awful boomed from menacing black speakers. I steeled myself, broke through the sound barrier and stepped inside. At first I could see almost nothing, but after a while I spotted a creepy-looking person, clothed in black latex, sporting a large Afro and wearing rings in its ears, eyebrows and septum. I couldn't figure out whether it was male or female, and that made me unsure of myself.

'Would you have fluorescent nail polish?'

'Yes,' said the apparition, 'red or green?'

'Red,' I said.

Without looking, the apparition reached behind itself and put a small container of poison-green polish on the counter. In the darkness it seemed very bright.

'This is green,' I said.

'That's quite possible,' said the apparition, 'I'm colour-blind.'

Another backwards reach. Another little bottle of poison-green.

'Missed again,' I said.

'Then the red is probably sold out.'

Jewellery tinkled as the apparition got up, turned around, made another grab and asked: 'Is this red?'

'This is red,' I said.

'Fifteen guilders.'

I couldn't bring myself to say that I didn't really want it, had only wanted to know whether it existed. I parted with fifteen guilders. The apparition pressed the bottle, which it had neither wrapped nor put in a bag, into my hands, and I left the shop. Even outside in daylight, the colour resembled that of a very bright traffic light. 'Rose,' I muttered, 'Rose, Rose, Rose.'

Once I was back home I first removed all her rings from my fingers. Then I carefully pulled off one fake nail after another. Thanks to the Tip Stickers they did come off; they were not stuck on as tight as the first time. Nevertheless I uttered so many cries of pain that all three cats came to watch me, their tails waving. I took off the earrings and her beautiful sweater, got out of the corset, put her sweater back on. I didn't have much choice, for I had deposited pretty well all my own clothes in a Salvation Army bin. I took off her boots and put on an old pair of mine. Fearful of blisters, I had not yet thrown out my own footwear, thank God. She had the same size but always wore much higher heels.

I wiped the makeup off my face and contemplated my own ageing features. Even with her makeup, I evidently had the appearance of someone whose facelift had gone wrong. If I wanted to keep on looking like Rose I would need another haircut soon. But I no longer wanted to look like her, and, feeling bitter, I said to the cats: 'The hairdresser called her son a revolving-door criminal; it figures someone like that and Rose would be attracted to each other.'

I went back out, bought a few bags of potato chips at Digros and returned home, the bags under my arm. It had stopped raining, the sun was out, Mijna would be able to tell what time it was by looking at the sundial. I saw myself reflected in shop windows. How dearly I would have loved to say farewell to the person I saw: a timid frump who could lose her composure simply from seeing a baby carriage. Fortunately I didn't see the tall carriages much anymore, those hard-to-manoeuvre mammoth vehicles of my childhood. They had been replaced by strollers that could go into an elevator or, folded up, into the trunk of a car. If the original baby carriages were to be seen at all, it was in neighbourhoods where lots of recent immigrants lived, so I avoided these areas to save myself distress. But there was always the chance of crossing paths with a father or mother on a bicycle, pulling a cart covered by a plastic top in which a toddler lay, sucking its thumb. Just as baby carriages had once tended to destroy my composure, nowadays those carts had the same effect on me.

How dearly I would have liked to say goodbye to myself for good. *One* thing I did know: I could go an astonishingly long way with someone else's accessories. Earrings I had to attach with glue that irritated my ear lobes. High heels that caused me to stumble. A corset whose stays stabbed me in the back if I relaxed my posture for even a moment. Artificial nails that caused me physical discomfort at every turn. When I wore accessories like these, I could not forget that I was playing a part. And even though it might have aspects of a penance: I had become someone else. Using Mandelstam's words, I had 'risen out of deep grieving', I had become a woman who remained unaffected by the sight of baby carriages and thumb-sucking toddlers in two-wheeled carts, and for that reason I had experienced the penance less as a punishment than as an unexpected form of liberation.

17.

'Tiger,' I said, 'I wish there was somebody I could talk to about all this. Graafland? *Ach*, no, that joker with his moustache and his roving eye...no, someone I can trust. I'm paying the price now for abandoning my girlfriends. Every time one of them had a child I let the friendship slip. That fussing over a baby, I just couldn't stand to watch it. It made me sad. Now they're becoming grandmothers, one after another, and I imagine they hardly talk about anything else. I can't say I blame them, but I don't want to hang around with them either: it hurts too much.'

Tiger lifted a paw like a preacher preparing to pronounce the benediction at the end of a church service, looked at me then closed his eyes, turned his head and gazed out the window.

'You're no use either,' I said. 'Even though you meet one important condition: you knew Rose. I need someone who knew her well.'

As happened every so often, I ran into Riet Goudsblom in the produce department at Digros late that afternoon.

'This *is* a coincidence, child,' she said. 'We were just talking about you during the coffee break this morning. A pharmacologist from Canada is coming to work with us for a month. We wondered if perhaps she could stay with you?'

'Stay with me? Why me?'

'This has happened several times before. Usually they stayed with Rose.'

'If she's pleasant...'

'I met her at a conference once. Charming girl.'

'And when...?'

'Soon. Give it some thought. She could stay at my place too, but visitors tend to find me a bit off-putting. At your place she would undoubtedly feel at ease right away.'

'I'll think about it. By the way, would you like to come and have a bite at my place tomorrow evening? Or the day after? You knew Rose quite well, I'd like…'

'Tomorrow evening would be fine. What time?'

'Right after the lab closes.'

'I'll be at your place at five-thirty.'

I prepared a leek-and-mustard soup and baked my special quiche with mushrooms, grated celeriac root, onion, tomato and cheese.

'You can serve this to that Canadian girl too,' said Riet Goudsblom appreciatively as I placed the quiche on the table. The rain clattered against the windows at irregular intervals.

'Oh, so you're already operating on the assumption that she'll be staying here?'

'Yes,' she said. 'Right now you're not looking forward to it, but when you meet her you'll love her. So what's troubling you about Rose?'

'I suspect she was moonlighting in a lab where they made Ecstasy and all that sort of garbage.'

'Heavens! Eduard thought so too, he wanted to call her to account. Not long ago he said to me: "Someday she'll destroy our Institute's excellent international reputation." I believe he even hired someone to check on her comings and goings. As far as I know, this person didn't find anything. You'd have to ask Eduard about it.'

'I'd find it hard to do that,' I said, but I remembered that he had redeemed himself in my eyes with his kind words at the memorial service. He had cited that beautiful Bible verse: "In the noontide of her days she had to go to the gates of the grave and be deprived of the residue of her years." I still didn't know where that was from. How could I find out? I couldn't very well reread the entire Bible.

'Eduard's not so bad when you get to know him better,' said Riet.

'So he thought…?'

'Not just him: me too. She was swimming in money. "How can you afford all that?" I asked her once. "My parents left me a bundle," she said.'

'But could that not be true?'

'They were Hungarian refugees who arrived in Holland without a penny to their name.'

'Once they were here, maybe her father…'

'Could be, but I'm more inclined to think…no, I'm not at all surprised, but never mind: what's the problem?'

'She left me everything. What should I do, Riet? Tainted money, filthy lucre; kids die taking those pills.'

'That's their own fault.'

'No doubt, but I think… I always really looked up to her, but now… I honestly don't know what I ought to do, most of all I'd like to get rid of it all, but I've signed for everything, and what will happen to the cats?'

'Get rid of it all? Happens automatically. The taxman will grab sixty-eight percent or thereabouts. Then most of it will be gone.'

'Yes, but she had so much, she had a whole bunch of shares… I told the notary I wanted to sell them, and a while ago I got the transaction slip; your head would spin if you saw how much money has been credited to the Berczy estate.'

'That'll be taxed as well.'

'There's going to be a lot left over, and what should I do with it? It's blood money earned from all those users, I don't want to have anything to do with it. If only I had held on to those shares; almost as soon as I sold them their prices began to plunge.'

'Some people have the rottenest luck,' Riet said cheerfully.

'Yes, you can laugh about it, but…'

'Look at it another way, child. Perhaps Rose was bothered by a bad conscience. I mean: we don't have to sit in judgement over her, but the way she lived… So she may have thought: I should leave my money to someone who, unlike me, lives a decent life, a straight arrow. Then I'll be sure that, after I die, nothing will be done with it that I would need to be ashamed of.'

This was such a novel point of view that I didn't immediately know how to respond.

'Give the money to good causes,' Riet continued. 'Adopt some poor little wretch in Afghanistan. Give it to SOS Children's Villages. Send it to Leprosy Relief. Make a donation to Médecins Sans Frontières; I have a couple of donation forms at home you can use.'

'That's how we salve our consciences,' I said bitterly.

'Ecstasy and crack are terrible things, but you shouldn't think what's done in our lab is that much better. Let's say you're doing really great research. What happens next? The pharmaceutical industry is a jungle, and your results get thrown into it. It's a safe bet your work will get caught up in a life-and-death struggle for market share. The other day I read in a professional journal about calcium channel blockers. They're taken for high blood pressure. There is English research showing that if the patient eats grapefruit the combination can finish him off. So what happens? The manufacturers of the other blood-pressure drugs trumpet this finding from the rooftops. Exit the makers of calcium channel blockers. Nobody wants their pills anymore.'

'What nonsense, people can just stay away from grapefruit, can't they?'

'Of course they can, but people don't pay attention. All they hear is "calcium channel blockers, bad stuff" and they ask their family doctors for some other medication.'

'All right, but surely that's nothing compared to Ecstasy?'

'You think so? I found out afterward that the grapefruit research was financed by the manufacturers of other kinds of blood-pressure drugs. And that's just *one* example, I could give you dozens.'

Even before she had finished speaking, the doorbell sounded. The peephole revealed the distorted shape of Fred Volbeda. One could not describe the building's security as airtight. I opened the door. Fred pushed me aside, walked in, slammed the door shut and said angrily: 'Sorry to show up without any warning, Leonie, but you told me some Goddamn cock-and-bull story. You're not her sister.'

'I never said we were related.'

'You said you were her sister, and I believed you… I swallowed it hook, line and sinker, I just heard from Piet van Stenis and I thought: I've got to get the story straight at once.'

'I tried to tell you a couple of times there was a misunderstanding, but you wouldn't listen.'

'You've bloody well taken me for a ride.'

'Come on in for a moment, I've got a visitor, but that's all right.'

We went into the living room, I introduced Riet and Fred to each other then said to Fred: 'You said she was always talking about her sister.'

'What about it?'

'She had no relatives. When she was talking about her sister she had me in mind.'

'I can confirm that,' Riet said. 'In the lab, when Rose talked about her sister she always meant Leonie.'

'So you work in that crummy lab too? Did you maybe give her some nasty little smart pill that caused her so-called sunstroke?'

'If we could make pills like that we'd all be filthy rich. There would be more demand for them than for wholemeal bread.'

'It's driving me up the wall. Rose gets murdered, but nobody wants to believe it. So I put Piet van Stenis to work on it, and what do I hear? There's nothing to be gained from pursuing this matter. The only thing he can tell me is that this so-called sister isn't a sister at all. Which I just don't get, because you look...you looked exactly like her. True, your hair is different now, but still... I'd really like to beat up everyone in that bloody lab so I could get at the truth...'

'We make tranquillizers that would certainly benefit you right now,' said Riet.

'Tranquillizers for me?' Fred raged. 'I'm calm, I'm perfectly calm!'

'Yes, calm like the calm in the eye of the hurricane,' Riet said.

Fred glared at her then, without being invited to, dropped into a chair.

'Nobody can convince me that she wasn't murdered. Piet told me she drank a big mug of coffee just before she left. I'm willing to bet my last guilder there was something in that coffee, some really sneaky stuff...'

'If *that* is what you're thinking, I can set you straight,' said Riet. 'I came down with her. Mijna had just made fresh coffee. I poured a mug for Rose because she was doing something with her nails. Then I poured myself a mug. If there had been anything in that coffee I would have been dead too.'

'Or, while she wasn't watching, maybe you...was anybody else there?'

'Anybody? Six of us were standing there. Two students, a research assistant and our secretary helped themselves right after me. Not only are all of them still alive, but they were watching me at the time.'

'You're probably right,' Fred said dully, 'but...'

'Would you perhaps know whether she was moonlighting as a researcher in some Ecstasy lab or other?' asked Riet.

'Her? Rose? What the hell made you say that? How did you hit on that sick idea?'

'Many bicycle racers and soccer players say the same thing when they're asked whether they've been using banned substances,' Riet said coolly.

Fred hardly heard her, screamed right through what she was saying: 'Her? Make Ecstasy? What bullshit, what crap, what garbage, what...!'

'You can stop now, Mr Volbeda,' said Riet, 'you've made your opinion abundantly clear.'

Fred glared at us in turn in a manner that suggested he wanted to strike us and snarled through clenched teeth: 'Couple of slimy dung beetles! Sitting around some miserable concoction the two of them, eating foul gooey mushrooms, besmirching Rose's name. Rose! A fantastic broad like that, someone super-special! Enjoy what's left of your meal.'

He hurried out of the living room. A moment later the front door slammed shut.

After we had recovered from the shock, Riet said: 'It's unbelievable that Rose went around with a hooligan like him. That was just asking for trouble.'

That night I dreamed that Riet and I were walking past a windmill. We saw several ambulances with flashing lights parked around it. 'That's what happens when you lengthen the vanes,' Riet said. 'Everyone who walks underneath them gets hit.'

'Shouldn't we warn the miller?' I asked.

'That's pointless,' she said, 'the miller is that hooligan.'

18.

The telephone chirped like a cricket with a throat infection. I picked up the receiver.

'Hello,' I said.

'Hello, it's Bas. I believe Riet already told you we're expecting a visiting researcher. A Canadian this time, from Quebec. In the past Rose always took care of visitors. Would you be willing…?'

'But why? After all, I'm not a member of the lab, am I?'

'You *are* one of the family, aren't you? Besides, your French is excellent. French is supposed to be her native language.'

'Undoubtedly she also speaks excellent English.'

'A few words of French would immediately make her feel right at home. Besides, you have the time to entertain her, show her the city, go shopping with her and so on.'

'Come off it, you're not going to tell me you don't have time to walk into town with her?'

'Listen,' he said, lowering his voice. 'You know Marjolein, unfortunately she happens to be insanely jealous. This researcher is remarkably easy on the eyes. If I go for a walk with her, it'll be raining fire and brimstone at home. You'd be doing me a great favour if you were to entertain her.'

'I never knew Marjolein was that jealous.'

'I could tell you stories! She kept thinking I had something with Rose.'

'You *did* have something with Rose.'

'Long ago, when we were both young and foolish, years before Marjolein joined the lab.'

'You still had a key.'

'That was Rose's own copy. She kept it in a pocket of her lab coat. In case

121

she ever accidentally left her place without her key. But back to the Québécoise: won't you please help us out?'

'Can't she check into a hotel?'

'There's no budget for that. Besides, she would be there all alone.'

'I'll have to take a look at the guest bedroom first.'

'You do that.'

Rose's apartment included a living room of no less than sixty square metres, an open-plan kitchen, a hall, plus a large and a small bedroom. Since moving in I had hardly ever gone into the small bedroom. Lellebel spent most of the day there, and it contained a digital scale. Can you imagine avoiding a room just because it contains a scale? Was I trying to avoid being reminded that I might have gained weight?

Whatever the reason, it was only with great reluctance that I went into the guest bedroom after hanging up the phone. The scale stood there, aggressively shiny. If I were to get on it, the judgement would be meticulously rendered not only in kilograms but also, behind the decimal point, to the exact gram.

I got on it gingerly. Hateful black numbers promptly appeared. More than a little bit startled, I got off at once. Had I eaten that many potato chips since my trip to the *Poseidon*? But what did it matter? It was unthinkable now that I should go through life as Rose's look-alike.

'Lellebel,' I said, 'are you in here? Are you on top of the wardrobe?'

I got on the chair that stood next to the wardrobe and cast a glance over its dusty top. A rolled-up poster lay there. I couldn't get a proper grip on it, but I was able to tap it so that it fell off. It landed on the bed. I got off the chair, picked up the poster and unrolled it carefully. What appeared first were three enormous yellow capital letters and a question mark: FUR? Below this, a woman's arm was visible, the wrist encased in a strip of light-brown fur. The hand itself, a beautiful girl's hand, was equipped with incredibly long, curved, jet-black, pointed nails. The implicit message was: only women with raptors' claws like these would wear fur. For those who hadn't got the message, yellow capital letters at the bottom spelled it out: 'FOR BITCHES ONLY!'

The sliding door of the wardrobe was not quite closed. I pushed against the door with one finger. It opened smoothly. I looked inside, straight into the glittering eyes of Lellebel.

'Are you comfy here?' I asked.

She had made a sort of nest of unidentifiable dark objects. I opened the door as far as it would go. Lellebel stretched herself, withdrew a bit, settled on a shiny black thing.

'Let me have a look, Lellebel,' I said.

I tugged cautiously at the object. Lellebel rose up angrily, hissed, slashed at me with a paw, jumped out of the wardrobe and disappeared under the bed. What I had got hold of seemed to be a kind of hip-boot with an improbably high stiletto heel. I didn't realize at once what I had found, or perhaps I didn't want to realize it, and even after I had extracted a second boot, as well as a laced corset made of gleaming black latex, I did not really grasp precisely how versatile Rose had been. I reached in once more and thought I had found another item of clothing with long laces, but it turned out to be a whip.

Only when everything lay neatly arrayed on the bed – boots, manacles, foot shackles, a neck shackle, two corsets, a mask, long, black latex gloves, a spiked collar and a formidable-looking dildo to which not only all kinds of belts and buckles had been attached but also three smaller satellite dildos – was I forced to conclude that Rose, to put it bluntly, had been mixed up in sadomasochistic practices.

'Well, Tiger, we'll just add it to the list of things to be dealt with,' I said, but Tiger wasn't there. Eager to put everything back in the wardrobe, I pulled wildly at the door; but it was already open as far as it would go. I threw the manacles and shackles in then noticed a few photos lying on the wardrobe floor. I got them out and arranged them on the bed. The largest showed Rose, with black boots above the knee and wearing one of the laced corsets, towering high above a masked man who was chained to a pillory. Rose wore the spiked collar and held a whip. A hood had been put on the man's head, hiding his face.

'Jesus, Rose,' I whispered, and I left the guest room in search of Tiger. 'Who was she with, Tiger?' I asked when I saw him lying stretched-out on the windowsill. 'Who did she do things like that with?' I walked back into the guest room and examined the other photos. Was it the same man? It was impossible to say. Each one seemed to be of the same naked hairy fellow with the same hood on his head. I took the photos into the living room and looked at them intently by the window. 'Would it be Bas, or Fred? Or Piet Mastenbroek? Or someone else? What do *you* think?' I asked Tiger. But Tiger didn't seem to think anything, basked peacefully in the weak October sun, had never heard of SM. That formed no part of his innocent feline world.

I kept gazing at the naked hairy arms of the victim, the 'slave' as I believed he was known in SM jargon. Why was I so keen to know who the man in the photo was? I had the feeling that, if I were to know *that*, it would immediately become clear to me who had murdered Rose. Because, with the discovery of the photos, the conclusion that she had been murdered seemed suddenly unavoidable.

'I think I'll make myself a cup of rooibos tea first,' I said to Tiger. He followed me into the kitchen, perhaps labouring under the false impression that a shocked mistress would be more likely to supply him with a cat treat. When that turned out to be a mistaken assumption he peacefully followed me back into the living room and lay down on the windowsill as soon as I settled into a chair by the window, nursing my tea and staring at the huge unmoving cumulus clouds. Perhaps this was the most blissful aspect of that wonderful apartment: the wide sky with its cloudscapes, high above the surrounding roofs.

Beating men, all right, that I could understand. I knew more than enough specimens whom I'd be glad to give a really good whack. Handcuffing and shackling them to a pillory, fine, I could kind of see that too. But mounting them from behind after you had buckled on a dildo, that was really gross! And what purpose did those satellite dildos serve? Did you have to insert one of them into your vagina to get off while you were riding some man?

Cautiously sipping my piping hot rooibos, I realized I was less shocked than after my journey to the *Poseidon*. Would it have been different if I had discovered this first? I asked myself. If you have already heard that someone is a murderer, then the revelation that he also kicks lapdogs now and then seems less disturbing. The big shock muffled the second. If I had happened on her dildo in the pre-*Poseidon* period, would I have ripped off her earrings and rings and nails? 'Yes, I would,' I muttered, but I didn't feel altogether sure. In any case the moral dilemma I faced would not have presented itself.

I was going to say: when I was young, Tiger, we used to sing 'I want to be like Jesus,' but I stopped myself. I really had to shake this habit of speaking to Tiger all day long. So I hummed the children's hymn to myself: 'I want to be like Jesus, his deeds were ever meet, his words were ever friendly, his voice was ever sweet.' Ever sweet? Even when he used a homemade whip to drive the moneychangers from the temple? Even when he had spoken approvingly of torturers? Even when he had said: 'But those mine enemies, which would not that I should reign over them, bring hither, and slay them before me.' As a child it had seemed to me less than appealing to be like Jesus, if only because he was a man. Besides, being like Jesus didn't square with the message of another hymn: 'Jesus bids us shine, with a calm clear light, Like a little candle shining in the night.' Was flickering like a candle being like Jesus? If so, was Jesus a little candle? That couldn't be right, could it? And what did the hymn's reference to being in 'a small corner' mean?

You had to be yourself: that was the great command. 'Be yourself, I said to someone, but he couldn't, he was no one.' Was that line P A de Genestet's? It contained more truth than perhaps De Genestet had realized. Yourself – there was no 'yourself', you were playing a part you had chosen for yourself, and, Schopenhauer notwithstanding, *if* you identified yourself with someone you admired, you could radically change that part. You were skating on dangerously thin ice, but the greater the admiration, the stronger the breeze at your back as you rocketed along on your skates.

But what to do when that admiration was put to the test? What should I do now that it turned out that the person I admired had assisted in the manufacture of illegal drugs and had worked men over with a dildo? A challenge like that indicated very precisely what my own limitations and prejudices were. Could I make another person's concept of good and evil my own? No, not where drugs were concerned, of that I was sure. Could I escape from my own limitations and prejudices about sadomasochism? Probably I couldn't do that either, but no matter how disgusting and outlandish I considered SM to be, it couldn't be compared to the fantastically profitable trade in Ecstasy. Add to this the fact that SM had a slightly familiar aspect to it because as a child I used to hear all those Bible stories about torture and shackles and whipping. So whether it was all *that* disgusting...how dreadful was it, anyway? Should I try on the boots and corset? Maybe I should do that first. If I wanted to keep on loving Rose, it might be better to reach a compromise than to moralize.

A bit later, when I looked into the big mirror in the bedroom, I noted with surprise that all that shiny black stuff looked just as good on me as they looked on Rose in the photos, precisely because I had put on a few pounds. What I saw had less to do with sex and cruelty than with toughness and motorcycles and unapproachability and the advantageous presentation of flesh that was just a touch too ample. Nevertheless I practically had a fit when the doorbell buzzed just as I was fiddling with that scary-looking collar. It was unthinkable to open the door, of course, but the caller kept on pushing the bell, and so I tore off the mask and got into one of Rose's long white dressing gowns. Wrapped in that, I walked to the front door. All I could see through the peephole was a big bouquet.

A big bunch of chrysanthemums, very probably sent by Bas to soften me up on the subject of that Canadian woman. Never mind, I could manage taking delivery of a bouquet.

I opened the door a crack. The bouquet began to move, pushing the door open, and a voice said: 'Sorry I've turned up without warning once again, but I have to make amends for something. I behaved rather badly last time. Hopefully you didn't get rid of Rose's beautiful vases.'

'I don't understand,' I said in confusion, 'how you always manage to slip in with someone else every time you're here.'

'No, no, girl, there is a different explanation. I built Grimburch Estates, and it struck me as useful to keep a copy of the passkey to the main entrance just in case the owners had complaints.'

He wanted to come in farther, but I stood in his way and said: 'Just give them to me, I'll put them in a vase; I'm not dressed yet.'

'You must have gone to bed late. Fine by me, I'll leave now.'

He pushed the huge bouquet into my hands, and as a result I lost my balance. He caught me before I fell to the floor, fortunately letting go of me as soon as I was solidly on my feet again.

'You're not very stable on high heels like that,' he said. 'Didn't you say you weren't dressed yet? Do you wear these in bed?'

What a pity I'm not quick-witted. A playful answer, for example 'heels like that are as good as a hot-water bottle,' a push through the door, and he would have been outside with the front door safely between us. Instead I stood there, clutching an unmanageable bouquet, wobbling on miserable stiletto heels, and quite at sea as to how to escape from the situation. One piece of luck at least: I had used the white belt to close the dressing gown tightly.

When I feel ill at ease I can be very tactless. So I said bluntly: 'That little club of yours is an SM club, right?'

'How did you guess?'

'Is that you in the photos?'

'What photos?'

'The ones I just found.'

'You'll have to show them to me.'

When I didn't immediately know quite how to respond to that, he said: 'Come, give me the bouquet. Then I'll put the flowers in a vase for you. Meanwhile you go put on some jeans and a T-shirt, and after that you can show me the photos.'

When I did show them to him a few moments later, he said nothing. Calmly he pulled up his close-fitting sweatshirt, pointed at his hairless chest and pulled his sweatshirt down again. So it couldn't have been him, and I was glad about that because even though I couldn't see the face of the man in the photo, I found him distinctly unsympathetic.

Fred didn't know who he was. 'It isn't someone from our club,' he said. 'It's an older guy, that's obvious at once, and it's also an old picture.'

'How can you tell?'

'How can I tell? Rose's hair, I think, or her skin. Her skin looks so young. No cellulite at all. *Ach*, yes, that dumb sun-tanning, it doesn't do your skin any good. To say nothing of other things.'

'So sunstroke, after all? When *I* saw these photos, I thought: Fred is right: she was murdered.'

'What made you think that?'

'Because...well, I associate SM with cruelty and torture and beating and...and...killing.'

'Are you out of your mind? It's all so damned innocent, it doesn't mean a thing, it's fun and games, a flying fuck on a scaffold, as we say in the construction game.'

'I don't care for it.'

'And yet I could swear you were wearing her outfit just now.'

'I wanted to see how I looked in it.'

'And?'

'It looked better than I had expected.'

'You should join us on a Saturday evening sometime,' he said. 'We always start at the Kaag Club. We have a drink by the open fireplace there, and then we have a bite to eat. After that we all go together to our secret address.'

'It doesn't sound like my thing at all.'

'Come along some time, without any obligation, you can just sit in a cosy dark corner and feast your eyes. You really don't need to be afraid that we'll be pleading with you to start using the whip right off. You'll see: it's all very innocent. It's a crying shame Rose is gone, she was a fantastic dominatrix, we won't find another one like her in a thousand years. But you...you've got her figure, and if you wore her mask and her other things we'd almost have the feeling Rose had come back. It's all so makeshift with these sly slippery bitches we get from escort services.'

'Plus they cost an arm and a leg,' I said snidely.

'Oh, but we paid Rose too,' he said. 'That happens to be part of it, that's part of the kick, you've also got to feel the pain in your wallet.' And he smacked his bulging right rear pocket.

19.

'She'll be coming straight from the airport tomorrow,' Bas said. 'She should be here in time for coffee, so it would be convenient if you were here as well to make her acquaintance. At the end of the afternoon or, if we take her out for dinner first, in the course of the evening, I'll take her and her luggage over to Grimburchstraat.'

'Everything has already been arranged,' I said. 'It's almost like I don't have any say.'

'Come on, we've been through all this, besides, Rose always loved it when someone like this showed up, so you ought to feel the same way.'

'You're the one who "forbade" me to follow in her footsteps! And now I'm supposed to be elated about having a complete stranger as a house guest for a month!'

'You looked like Rose, you talked like Rose, it was downright creepy, thank God you've been yourself again for a while now. Marjolein saw you in Digros the other day, and in bed that evening she said: "She's rejoined the human race."'

'I'll be there,' I said sharply. 'See you tomorrow.' Then I put down the receiver.

If it hadn't been for the Ecstasy problem, I would have liked nothing better than to sit down at Rose's dressing table right away and make myself up like her. What business was it of Marjolein's? Who did that bitch think she was, anyway? If *I* ever murdered anyone, it would be her.

I cleaned out the guest bedroom, hoping to find a few more SM photos that would reveal to me who her hairy slave was. All I found were photos of Florence Griffith and Gail Devers, the champion sprinters, both equipped with insanely long fingernails. On Gail Devers's picture, Rose had written YES in big letters right below the formidable claw-like nails.

The next day, feeling unhappy, I walked along the high-ceilinged corridor of the laboratory. My footsteps rattled across the marble-and-concrete composite floor. I came to a halt outside the door to the room where the coffee was served. I heard voices. People were speaking Brenglish, Thomas's term for broken English. Naturally Bas dominated the discussion, talking about research into temperature regulation in rats' tails. Whereupon I heard Riet say with nearly perfect pronunciation: 'You see, this laboratory…I tell you, only lunatics.' Then I heard the newcomer laugh. Was it Georges Buffon who said: '*Le style c'est l'homme même*' – 'the style is the man'? Given that most people don't write poetry or prose, so that in their cases one can hardly speak of style, the remark has always struck me as rather inappropriate. It would be much more accurate to say: '*Le rire, c'est l'homme.*' Laughter expresses the deepest essence of human beings. There are people who laugh hatefully, people who never just laugh but always laugh *at* someone else, people in whose laugh one always hears malice, people whose laugh is phoney, people who laugh like children. You can charm people with your laugh, but you can't fool them.

Cheerful, carefree, untroubled. Her laugh reminded me of Rose's, reconciled me for a moment to the entire world, to existence, to this incomprehensible universe in which we wander around ignorantly and live for such an astonishingly short time and are dead for such an incredibly long time. I stayed there, I was afraid that after a laugh like that she would disappoint me. I also thought: I can't compete with that. I can't laugh without a worried note revealing itself. If you're looking at me for warm spontaneous laughter, you've come to the wrong address.

Loud footsteps were approaching. It would have seemed strange if I continued to hover outside, so I entered the room and saw her a moment before she saw me. She was standing with her back to the window. The sunlight bathed her, lighting up her platinum-blonde hair. She was wearing a white turtleneck and dark-blue jeans. She was fragile, slight; for a moment I even thought: what's this, she's a child.

Anyway, all my reluctance, resentment, anger vanished. When Bas introduced me to her, and I shook her hand, I felt an itch in my nose as if I were going to sneeze. I looked at the sun for a moment to release that sneeze, but it didn't want to escape, it kept on itching devilishly. That put me at a disadvantage; I had to keep rubbing my nose. Not that it mattered. Bas was monopolizing the conversation and didn't want to let go.

Only late that evening, seated by the living-room window, was I able to exchange a few words with Claire undisturbed. She informed me, as if I myself were employed in the lab, that in Canada she had been monitoring 'your Institute' for years and admired 'the amazing investigations' enormously. She had come to see how all that research was carried out and to learn from it. Then she said: 'We've carried out a number of your most noteworthy experiments in Montreal, but we got different results.'

'Thomas, my ex-husband, told me that's what always happens,' I said. 'It seems experiments can't be replicated exactly.'

'But it's got to be possible to do that.'

'Yes,' I said, 'and yet in practice it's otherwise.'

'In every lab, sodium hydroxide reacts with sulphuric acid in exactly the same way,' she said.

'A simple experiment like that…sure, but if the experimental elements are more complicated…well, conditions differ from lab to lab. Different climate, different degrees of humidity, different test animals, different researchers, different lab technicians.'

'That's why I want to replicate a couple of your most sensational experiments over here to see whether I can get the same results as you.'

'"You",' I said. 'That does sound strange. I don't work there, my ex and my best friend worked there, but that is the extent of my connection to the Institute.'

'At the time the arrangements were made I was given to understand that I would be staying with the person who had done the research,' she said. 'That would have been fantastic. Then I could have gone over everything very thoroughly with her.'

'Well, I'm sorry, but you'll have to make do with me instead.' I said this in French to show my versatility.

She frowned, said in broken French that she spoke that language badly and continued in English: 'She had an accident, didn't she?'

'Yes, she did,' I said, and I told her about Rose and the sunstroke, but of course I didn't mention that some people doubted she had died a natural death.

We talked about those doubts a good deal later when she had been staying with me for three weeks and we had become so close that, like schoolgirls who are visiting out of town together, we would often sit by the living-room window until the wee hours, looking at the starry sky, talking to each other.

On Claire's last evening at my place, an evening with an unusually clear sky and boldly sparkling stars, she said she had to confess something to me. She emphasized that what she was going to say should go no farther. 'I trust you,' she repeated several times, and she also said that, since I did not work in the Institute, she felt able to take me into her confidence. She said she had entered the Institute under false pretences. An ever-stronger suspicion had developed among researchers in her university lab that for years the results of scientific research 'at the Institute here' had been 'cooked' on a large scale. All those sensational results seemed to be unique, and it had never been possible to replicate them in Montreal. For that reason, and probably also because she looked so 'innocent' as she said, laughing cheerfully, she had been dispatched to try to find out, very cautiously, whether those Dutch scientists might perhaps be highly skilled at fiddling with numbers. Figures don't lie, she said, but liars do figure.

'It's too bad that research assistant had an accident. She was always given credit, so she must have done a lot of the research. She knew what the real results were and whether the senior academics had massaged the numbers in such a way that what came out seemed spectacular and got worldwide attention, even though *we* think it is fraudulent. How I would have loved to speak with her! It must have been awfully convenient for them that she had an accident.'

'Could they have known you were coming to investigate whether fraud was being committed here?'

'They might have been able to guess it.'

'Was it known for a long time that you would be coming?'

'Oh sure, that was settled at a conference a year ago. All your research staff were there.'

'God almighty,' I said.

'What's the matter?' she asked.

'I didn't want to tell you, because, well, maybe they're idiotic fantasies...but...well...Rose...'

'What about Rose?'

'Some people think she may have been murdered.'

'That's what *I* keep thinking.'

And then we sat there for a while, staring at the dark starry sky, not saying anything. After a minute or so had passed I asked: 'Could fear that scientific fraud would be exposed be a motive for murder?'

'Just think of the terrible loss of scientific face,' Claire said. 'You're drummed out of the scientific world, your name is removed from all the textbooks, you're reviled, you're derided, not one of your colleagues ever wants to have anything to do with you again. It's definitely the end of your career.'

And your name doesn't get inscribed on the base of the sundial, I thought, and I said: 'If she was murdered, which of the people here might have done it? Who was the fraud artist?'

'Hard to say, there are always at least three or four authors listed, they always published as an institute, not as individuals.'

For a while we contemplated Cassiopeia and Ursa Major. Then she said: 'It was weighing on my mind; I thought you should know. Otherwise when I get back and write my report, and you should hear about it, you would think I hadn't been straight with you. But let's change the subject. Let's talk about kids.'

'Talk about kids?' I asked, bewildered.

'Yes, you said you don't have children. Didn't you want kids? Or were you unable to have them?'

Although I knew very well she was saying this to make a radical change of subject, I cringed. To be asked so frankly about the one thing that had thoroughly messed up my life was hard to take.

I told her as neutrally as possible that I would have loved to be a mother, but that gradually I had realized I would never become pregnant, then had gained renewed hope because in situations like Thomas's and mine there had been successful in-vitro fertilizations, that embryos had repeatedly been implanted in me, and that in every case my womb had rejected the embryos after a few weeks. ·

'It also wrecked my marriage,' I said.

'I'm very, very sorry I asked you so bluntly,' she said.

'Don't apologize,' I said. 'It does me good to talk about it.'

'Do you still have a lot of regrets?' she asked.

'For a while I was all right,' I said. 'It seemed like I had got over it, like I had come to terms with the feeling that my whole life was a failure because we hadn't had kids. For a while I was out of the wind, in the eye of the hurricane as it were, but then the wind kicked up again, the girlfriends who had become mothers became grandmothers, one after another. A second round began, everything I had gone through I had to go through again, and I was older, more vulnerable, my resistance had gone down. On top of it, these grandmothers...not only do they almost keel over with joy when they get to hold their first grandchild in their arms, but they shout their joy from the rooftops.'

'What about Rose?' she asked. 'Did she have kids?'

'No,' I said, 'she didn't want any, she used to say: "Nuclear missiles with multiple warheads are aimed at us; whoever has children these days is irresponsible."'

'She was quite right,' Claire said.

'So that's the reason you don't have children either?'

'We want kids very badly, me and my hubby,' she said, 'very, very badly. When I get back to Canada I'm going off the pill.'

With the use of that curious word 'hubby' she created a barrier, distanced herself from me. I got up.

'Time to get some sleep.'

'Yes, I've got to be up early tomorrow. I still have to pack. And then…yes, I'll miss you, but we'll stay in touch, won't we?'

'What did you have in mind for tomorrow morning?' I asked.

'I'll take a cab to the Institute. Then my luggage will be there, and I can go straight on to Schiphol in the afternoon. Do come along, please. I very much want you to meet my hubby. I'm so glad he's got to be in London for a botany conference and is travelling by way of Amsterdam. This way we can fly back home together.'

20.

At eight-thirty the next day, on a pale Monday morning, Claire's 'hubby', as she affectionately kept calling him, arrived at Schiphol.

He phoned and said he would leave his luggage at the airport, then would take the train to Leiden. Claire and I took a taxi to the lab, left her suitcases with the porter and went on to the station.

Twenty minutes later he came bounding up to her in tennis shoes. By way of greeting he lifted her high into the air then embraced her, kissed her, ran his hand through her hair, patted her on the back and, after I had been allowed to shake his hand for a moment, took her in a kind of hold that struck me as distinctly uncomfortable for a walk to the laboratory. But they strolled, ardently entwined, looking like a quadruped with two heads, along sidewalks and pedestrian crossings, all the way to the entrance of the Institute. I walked at a suitable distance behind them the entire time, feeling out of place, inappropriate, superfluous. I could have been walking there a century earlier or a century hence, but it wouldn't have mattered. They could manage without me, I might just as well not be there, and if after lunch I should cease to be, not a soul would lose sleep over it. 'Oh, the needs of unborn life,' Martinus Nijhoff once wrote, but the needs of the unborn don't exist. Even the needs of the already born barely count; they are replaceable, exchangeable like everyone who comes into this life.

As I strolled along behind the intertwined couple, existence seemed to me neither meaningful nor meaningless, but rather completely unnecessary. Earth might just as well have been a barren planet, as bare and empty as the moon, and no one would have shed a tear.

But discouraging thoughts of this kind don't get you anywhere, so I was glad when we reached the laboratory and walked into the coffee room halfway through the morning break. Claire's husband got a huge mug of coffee and leaned against the long table, his back to the quadrangle and sundial. What if he had continued in that position? That might easily have happened, for it looked as though he were a one-man receiving line. He met everyone, shook hands with them and could have very well have kept on doing so until the end of the coffee break, in which case he would not have seen the Datura.

The medium-sized star that governs our solar system shone wanly on the sundial. Out of the pale, soft-blue, somewhat misty sky a small green bird with ragged slate-grey wings came flying down.

'Hey, a ringneck, that's bound to be an escaped parakeet,' one of the handymen said.

For an extraordinary event like that, everyone interrupted their conversations, turned their faces to the quadrangle and looked at the little bird, which flew around in confusion. From the look of things, it didn't know what to do with its newfound freedom. It landed on the sundial, allowed itself to fall off as if to test whether the law of gravity applied around sundials, rose up again, then shrieked and plummeted to the ground. There it lay on the grass, breathing heavily.

'We've got to catch it,' the other handyman said. 'We can put it in a rat cage for the time being. Then we can put a note in the mailboxes of all the houses in the area: "Ringneck parakeet found, to be picked up at the Pharmacological Laboratory."'

'I'll bet no one turns up to claim it,' Riet said. 'Ringnecks have been getting quite commonplace in parks and gardens.'

'It's a lovebird,' said Claire, who of course hadn't understood the Dutch spoken by the handymen and by Riet, but who nevertheless wanted to add something to the conversation.

Claire's husband had turned around as well. He looked around the quad and said in a delighted voice: 'I see you've got a unique old-fashioned equinoctial sundial here. You should take good care of it; you just don't see this kind anymore. And look at that, what a marvellous number plate. And so beautifully embedded in the lawn. Too bad the sun shines so rarely in Holland, and even when it does shine, like right now, you can hardly see the shadow of the rod because the intensity of the light is so low.'

'In summer we have the most beautiful clock anywhere,' Riet said crustily.

Claire's husband didn't answer, gazed attentively at the quad, muttered half to himself: 'That's a very interesting plant.'

'Which one?' asked Riet.

'The Datura. Its flowers have faded, of course, but from the way it looks it's not the common Datura. In my opinion that's a *Datura fastuoso*. How did you people get hold of one of *them*?'

'We got seed from someone who works in a university institute where they study the languages and cultures of India,' Bas said. 'The people there regularly travel to Madras, and they return not only with various artefacts but also with seeds. Through connections we obtained some seed; most of it didn't come up, but this bush did...and, well, as you can see, it is gorgeous, it flowered magnificently this summer, we were all mighty proud of it.'

'I can relate to that,' said Claire's husband. 'It's a wonderful specimen, but watch out, it's far more poisonous than the common thorn apple. The Thugs used to use this plant to commit crimes. For all I know they're still doing it.'

'I think I heard about that once,' said Bas. He didn't like to admit there were things he didn't know, and he is not alone in that.

'The Thugs used the seed,' Claire's husband said. 'You pound it into a very fine powder that is both odourless and tasteless. You can mix it into anything at all: flour, sugar, you name it. When someone puts a spoonful of this enriched sugar in his coffee, he tastes nothing and pours it down the hatch without noticing.'

'So then you die?' Riet asked cheerfully.

'No, nothing happens, nothing at all.'

'So what is the point?'

'What makes Datura powder so effective in a country like India is the sun. When somebody has taken a dose of that powder and goes outside, into the bright sunlight, they lose consciousness after a while. Even then, there doesn't have to be a problem. If you get them out of the sun in time they will recover. If you don't do that, and the person stays outside, sitting or lying in the sun, then they go into a coma...and, yes, in that case the outcome may be fatal.'

He looked as though he were giving a lecture about orchids and their attractions. With the gestures of a seasoned lecturer, he continued his account: 'The powder is highly soluble in water. Or in coffee. You could put some in your coffeemaker, it dissolves nicely, and then everyone who drinks coffee here gets a dose. It's a magnificent poison. It leaves no trace to be found in an autopsy. Yes, it's one of the great poisons, a king among poisons. There's just one problem: you need bright sunlight. You can't use it in Holland or England. You need the sun to finish the job.'

He looked around triumphantly, gestured once more at the nearly bare shrub, repeated softly to himself, the way people do with the punch-line of a joke, the crucial sentence: 'You need the sun to finish the job.'

The room had become deathly silent, so silent you could hear the restless gurgling of the water in the old-fashioned pipes of the central heating. Weak cries came from the messy pile of feathers that still lay on the lawn, looking little like the parakeet that had fallen there.

'Well, what's the matter?' Claire's husband asked in surprise.

Nobody answered, the water gurgled in the pipes, the parakeet shrieked pianissimo. Nevertheless the sound boomed in my ears. As well, I heard the grating sound of the breathing of the faculty members, students, and technical and administrative staff of the Pharmacological Laboratory.

'Did I say something wrong?' Claire's husband whispered. He paused a few seconds then asked again: 'Did I perhaps say something wrong?'

No one among his listeners seemed capable of saying anything. It remained unbearably silent. One of the handymen, unable to stand it any longer, said softly: 'Everybody's speechless.'

Claire's husband looked at his wife in desperation. She took his arm, pulled him out of the circle, whispered: 'You really shook them up.'

'But how?'

'By what you said just now.'

'But why?'

'Somebody here died of sunstroke last summer.'

'Sunstroke? So what? That's got nothing to do with the Datura, does it? Sunstrokes happen more often than you think. A lot more.'

She pulled him farther away from the coffee-drinking pharmacologists. As she led him out of the room he looked back in despair a couple of times. Even after they had left the room no one was able to utter a word. Their footsteps sounded awfully loud in the long laboratory corridor.

I couldn't stay there either. I put my mug down on the table as carefully as possible – it sounded like an exploding bomb to me – and shuffled slowly backward, step by step, keeping my gaze fixed on the sundial. I didn't belong there, after all, I didn't work there, so I was free to withdraw; they would have to deal with this among themselves. At long last I reached the door. As soon as I had slipped through it I hastily took off my shoes and ran along the corridor in my stocking feet. Even when I was outside, having put my shoes back on, I kept on running until I reached a residential street. Only then did I slow down. I had to, I was out of breath, I felt queasy, I had a stitch in my side. I pressed my hand on the stitch, it was no use. A man stopped his car, rolled the window down, asked: 'Excuse me, please, would you happen to know where Laat de Kanterstraat is?'

'Sorry, I don't,' I said. Here I was at the epicentre of an emotional earthquake, and someone was asking me for directions. Jesus!

The cats, I thought, I'm almost out of Sheba, I should buy some Sheba, have I got any money on me? Otherwise I'll have to go home first. Jesus, that hurts, stupid to run so hard, it makes you feel like throwing up; she took a petal of it to Ici Paris: do you have this colour nail polish, how in God's name is it possible, now it's certain not only that she was killed but also killed exactly the way Fred Volbeda thought it must have happened, something in her coffee or in her sugar, no, not in the sugar, because she never used sugar, so something in her coffee, someone could have put it in her mug ahead of time, everyone there had their own mug. Or even, just to be sure, into all of the mugs, because only those who went out into the sun were at risk; or someone could have put it in the coffeemaker too, or in the coffee, it is soluble, after all, so you let the water drip on the coffee in the filter with powder at the bottom, that way you flush the poison through, child's play, anyone could have done it, the only thing needed was the information that the crushed seeds make such a nasty poison. Who in God's name would have known that, wouldn't he almost *have* to be a botanist, like Claire's husband, or would the information be available in pharmacological handbooks? It should be possible to find out, sure, but knowledge is like water, it spreads everywhere; white Datura powder, you swallow it, you lie in the sun on a large beach towel, and you're done for.

As I entered Grimburchstraat, I half-expected to see Piet Mastenbroek standing by the fence, but fortunately he wasn't there. And on second thoughts there seemed to be no good reason why he should have chosen this particular pale Monday morning to hold onto the bars of the fence. With trembling hands I gave the cats their Sheba, and something happened that had never happened before: they sniffed at it but wouldn't eat. They meowed, retreated from me, almost seemed afraid. I sat down by the window, got up again, walked through the apartment, sat down again, got up again, got out the photo of the hairy man, looked at it. If only I knew who he was. Then I thought: what nonsense, that man has got nothing to do with it, someone in the lab did it, that has to be it, and yet I couldn't shake the feeling that the man in the picture was somehow connected to it all. I put the photo away, didn't know what to do to allay my terrible restlessness. I picked up her telephone directory, leafed through it, hit on Salon Marquise, put the directory down and keyed in the number.

'Salon Marquise.'

'It's Ro…it's Leonie Kuyper, would you be able to cut my hair today?'

'Today? Monday? Oh, I've had such a dreadful weekend, they picked up my son yesterday, Sunday of all days, couldn't they have waited *one* day, and early this morning when I was putting out the garbage I had such a terrible fall. I slipped, I think I've broken every bone in my body, I can't stand up, I can't sit down, it's awful, maybe I'll have to go to the doctor, I…'

'Oh, so cutting it today…'

'Sure, of course, I'll do it, it'll distract me, why don't you come?'

I put on a parka of Rose's that I hadn't worn before, walked to the station, took a train to Den Haag, got into a cab and went to Tureluurlaan and listened for more than an hour to complaints so bizarre that they distracted me and even cheered me up a bit. But on the train back I sat in an empty compartment, and because I couldn't convert my restlessness into motion and because nobody was chattering to me, I was afflicted by the chaotic stream of thoughts running through my head. It was almost as if I had a fever.

Whatever fantasies presented themselves to me, *one* thing was crystal clear. For months I had been able to contemplate the possibility that Rose had been killed, had even been aware of a motive for murder, but that had meant nothing. In fact, all that time I had not really believed she had died anything but a natural death. Murder as a likely hypothesis or murder as fact, it was the difference between a ball hitting the post and an actual goal, a difference of a few centimetres but, for all that, the difference between everything and nothing, between winning or not. It was only now that I had to confront the fearful truth: someone had intentionally, fiendishly planned to poison her, using the seeds of a plant the colour of whose flowers she had cherished.

To *know* that she had been murdered changed the look of everything, it even meant that I could forgive her for having been associated with the manufacture of Ecstasy. Besides, her murderer could hardly be connected with the locked-up *Poseidon*, unless he worked in the lab but had been moonlighting in the houseboat, and that too changed my attitude to her involvement in the production of illegal drugs. No, her murderer must have been much closer at hand; just like her, just like me, he had often heard his own footsteps sound loudly on the Institute's worn old composite floor.

When I was home again, I soothed my restlessness at her dressing table. Slowly I erased myself, slowly she emerged in the mirror. She had been murdered, and therefore it might be bloody dangerous – to use Fred's words

– to crawl into her skin, but I couldn't do anything else, I owed it to her, and if the murderer wanted to kill me too, he would just have to do it. I had been warned: using Datura powder this time around wouldn't do the job. Anyway, broiling gently in the summer sun was altogether out of the question at this time of year.

I attached her earrings to my earlobes with a drop of glue, put her rings on my fingers, strapped myself into her tightest corset. Diet, lose weight: that was the message her corset gave me as I wormed myself into it, and I got this message for a second time, mercilessly and emphatically, when I put on one of her nicest suits. All right, I would lose weight, Curve Oval would help me do that, and I took the last set of nails out of the package. First I thought of applying them with the help of Tip Stickers, but then I thought: no, they've got to be firmly attached so I can scratch the murderer's eyes out, even though I knew a heroic deed like that would be unlikely, at least in the immediate future.

After I had applied them, first the right hand then the left, the question arose what colour to paint them. The Datura colour was out of the question, of course. I hunted for another suitable shade among her many small jars, couldn't find what I was looking for and then thought: didn't I buy some of that fluorescent polish a while ago? After I painted the right thumbnail, I had the fright of my life. It looked as if it was on fire. But what did I care? I wanted to be on fire, I had to be on fire, when I went shopping I could wear gloves. It was the season for them, after all.

If you want your nail polish to be perfect, you've got to take your time. You've got to apply three coats and give them plenty of time to dry. I felt too restless for this process but forced myself to sit quietly by the big living-room window. I was assisted by the enormous clouds that drifted slowly along the pale-blue afternoon sky. Whenever I couldn't stand it any longer and wanted to get up, another colossus came into view. Sitting there, simply sitting there, what a hard task that turned out to be. When at last I had enough, I picked up her directory and looked for a number. Moments later, using my knuckles, I keyed it in.

'Volbeda Construction, how can I help you?' a girl's voice sang.

'May I speak with Mr Volbeda, please?'

'I'm sorry, he is at a construction site. Can he call you back?'

'Sure; it's Leonie Kuyper, he knows the number.'

'Please let me have it anyway,' the girl said.

Ten minutes later the phone chirped.

'Hello.'

'It's Fred. This is the first time you've ever called me, what do I owe this honour to?'

'I just wanted to say you were right, there *was* a dose of very nasty powder in her coffee.'

I heard him breathe heavily; then he began to curse.

'Please don't swear,' I said, 'I grew up Christian Reformed, I can't take it.'

He kept on cursing for a while and then said: 'I grew up in the Reformed Calvinist Community, that's even stricter than Christian Reformed, that's why I curse and swear like a Philistine and an Edomite and an Amalekite all day long. Nobody can order me to stop swearing, not even you. Hold on, would it be okay if I dropped by for a moment? I'm right in the neighbourhood, I want you to give me all the details.'

Oh my God, I thought, I can't receive him with flaming nails like these. But he hardly looked at them as he sat on the couch a few minutes later, with Ober on his lap. I told him what had been revealed to me while I was drinking my latté that morning.

'You see, all the time I kept saying it, but nobody wanted to listen, they all made fun of this lad here, led by that bull-necked Van Stenis and that woman who was sitting here some time ago…couldn't she have done it?'

'No,' I said, 'she couldn't, because she and Rose never did research together.' And I told him what I had heard from Claire. Whereupon he cursed as I've never heard anybody else curse while stroking Ober almost ferociously.

'Flaming hell and Goddamn,' he concluded and immediately continued: 'People always thought I was a real dummy, it started in kindergarten, and in elementary school…well, okay, it's true, when we first started doing fractions, we had to add one half and one third and there was a brain who said three-quarters right off.…'

'I'm no math genius,' I said, 'but I don't think that adds up to three-quarters.'

'You see, when it comes to fractions I'm still no star, but what the hell difference does it make? It's only an example, all I want to say is: when we started doing fractions I was completely lost, *I* thought I was a moron too, a prize dimwit…and now I've got a business that's going great guns, and that brain who was so good at fractions: I saw him on the box the other day, he writes poems and sits there complaining that he's earning squat and drifting from grant to grant; I just want to say… Goddammit it, so I was right all along, it really *was* the coffee, now all we've got to do is find out who killed her.'

He gave Ober an affectionate little tap, resumed his vigorous stroking and said over the sound of loud purring: 'When I know who's done it I'm going to waste him, that's a promise.'

'I don't care for that kind of talk,' I said. 'You can save it for the construction site.'

He looked up in surprise from his self-imposed labour of stroking.

'Rose's voice,' he said happily. 'That was Rose's voice, *ach*, poor Rose…anyway, you look fantastic yourself, would you like to go have a bite with me?'

'I've got absolutely no appetite,' I said.

'No problem,' he said. 'You just order a small appetizer, that's cheaper too.'

'No, I still feel queasy.'

'*Ach*, sure, you're heart-stricken. Who wouldn't be? Fine, we'll go some other time, let's have a look, tomorrow…no, I can't go, the day after, Goddammit, the rest of the week is booked solid, Saturday…hold on. Come along on Saturday, of course, that's what you've got to do, you owe me one, you laughed at me too, just like the others, you thought: Fred and his dumb coffee, yeah, well, now you owe me one. A drink at the Kaag, a bite to eat and then…yes, that's what you've got to do.'

'It really isn't my scene.'

'For Rose it was life itself. She worked in a classy club in Den Haag now and then, in the Flower District. That's where I got to know her. You're living in *her* apartment, you're looking after *her* cats, you're wearing *her* clothes, you're using *her* nail polish, was she ever ballsy, a smashing colour like that…*you* would never have been able to get yourself to do that, it's *her* gutsiness that's inspiring you now.'

He took breath, said: 'You were brought up religious too, you remember Elijah, who went up to Heaven? And then his mantle fell down, and Elisha rent his own clothes… As a kid I always thought that was so fine, they're constantly tearing their clothes in Holy Writ, as a kid I would have loved to do that because I always got my brother's hand-me-downs…so Elisha rent his own clothes and cried: "My father, my father, the chariot of Israel, and the horsemen thereof", how marvellous that is, and then he put on that mantle. And he became Elijah. It's stated there so beautifully: the spirit of Elijah rested on Elisha. You received *her* mantle, the spirit of Rose now rests on you, so you *have* to come along with us, even if it's only once. Completely without obligation. You can sit in a corner, take a good look; if you pass this up and shy away from it, you'll never have the faintest clue what Rose was really like.'

'What a speech,' I said admiringly. 'You should have become a dominee.'

'There you go, it was a good thing after all I was a bungler like that fathead Gehazi, otherwise my father would have sent me to dominee school, just like my brother, and then now I'd be earning peanuts bullshitting from a pulpit twice every Sunday...so you're coming along on Saturday?'

'Twice every Sunday? Nobody has two services on Sunday anymore, do they?'

'At my brother's church they do, Reformed Calvinist Community. And no dinky little half-hour sermons either, no way, an hour-long sermon with a sung psalm in the middle. So are you coming on Saturday?'

I couldn't bring myself to give him a flat no. So I said teasingly, while thinking, this is safe, he'll never manage it: 'I'll come along if you can tell me where it says in the Bible: "In the noontide of her days she had to go to the gates of the grave and be deprived of the residue of her years."'

'Do I have to tell you right now?'

'No, you can look it up.'

'I've got the whole Bible on CD-ROM, so it ought to be a piece of cake.'

21.

Saturday afternoon at five he was on my doorstep.

'Did you find that verse?' I asked.

'I know where it is,' he said.

'So where is it?'

'I'll tell you once we're on our way.'

'If you're playing games with me, I'll go home at once.'

'I'm not playing games, so please come along.'

I put on her parka and stepped out the door.

'Aren't you bringing her things?' he asked. 'She had such a nice little case for them.'

'No,' I said.

'Come on,' he said, 'bring them along. Later, when you're there, you'll think: if only I had brought them.'

'I won't bring her things,' I said. 'You keep trying to get me to the point where I'll go one step farther.'

'Better to have it and not need it, than need it and not have it.'

'I've heard that line before.'

'I'll tell you this: later on we'll be buck-naked, and that lovely lady will be wearing a great costume. You'll feel really out of it because you'll be sitting there dressed in your street clothes.'

I had thought of that myself, but I didn't want to give in, so I said: 'Honest, it really isn't my scene, why not just leave me at home?'

'Stay home? "Prove all things; hold fast that which is good," said Paul the Apostle.'

I said nothing, went back inside, grabbed the handsome case and went back out again.

'Look at that, you had everything ready to go. In your case Bible verses make you move; that's very different than Rose.'

I felt deeply embarrassed, but when we had left the city and were driving alongside one of those typically Dutch waterways – with foam-topped waves and languidly waving reed tufts on the shore, a leaden sky above and briskly whirling windmills here and there; and Fred had to keep braking because groups of coots with outstretched necks were crossing the road like storm troopers – I began to feel better.

'I'm late,' said Fred. 'You can bet the others are already boozing it up. There's Arie, an auto wrecker but honest as the day is long, Cornelis, a tough guy who's in the driving-school business, and Simon. He earns his keep as a chief in the fire department.'

When we arrived at the Kaag Club Fred's pals were indeed already waiting for us. They wore expensive three-piece suits, but the cuticles of their fingernails were grimy. At their table sat a sturdy, big-boned blonde of perhaps twenty-five summers, who was gazing morosely into the middle distance.

'That's Sheila,' Fred said. The English name didn't really fit her; something ultra-Dutch like Nel or Coby would have been more like it.

When I introduced myself and shook her hand, she whispered: 'Are you coming along too, Mrs Kuyper?'

'That's the plan, yes.'

The girl looked as though she had just been told she had won the weekly lottery. I could see a great burden had been lifted off her shoulders. Heavens, I thought, she was utterly miserable because she was going out with four total strangers. Now she's happy as a clam at high tide because she's got a partner in misfortune. Gives you a sense of how tough an assignment something like this is. It's hard to grasp why girls let themselves in for it; they must be keen to get the money, no doubt only to blow it all in some disco afterwards.

In the meantime the four men were trumping each other with tales of derring-do. As the glasses emptied, the swaggering increased. Their glorious accounts of heroic deeds performed on construction sites, at fire stations and in scrap yards were interspersed with unsubtle jokes.

'Did you hear the one about the Frenchman, the Englishman and the Polish Jew?' said Arie, 'they took bets who could spend the longest time in a polecat's lair. First the Frenchman goes in. Within a minute he comes out and keels over. Then the Englishman goes in. After five minutes he comes out and keels over. Then the Polish Jew goes in, five minutes pass, ten minutes pass, fifteen minutes pass. "Why doesn't he come out?" say the Englishman and Frenchman, and then, after twenty minutes, the polecat comes out and keels over.'

I found it impossible to understand why they laughed so hard. It must be latent anti-Semitism, I thought, and I pushed my chair back a bit. The blonde pushed hers back as well, and I said softly: 'I've got no experience with this kind of thing, Sheila, I find it really creepy.'

'*Ach*,' she whispered, 'it's not that bad, you handcuff them and then nothing more can happen.'

'Yes, but you do have to give them a good thrashing, don't you?'

'Beating a carpet is a lot more tiring, here you don't have to hit nearly as hard.'

'And hoods? Don't you also do something with hoods?'

'Hoods?'

'Yes, I read in the newspaper the other day about hoods that go over the head. That way they don't get enough air and they get high...really scary stuff.'

'As far as I know, there's no hoods,' Sheila said grumpily. 'You beat them a bit, you drop hot candle wax on their backs, you put an ice cube between their balls...it's no big deal. Arie wears a collar with a chain. He always wants to be a watchdog, he gets a bowl of smelly dog food. Cor has to be strapped into a straitjacket. And Simon goes into the pillory. When he was a boy he used to see an ad for tobacco...'

'Oh yes, that ad for Van Rossum's pipe tobacco. A man in a pillory who's very contentedly smoking a pipe.'

'That's what *he* wants too, he spends the entire evening in the pillory, smoking a pipe, he's no bother at all. The only thing is the pipe keeps going out, that's a real pain. You've got to keep relighting it.'

'Oh, I can do that.'

'With *those* nails? Give me a break! You can barely hold a match. No, I'll work on Arie, Simon and Cor, and you can look after Fred, after all, he's your friend. He likes to be kicked and beaten, and at the end you've got to pee on him good and proper.'

'I'm not looking forward to it one bit, and those dildos...'

'Oh, but we won't get to them, I think; the trick is to make sure they've got off before they start thinking about the dildos, and when they've come the balloon deflates right away, then its game-over for them, all they want is to relax and talk while they're drinking a beer.'

'Do you enjoy doing this?'

'It pays an awful lot,' she said evasively.

'Ladies, would you care to rejoin us?' Fred said. 'I want to go and eat.'

'You were going to tell me where you found that verse,' I said.

'According to my CD-ROM it's *Isaiah* 38: verse 10, but it's written a bit differently. It says: "In the noontide of my days I shall go the gates of the grave, I am deprived of the residue of my years."'

'What's the context?' I asked.

'Context?'

'I mean: what's around it? How does it get to be the subject?'

'I haven't got the faintest. I typed "residue" into my computer, my CD-ROM hummed for a moment, and then it coughed up several verses with "residue" in them. I saw the right one at once: *Isaiah* 38: verse 10.'

'Would anyone happen to have a Bible available?' I asked.

Fire chief, auto wrecker, and driving-school owner all succumbed to great merriment.

'Do you have a Bible on you, Simon?'

'Normally I always carry one, you can't do without it in our line of work, but would you believe it? It happens to be in my other coat.'

'The Bible? No, not the Bible, but I do have the Koran here. Would that be of any help?' said Cornelis.

'When I went today out my wife said: "Arie, could you leave the Bible at home just this once? I want to look up a recipe for sweet and sour red cabbage."'

It was crazy to have asked for a Bible, of course, and the men kept on laughing and cracking lame jokes for some time. When they finally quieted down Fred said to me: 'I've got something else that may interest you. I got a report from Van Stenis, maybe there's something in it that will help us along. I brought it with me. Do you want to see it?'

'I'd love to,' I said, 'but how come he didn't send it to me? I paid him.'

'You paid him too? That scumbag! He sent me a bill as well, Goddammit, I'll give him hell for that on Monday, the dirty swindling rip-off artist.'

Once we were at the table, during that disagreeable dead time between ordering food and getting it, he gave me the thin report. More than anything else it resembled a neatly prepared student essay, with paragraphs and subheads. I didn't learn much. Van Stenis had taken great care to find out who had been in the lab between noon and one. One paragraph listed the names of all those who had seen Rose leave the lab at twelve-thirty (the coffee lady, Riet Goudsblom, two students, the research assistant and one of the secretaries), with the additional information that each of them had heard the black Saab start right after Rose walked out. Van Stenis also noted there had been a visitor after twelve-thirty: Marjolein Mentink. I contemplated this name for a while. She had dropped by the lab briefly. That was really nothing remarkable: when Thomas was still there she had often dropped in, and besides, she had worked there as a young woman. And yet her name kept running through my head while we ate a quintessentially Dutch meal – noodle soup, braised beef with cauliflower, crumbly potatoes and a thick brown sauce, and semolina pudding for dessert (and that before an SM orgy!). You could go blind staring at what seemed to be the most likely motive for the murder – fear of the consequences should it become known that there had been large-scale fraud in reporting research findings. But it was possible there had been another motive: jealousy, for example. Suppose the man in the SM photo was Bas. Suppose Marjolein had found out that Bas's former girlfriend had something going with him again and used the whip on him from time to time? Fantasies, sure, they were probably fantasies, and besides, I hated her and was deeply prejudiced against her. Moreover, she had entered the lab at 12:35 – five minutes after Rose had left.

What gave me growing concern during the meal was that the four men were washing the exotic dishes down with amazingly large quantities of wine. Whether they were fine wines I couldn't say, I don't know about wine and hope to keep it that way, but *one* thing I do know for sure: whatever wine you're drinking, each glass contains around twelve percent alcohol. Would Sheila and I have to hit the road with four drunks?

It turned out differently. After the meal, coffee was served, which did nothing to allay my fears because it is a myth that coffee sobers you up, but when the men had amply imbibed *that* liquid, each putting back a big snifter of cognac at the same time, Fred said: 'The time has come to set sail.'

At that moment it should have become clear to me where we were going, but I was in a state of, let us say, controlled panic. Even when, after a lot of merry hooting and hollering, the motor boat had cast off, and we were moving along a broad waterway named the Joppe under heavy cloud cover and in near pitch-black darkness, I still didn't realize where the SM event was going to take place. My entire being was in a state of protest, and I latched onto Sheila, who was seated on a small bench in a sort of deckhouse.

'This is really creepy,' I said.

'You'll see: it's not so bad.'

'Have you been there before?'

'Twice.'

'Were you all by yourself with these guys?'

'No, thank God, both times somebody came along, a cousin of someone else who used to go there with them a while ago, but she seems to be out of commission now. A real pity, because these guys were crazy about her.'

'These guys are hammered,' I said disapprovingly.

'Yeah, that's a real pain. The more they've drunk, the longer it takes before they come.'

'I hope you'll take charge of that department.'

'Oh, fine by me, I'll give it a good yank.'

What a cute expression, I thought, I must remember that, it might come in handy some day.

'The only thing is, you've got the right nails for it,' Sheila said. 'If you tickle them with those, it'll get them off in no time.'

She took my hand, caressed the plastic nails and said: 'Too bad they're so terribly impractical. Guys get really horny when they see them, and the hornier they are, the quicker they come, but, well, nails like that are pretty well useless for most things.'

'You get used to them,' I said, 'and they keep me from mindlessly eating potato chips in front of the TV.'

'Could be, but how are you going to do up your corset once we're there?'

I wanted to say: 'I'm not getting into any corset,' but then I thought: I can't let that poor lamb try to cope with these four lushes all by herself, so instead I said: 'Maybe you'll do it up for me when the time comes.'

'That goes without saying, at least, if my fingers are still up to the job; they're just about frozen. I hope it's going to be warmer over there, I'm freezing my butt off.'

Yellow, white, blue and red lights twinkled everywhere on the shore, but on the Joppe it was dark as could be. Even the reflection off the water's surface was barely visible through the copper-rimmed porthole. Time and again oncoming boats loomed up out of the darkness, and we were often only barely able to avoid them. Fred stuck his head into the deckhouse.

'Ladies, is everything okay?'

'It's cold as hell,' Sheila said.

'You should have worn your fur coat.'

'Don't have one.'

With a boozy catch in his throat, Fred sang: 'Jesus, Saviour, pilot me, over life's tempestuous sea; unknown waves before me roll, hiding rock and treach'rous shoal.'

He stopped singing and said to me: 'You know that one, don't you?'

'Indeed I do.'

'So why weren't you singing along?'

'Were *you* allowed to sing that when you were a kid?'

'No, of course not, it's not a psalm. In *my* church they called that kind of hymn a whorehouse ditty. That's how come I know it so well.'

And loudly he sang all three stanzas of 'Jesus, Saviour, Pilot Me', holding the tune well, but every note with a drunken quaver. If I hadn't been feeling so panicky, I would have burst out laughing at the lines: 'Boist'rous waves obey thy will when thou sayest to them, "Be still."' He blared the hymn out over the Joppe with total commitment and bravura then ended with a long sustained trill on the final note. 'You sing quite creditably,' I said.

'When I was a kid I really would have loved to join a choir,' he said, 'but I wasn't allowed to, it was sinful, worldly pleasure.' Then he exploded: 'Those assholes, they ruined my whole childhood with their fucking bullshit, their Goddamn Bible, their shit-face elders, their dickhead dominees, oh, how I'd love to go into church some Sunday with a machine gun, I'd mow down every last one of them, every filthy son of a bitch, I'd blast their balls off, right through the pews while they were sitting there and then I'd turn the muzzle on their Goddamn heads so that their brains would splatter over the communion table...'

'Stop it at once,' I said in Rose's voice.

His rage seemed to dissolve in an instant. Calmly he asked me: 'Don't you ever get worked up over what they did to you?'

'Why should I? It's often a source of pleasure to me now that I was kept on such a short leash back then. Our dominee used to say in his sermons: "Sisters, please don't ever wear trousers, it grieves the Lord so greatly."'

'And you enjoy remembering bullshit like that?'

'Because of that, it's really enjoyable to put on a pair of stretch jeans, for example. You would never sing that hymn with so much pleasure if it hadn't been forbidden when you were young. Forbidden fruit tastes sweet.'

Before Fred could reply, Simon shouted: 'Get ready to disembark. *Poseidon*, ahoy.'

'The *Poseidon*?' I asked, dumbfounded.

'Yes,' Fred said proudly, 'nice little houseboat. Picked it up for a song, fixed it up, turned it into a small palace. Rose was blown away by it, and so was her cousin.'

'I told you she didn't have any family, so no cousin either.'

'No cousin either? I'll be a monkey's uncle. That girl, little Fiona…the poor lamb is completely at sea since Rose…she wasn't her cousin?'

'She probably called Fiona her cousin, just as she called me her sister.'

'Oh,' he said, 'well, we'll just have to accept that; watch out, Arie, there goes that *Poseidon*-spotter in his penny-ante rowboat, the one who's always keeping track of us.'

Arie gave a small tug at the wheel. The *Poseidon* loomed up leeward. Psalm 100 rose up in my throat: 'Make a joyful noise unto the Lord, all ye lands.' At the same time I felt deeply mortified. When I first saw the houseboat I had jumped to the conclusion that it was a floating laboratory and that Rose had made Ecstasy pills there. As though I had been glad to believe it! Without any tangible proof, on the basis of the vaguest evidence, I had unquestioningly assumed that she had sold her soul to the drug trade. True, experience had taught me that people – 'that doesn't surprise me at all, I thought so all along' – can believe at the drop of a hat idle rumours that put good friends in a bad light. But that I myself had done the same thing, had in fact spread the rumour? I who had loved Rose so dearly? I would never be able to make up for that. They ought to put *me* in a pillory and whip me until my back bled.

While I was overcome by shame and simultaneously felt happy as a lark because Rose had been cleared of all Ecstasy-related guilt, our small boat moored alongside the *Poseidon*. Cor took a rope that had lain under cover on the deck of the boat and pulled it through a ring on the *Poseidon*. Because the bow was now firmly attached, the boat's stern drifted peacefully towards open water. Sheila had emerged from the deckhouse with her case and was up on deck. Cor, Simon and Arie were up on deck as well; Fred had taken the wheel from Arie. As I put my right foot on deck, a cabin cruiser of the kind that's bought by people with more money than sense loomed up out of the darkness and rammed us amidships. The force of the collision sent Cor, Simon, Arie and Sheila overboard on the windward side. I smacked against the deckhouse roof. On the cruiser, a woman's voice yelled 'Back up!' and the ship, which even had radar (raising the question how it had failed to spot us), backed up amidst turbulently churning water. Then it turned around and swiftly disappeared.

While I watched its board lights fade, Fred pulled Sheila out of the water. Cor and Simon hoisted themselves out and were back on deck even before I, shivering slightly, had got up and stepped out of the deckhouse, suitcase in hand.

'Arie's gone,' said Cor.

'Arie's gone,' confirmed Simon.

'Arie's gone?' said Fred.

The three men peered intently into the glistening black, peacefully murmuring water.

'His head hit the railing,' Simon said, 'I heard something crack. Maybe he's lying down there on the bottom, unconscious.'

'We have to get him out,' said Fred. 'You two are wet already, so in you go.'

Simon and Cor went overboard again while Fred yelled after them: 'We can't have it that later on he's pulled out of the Joppe dead. What the hell would we say to his wife? I don't know what story he told her, but he sure as hell won't have said he was going to get his rocks off on the *Poseidon*.'

These remarks seemed to help. Arie's deathly pale head appeared above the railing. Blood ran out of a large wound above his right eye. 'He's still breathing,' Cor said. Fred pulled him out of the Joppe without apparent effort, while Cor and Simon climbed back on deck. I was enormously impressed by the calmness and efficiency with which they acted.

'He needs help,' said Fred. 'There's nothing for it but to take him overland to some place where we can get an ambulance.'

'I'm dying of cold,' Sheila wailed.

'Why don't you two go into the *Poseidon*?' Fred said to Sheila and me. 'Here's the key, it's warm inside, we're going to take Arie away, and we'll come and get you later. If you think it's taking too long, just hail a passing boat, there's plenty of them coming by. One of them can take you to some place where you can get a taxi.'

Followed by Sheila, who was dripping, I walked along the *Poseidon*'s narrow gangway to the front door. When I opened it, warm air came billowing out. Evidently the heating was on high. But even after we were inside, Sheila continued to tremble and shiver. It was dark, and I felt around for a light switch. At last I found the round knob of a dimmer switch. I turned it, half-preparing myself for the sight of Erlenmeyer flasks, test tubes, beakers, Bunsen burners and exhaust hoods. In fact, a fairy-tale interior, lit by ceiling spotlights, slowly came into view. In the large rectangular space stood three horses of the kind I remembered from gym class, pillories, and chairs to whose armrests horseshoe-shaped manacles had been attached. The chair legs had also been fitted with shackles. Chains with various hooks hung from the ceiling. There were gears too. Apparently you could put a manacled slave in a harness, hang him from one of those hooks, and crank him up. In the corner stood a narrow bed covered with folded blankets and a huge bath towel.

'Take off your clothes, Sheila,' I said, 'We've got to dry them as quickly as possible.'

'I'm soaked,' she said, 'I'm freezing to death.'

Shivering violently, she took off her flimsy garments. Meanwhile I looked for something she could put on. I found a shiny leather coat, but after she put it on, having first removed her sopping wet underclothes, she shrieked: 'Oh, that's so cold on my skin!'

'Then wrap yourself in a blanket,' I said, taking one off the bed.

I picked up her wet clothes. 'You'll see, they've got all the niftiest stuff here, but a laundry rack? Forget it. And even if there were one, where would you put it? There isn't a space heater in sight.'

'Can't my things dry on the radiators?' asked Sheila.

'I don't see any radiators; it's a safe bet they've got forced air heating.'

'Next door, in the cubicle where we always had to change, there's an electric radiator on wheels, I think.'

I opened the cubicle. There actually was a small radiator. I plugged it into an outlet, walked back, took the bath towel from the narrow bed, put it over the radiator and then draped her wet clothes on the large towel.

'All we can do now is wait until everything has dried,' I said.

I settled myself in a chair with manacles on the armrests. Sheila first sat on the bed then tried to lie down, but the folded blankets were in the way. She pushed them off the bed, lay down and asked: 'Leonie, could you please put a few blankets over me?' I did so and then got back into my manacle-chair. Sheila sneezed.

'You've caught a cold,' I said.

'I'm allergic to dust mites,' she said.

Then we both stopped talking, and I just sat there and stared at the pillories and gears. A spotlight was mounted on the ceiling; it pointed at a large cage. Its bars cast a fan of shadows on the floor. They looked like a lot of sundials, I thought, and as I peered into the shadows the warmth made me languid and dozy. No Ecstasy, thank God there had been no Ecstasy but in that case where *did* all that money come from? These outings? Whipping men part-time in a classy club in Den Haag's Flower District? I wanted to ask Sheila: 'How much does a session like this pay?' but she had closed her eyes. Maybe she was sleeping. I felt nice and sleepy myself, but I didn't altogether pass out, I sank into a somnolent doze. It seemed as if my wrists had been shackled to the armrests with the horseshoe-shaped manacles and my legs had been shackled to the chair legs. I couldn't move any more, I felt as if I had been anaesthetized, drugged. The sundial arose slowly before my mind's eye. 'He brought the shadow ten degrees backward, by which it had gone forward on the dial of Ahaz.' How many minutes would that be, ten degrees? A full circle was 360 degrees, a full day was twenty-four hours, so you had to divide 360 by twenty-four. Was that fifteen? In that case ten degrees were forty minutes. If at 12:45 the sun were to turn back ten degrees, it would once again be five past twelve.

Five past twelve wasn't necessary: twenty-five past twelve would do the trick. Marjolein had shown up at the lab at 12:35. Was the clock in the porter's office fast, perhaps? Would the sundial perhaps be slow? No, it was always on time, it gave the only correct time, not the Central European compromise time of clocks and watches. Could that account for a difference of a few minutes? Too bad I was too sleepy to be able to think clearly.

I woke up with a start, feeling stiff and shivery, when Fred opened the front door of the *Poseidon* and announced that unfortunately it was too late for fun and games. I remember little of what happened after that. I continued to feel drowsy when we sailed back over the Joppe and when we took the little ferry from the Kaag Club to the parking lot. For example, I can't remember where Fred dropped off Sheila. Or was that because the night was so dark? What I do remember is that Sheila and I sat in the backseat of the car and that she said to me: 'I will get my money, won't I?'

'It would be the limit if you didn't,' I said. 'At the least you should get damages in lieu.'

So when Fred opened the door to let her out and made no move to pay her, I growled: 'Doesn't she get her money?'

'Why should she?'

'You engaged her. Can she help it if she wasn't able to do her work?'

'We *can* help it, I suppose?'

'You've got to keep paying your workers even when there's heavy frost, don't you? She has a right to her money. She almost drowned, for Heaven's sake.'

'It's just like I hear Rose speaking,' he said contentedly, pulled a billfold from an inside pocket, then said: 'Five hundred each was the agreement; I'll settle with Arie, Cor and Simon.' He gave her two thousand guilders then said to me: 'And you? Do you want to be paid, too?'

'You must be out of your mind,' I said.

155

22.

Before I went to bed that night, I opened her Bible to look for Isaiah: 38 verse 10. If only I hadn't done that. As I was turning the thin rustling pages a thousand-guilder bill fell out of the Lamentations of Jeremiah. 'All that money,' I groaned. Isaiah 38: 10 turned out to be the first sentence of King Hezekiah's song of thanksgiving. I really should have known that, for just above it verse 8 read: 'Behold, I will bring again the shadow of the degrees, which is gone forward in the sundial, ten degrees backward.'

So I couldn't get to sleep, and I lay there, tossing and turning feverishly. What to make of this? Coincidence? In his funeral eulogy the Professor Emeritus, the boss as he was still called, had referred to Hezekiah's song of thanksgiving. That song pointed to Hezekiah's recovery and the miracle of the sundial. It was only a step from the sundial to the shadow cast by the bush next to it, the South Asian thorn apple with its purple flower petals.

I don't have much use for Freud. Still, it seemed not impossible that the Professor had unconsciously chosen this particular text for a reason. If he *had* killed her because of the fear of exposure as a scientific fraud and the dreadful loss of face that would result from it, the image of that shadow must have been buried in his unconscious mind. And the result was that at the funeral service he had, by way of Freudian alchemy, implicitly pointed to the sundial without realizing it.

In any case, after a sleepless night, that was the conclusion I came to. I dropped off at the crack of dawn. When the cats woke me up, meowing indignantly because they hadn't been fed yet, everything my mind had conjured up during the night seemed like a chimera. Had Wehnagel actually *been* in the lab that fatal Wednesday? Van Stenis's report said not one word about it.

'Be patient,' I said to the cats. 'I'm facing this all alone, whereas a professor always has a lab technician available to take care of the dirty work.' For example, had Marjolein, who once worked there as a research assistant, ever looked after Eduard's dirty work? She hadn't entered the lab until 12:35, of course. But was 12:30 on the sundial perhaps equivalent to 12:45 on the clock in the porter's cubby-hole?

My thought processes began to grind once more. Did the regular clock run ahead of the sundial? But how did that fit with European Summer Time and standard time, and did the clock advance in the spring or did it go back? When European Summer Time started, didn't you have to get up an hour earlier? That must be true, because most of the complaints came in the spring. So didn't that mean that the regular clock ran way ahead of the sundial? In that event there was no point talking about a difference of, say, fifteen minutes, in that case the difference had to be a multiple of that, unless the people in the lab took account of the fact that, in summer, sundial time diverged sharply from Central European Time and silently corrected for it. I would have to go there when the sun shone and ask Mijna for the time and then run over to the porter. Of course Bas would give me a rough time because I was walking around looking like Rose again. So what? He could go straight to hell, I thought.

At the end of the afternoon the telephone chirped.

'Hello.'

'Fred here, you haven't caught cold?'

'No, but I didn't sleep all that well.'

'Feel like a little cuddle?'

'Have you gone completely crazy?'

'No, I'm horny.'

'So give it a good yank.'

'Done that already, didn't help.'

'A little cuddle, what an expression!'

'So what *should* I say? Will you go to bed with me? I've always thought that was such a dumb thing to say. As if you absolutely need a bed. Doing it standing up is often most fun.'

'Lay off, please; sex is just like yarn.'

'You mean yarn for knitting? What the hell are you burbling about?'

'It can be nice and warm, but it gets tangled up awfully quickly.'

'I'm glad you expressed yourself so clearly.'

'So did you.'

'Yes, and why not? If you *had* felt like it and I hadn't asked, maybe you would have thought: am I that old, am I no longer attractive? I didn't want you to think that.'

'Thanks for the compliment,' I said.

'Thank you too. We've now discussed the topic fully, and henceforth it is closed. From now on we can deal with each other without feeling that sooner or later we'll have to get it on together.'

After I had put down the receiver, I thought contentedly: well, look at the new, the authoritative woman. Then I thought: would Rose have spoken so bluntly to this contractor? Had she ever slept with Fred? It struck me as less than likely, she used to say: 'All that stupid, moist messing around between the sheets, and then they have to go straight into the washing machine, it's so enormously overrated, people get terribly worked up over it and yet it means so little, it's a need, just like eating and drinking and shitting and sneezing. Shopping is a thousand times more fun.'

So I went out with my Biblical thousand guilders (long live Sunday shopping!) and tried to buy a breathtaking sky-blue pants suit with a short fitted jacket. But the salesman didn't want to take my thousand-guilder note, and since the banks were closed I couldn't get it changed. I could have used my debit card or other, smaller bills, but I absolutely wanted to spend this particular thousand, so I went back to the store and said to the salesman: 'I can't get this thousand changed anywhere, and I don't want to pay any other way. Why don't I give you my name and address? You can go to the bank tomorrow; if the bill is a fake, you'll know where to find me.'

He badly wanted to make the sale and gave in, and so I had acquired something Rose might have worn but that I could nevertheless wear to the lab, because of course she had never been seen in it there.

That turned out to be a serious miscalculation. The next day was cloudless, and when I walked through the corridors, my heels clattering on the composite floor, I startled everyone I met. The porter stared at me as though I had come to take his life. A student who met me in the hall demonstratively turned his head away. Mijna barely looked at me when I asked her: 'What time is it?' Promptly she answered, without first looking outside: 'Half-past nine,' the very same answer the discombobulated porter had given me twenty seconds earlier.

I tried to imagine how it must look from their point of view. Here was a woman who was doing her level best to look exactly like someone they had seen every working day for years and whom they had liked a lot. Would the sight of this look-alike be a shock? Or would they think: she's gone bananas, she ought to go see a psychiatrist? Or would they get angry? No, they didn't get angry, they were simply pained by the sight of me.

I looked at the sundial and tried to figure out the time. Ten past nine? Then would it…?

I walked out of the room. In the corridor I ran into Riet. She cast a disapproving glance at my nails, came to a halt and said: 'What brings *you* here, child?'

'I just came to check the clocks.'

'Come again?'

'It may be that the porter's clock indicates a different time from the one in the coffee room. According to the porter, somebody came into the lab at 12:35. By that time Rose was supposed to have left, but I keep thinking: maybe the sundial indicates a time that is different from normal Central European Time, maybe this somebody was already here before Rose left.'

'As if someone who knew this place and had evil plans wouldn't also know that there's a back entrance.'

'You're right! That didn't occur to me. But then you'd have to sneak through the old morgue.'

'Just the sort of thing a murderer would do, I should think,' Riet said sarcastically.

'I get the impression you don't put much stock in that theory.'

'Come along to my office; we can talk there undisturbed.'

After she had shut the door carefully and had sat down behind her desk, she asked: 'Did that young lady from Canada try to tell you people have been committing fraud here for years?'

'How did you know *that*?' I asked in surprise.

'"Know" is a big word; I suspected it. That research team in Montreal is working in the very same area as us. They've been trying to do us one better for years now. Not long ago they decided to change their tactics: now they want to crush us. It started last year at the big pharmacological conference. Whispering in the corridors. That wonderful research in Holland? Maybe it's all a swindle, a fraud? This time they sent us a cutie-pie who wound everyone around her little finger while she spied on us. Outside the lab she let it be known here and there that we've been fudging data for years. She said it to you, she said it to the director of the university hospital at a reception, and I'm willing to bet she said it to ten or twenty people on whom our research financing depends. She has sown the wind. Now she's gone back home to Montreal, where in time they hope to see *us* reap the whirlwind.'

'I don't get it,' I said. 'You insisted she stay at my place, you spoke very highly of her, and now...'

'Bas and I wanted to put her up someplace where she couldn't do a lot of damage.'

'So the reason you told me she was so nice was that you wanted me to cooperate.'

'A little white lie. I apologize. You can ask Bas for an apology as well; he's the one who thought of it.'

She sat there for a few moments, looking sombrely into the middle distance, then said: 'What a stroke of luck for those guys in Montreal that there seems to have been a murder here! They can make it part of their rumour-mongering campaign. I keep asking myself whether maybe it was all a put-up job, it was so amazingly convenient for them.'

'Do you mean to say that those guys in Montreal...?'

'No, no, they had no part in *that*. That strikes me as being out of the question; it would be far too risky. No, my mind is on a different track, I believe the girl told her husband...if he *was* her husband, they acted so exaggeratedly devoted to each other that I can hardly believe it...I believe this girl told the so-called botanist, by phone or email or letter, that there was an exotic Datura in the quad here, and then he made up some wonderful-sounding story about seeds you can use to make a deadly poison.'

'I find that hard to believe. In fact, I don't believe it; it should be possible to check that out.'

'I *have* checked it out, I've looked up all the literature on genus Datura I was able to find in the library of the State Herbarium. For starters, that stuff about sunshine seems to be full of holes. Even if you don't go out in the sun, you're in danger. It also appears that the white variety is more poisonous than the purple one we have. But if you swallow the powder, you can be in trouble within five minutes.'

'Good Lord,' I said, 'but there's something I still don't understand. How would it benefit the team in Montreal to have this man tell a tale like that over coffee here?'

'Don't you get it? Something like this spreads like wildfire. You can bet the entire academic community knows by now that a woman was poisoned in Pharmacology. You can guess what the outcome will be for *our* team.'

'But was Rose not poisoned, then? Would that man...? He seemed such a nice fellow...he practically had to be carried out of the room.'

'A great actor, that's what he was. Since when did *you* go by appearances?

You yourself are a shining example of how they can be adapted to one's wishes. But remember what Goethe has Mephistopheles say to Faust: 'You are just what you are. Do what you will; wear wigs, full-bottomed, each with a million locks, stand up yards high on stilts or actor's socks – you're what you are, you'll be the same man still.' Believe me, child, that performance served and serves one purpose and one purpose only: to destroy the pharmacologists in Leiden.'

'So that story about the Datura...'

'I have serious doubts about it.'

'But in that case... Sunstroke, after all?'

'There's nothing to suggest otherwise. That's what I keep saying, and I pretty well have to, because morale here is lower than low, it's like the death knell keeps ringing all day long.'

'I'm not the least bit surprised...that man, he really shook me up, too.'

'Not me. Right away I thought: there's something fishy here, a story like that about a dash of powder in the coffee...come now, things would never be done that amateurishly in a place like this. You wouldn't even know the LD 50 of a substance like that: the dose that would kill half the subjects taking it.'

'And what about the fraud?'

'Fraud? I would put both arms in the flames for Eduard, up to the elbows. It'll be the death of him if he hears what they're cooking up in Montreal. I've been there. I've seen how they work. They're bunglers, terrible bunglers, so it doesn't surprise me one little bit that they can't confirm our results. Since Rose's death his health has been a problem. No, fraud...'

She looked at me like an offended schoolmarm.

'Shall I tell you something? Scientific research is just like playing the piano, you've got to be awfully precise, you've got to weigh and titrate and use a pipette and filter and distil, and for all that you need your fingertips, just as when you're playing the piano. Ever seen a woman with long nails who plays the piano well? I always used to say to Eduard: keep Rose away from my research. It's impossible to work carefully with claws like that. He used to laugh at me. I'm telling you: if there's anything the matter with the results of his research it is *her* fault. It's all because of those misshapen fingernails.'

She closed her eyes for a moment, said resignedly: 'And because you identify with Rose you are actually wearing... May I ask you something you may not wish to answer? Are you also turning against Mozart and Schubert these days? Since you've moved, do you prefer her music too, Bill Evans and Miles Davis?'

She didn't give me an opportunity to answer, which suited me just fine. Apparently she knew the answer already. She raged on: 'Please cut off those nails as soon as you get home, child. They look like nothing on earth, they're vulgar, they're ugly, they serve no purpose; you're not a bird of prey, are you?'

'They help me lose weight.'

'Help you lose weight? What kind of idiocy is that?'

'Thanks to these nails I can't pick up anything or cook anything delicious. Before I had them I used to sit in front of the TV and empty a bag of potato chips without thinking.'

'As if you need nails like that to keep from eating potato chips. Cocaine is banned, but the supermarkets are crammed full with wagonloads of horrible greasy chips and salted snacks full of carcinogenic acrylamide and all kinds of other garbage…it's Godawful. If you're not disciplined enough to stay away from potato chips, keep walking around with those claws with my blessing.'

When I was back out on the street, I felt strangely light-headed. After Riet's astonishing verbal assault on Rose's nails it seemed to me as if everyone was staring at mine, and so I put on my gloves and kept them on when I entered the State Herbarium. Once in the library, I said to a man who looked as if he had been laid out to dry between two pieces of parchment many years ago: 'I'm sorry I can't be more specific, but do you perhaps have some literature about the genus Datura?'

'That plant has been enjoying a remarkable amount of interest lately,' the librarian said.

'So everything is out?'

'No, one volume was returned very recently. It's still lying here, I can let you have it in a moment.'

When I went out again, the book loosely under my arm, a borrower's slip fell out. I bent down, picked it up, and, since I didn't know what to do with it and couldn't see a refuse bin anywhere nearby, I put it back into the book. Waste not, want not; I could always use it as a bookmark.

23.

Towards the end of a windless day in December, I cycled along Uiterste Gracht through fallen oak leaves. Because Digros was out of Sheba, I had gone to buy it at a pet store. A heavy, dark-grey blanket of clouds had been hanging overhead all day. Oddly enough it wasn't raining or even drizzling. When I still used to drive I had noticed that, after sunset, cyclists dressed in dark clothes became visible only at the last moment, even when their front and rear lights were both on. That's why I had chosen Rose's light-brown muskrat jacket from among the many possibilities in her ample collection. I wanted to save drivers from what I had so often experienced myself: being frightened witless by a cyclist suddenly looming up out of the darkness.

I thought I could wear that fur jacket without feeling guilty. As far as I know, muskrats aren't raised for their fur but are trapped by the tens of thousands because they constitute a huge danger to dikes and dams. In my opinion, it's all right to make coats from the skins of animals that have to be killed anyway. With the jacket I wore a matching muskrat cap, which reduced my face to a smallish oval.

Slowly I pedalled along. A bicycle doesn't go very fast, but what a delightful way of moving around it is compared with an automobile, in which you sit all hunched up and you constantly have to worry about getting into accidents. And it's not even that you're afraid of getting hurt yourself but of killing somebody else. Anyway, I guess not very many people share that fear, because even on Uiterste Gracht there was the beginning of a traffic jam.

As I wriggled my way past the cars, I saw a black Saab waiting between a Peugeot and a Honda Civic. Moments later the Peugeot passed me, and right behind it the Saab slipped past me almost noiselessly. To be honest, I paid no attention to the licence plate, but when I passed the three cars a short while later, the driver of the black Saab honked his horn. It almost seemed as if he was honking at me in greeting. I stood out in my light-brown fur jacket, but I thought it rather strange that I was being greeted from inside a car. When you're on a bicycle it's hard to see people inside a car. It often happens that a driver waves at me enthusiastically and I think: who could that be, for Heaven's sake? And then I just wave back. At night it's almost impossible for a cyclist to see who is behind the wheel. So I waved a couple of times and rode on, and a few moments later the three cars passed me again. The Saab honked a second time.

Who could that be? I wondered. As the car speeded up I looked at the licence plate: NJ-JN-25. Because I hadn't expected this, a few seconds went by before I realized it was Rose's car that was disappearing into the December darkness.

Who was driving Rose's Saab? The question fascinated me. It must be somebody who didn't feel ashamed that he had appropriated, no, let's call a spade a spade, that he had *stolen* the Saab. The thief had used the horn, bold as brass. As though he knew who I was and wanted to say: look at me, here I go, you can eat my dust. Sure, but that couldn't be it; the thief couldn't possibly know that the cyclist in the light-brown jacket he had passed on Uiterste Gracht had inherited all of Rose's possessions, the black Saab included. Or was it possible that the thief had known Rose well enough to know that she often wore a muskrat jacket in winter?

I pedalled harder. Maybe I could catch up with the Saab and find out who was at the wheel. When I reached the boulevard I spotted the Saab standing in a line of cars up ahead. This time it was not a mini-jam but one that extended all the way from one bridge to the next, a considerable distance farther on. The darkness was brightened by the taillights of the slowly advancing cars. Even the pedestrians on the sidewalk were making better time, and the cyclists on the bicycle path were simply flying past the long line of vehicles.

I halted on the first bridge. If I were to ride alongside the virtually motionless cars, I could stop next to the black Saab and look into it. Whether I would be able to figure out who the driver was remained to be seen. I could brazenly tap on the window, of course. The question was whether the driver would have the nerve to open the window and speak to me. What if, as seemed altogether likely, it turned out to be someone I didn't know? Some idiot who was turned on by women in fur jackets and who had honked at me for that reason? Someone like that would certainly open his window if I drew up alongside and tapped on it. A man like that might even think I was responding to his car-horn overtures. Yuck! No, that was not exactly the best way to discover who was driving Rose's Saab as though it were his own.

Suppose I was able to follow him until he got home. Then I would know where he lived and could consult with Graafland and decide what we should do next.

I pedalled slowly past the lined-up cars. The Saab was a fair distance up ahead. Would the driver see me approach? Surely not, because he was on the left side of his car, while I was riding past the cars on the right. And yet, as I drew closer, the chances of him spotting my fur jacket in his rear-view mirror, for example, would increase. What had seemed like such a good idea, wearing a light-brown jacket in the dark so as not to startle drivers, had turned into a disadvantage. But didn't I have my dark-blue plastic raincoat with me in my carrier bag? I could put that on.

I stopped at a curve. Houseboats were moored in the canal, and in the narrow strip of green between water and road stood some spindly trees. I hastily donned my dark-blue coat behind one of them. I released the dynamo from my front tire. From now on my light would not be able to betray me either.

I got moving again, pedalling past the long line of cars, the Saab among them, firmly resisting the temptation to look back at it after I had gone by it. I rode until I reached the next traffic light, where one could go in two directions. Passing between two stopped cars, I crossed the road on foot, looked for a dark spot near some tall trees and waited patiently until the Saab showed up. It seemed unlikely that I would manage to keep tailing the Saab. As a cyclist, I enjoyed the advantage as long as there were traffic jams, but as soon as the Saab hit a piece of open road it would be gone from sight. Still, it was worth a try. Waiting was hard. Every time the light turned green four or five cars succeeded in getting through. Then everything ground to a halt again, while the traffic at other lights came slowly into motion. As I watched, I marvelled that every day millions of people subjected themselves to this ordeal all over again. Advance, come to a halt, advance, come to a halt, pass through a green light, crawl a hundred metres to the next set of lights and then go through everything again: advance, come to a halt, advance, pass through another green light until they reach the next set of lights, the sequence repeating itself relentlessly. *Ad infinitum.* All right, not quite yet, but that's only a question of time. One day the roads will be so full that the traffic jams will not dissolve, and the cars will be in gridlock, forever facing traffic lights that promise much as they change from red to green, but whose promises are empty.

It hadn't reached that point yet on that dark December afternoon. The black Saab reached the lights at last. When they turned green the Saab turned left, and I followed at a suitable distance. The next lights were two hundred metres away. There the Saab could either go straight on or turn right. So at that point I had to wait again. Fortunately right by the stoplights there was a flower-stand on the broad sidewalk. I took cover behind it.

Some four minutes later, the Saab passed through the lights and picked up speed as it moved along Hoge Rijndijk. Before it reached the big bridge over the canal, it might turn right at Kanaalweg, in which case I would have to abandon the chase. The traffic jam at the bridge consisted mainly of cars that wanted to get *off* Kanaalweg and *on* to Hoge Rijndijk. If at that point the Saab turned right, it had an open road as far as the eye could see.

When I neared the bridge I saw the Saab in a line-up of cars waiting for the light at the bridge to change. A bell rang, and the bridge span went up. As a result, within a couple of minutes the line of waiting cars on Hoge Rijndijk stretched back to Hogewoerd, and the line on Kanaalweg back to the next province. I saw nothing but the headlights and taillights of hundreds of automobiles. As a cyclist, when I find myself in the middle of something like this I can only shake my head over such a grossly impractical and at the same time very costly means of transportation. Even a person shuffling along behind a Zimmer frame moves with greater speed.

I concealed myself near the barriers, on a strip of grass behind the cars that were lined up along Kanaalweg. When, after an almost unbearably long wait – four long river-vessels passed slowly through – the bridge began to close at last I positioned myself right at the barrier. I had to reach the next traffic light as quickly as possible. The Saab could go in any of three directions there, so I had to find a place from which I could, without being observed, see which way it went.

With a hollow, almost macabre, sound the bridge closed. The barriers opened, the cyclists started to move, but the cars were still jammed up. I spent at least three impatient minutes at the next light waiting for the black Saab to show up. Before it did I had plenty of time to look for a dark spot where I could wait for it. If the Saab drove straight on at this point, many more traffic lights awaited it, which would make following it a piece of cake. Only if the driver were to turn right at the fifth light, onto the highway, could I kiss him and the car goodbye. If he turned right where I stood waiting, he would find himself in a shabby residential area that he could only leave the same way he had entered it. No matter how quickly he disappeared into that neighbourhood, I would certainly be able to track him down. If he turned left, he would be on Waard Island. There too, he would never be able to escape me.

He turned left, onto Waard Island. Braking for each speed bump, the Saab crept along. I followed at a prudent distance. Finally the car stopped at the head of the island, where the most expensive of the linked villas enjoyed the most expansive view over the Zijl River. I chained my bicycle to a traffic sign. Then, staying in the shadows as much as possible, I walked slowly towards the Saab. The taillights went out, the door swung open. A slender person wrapped in a long dark cloak got out. Beyond any doubt it was a woman or, perhaps I should say, a girl. Curious how you can tell, even when the distance is great, even when you see nothing but the curve of a back, whether you're dealing with a man or a woman.

While the girl got her handbag out of the car, I took a few more steps in her direction. I think I already knew who was slinging her bag so gracefully over her right shoulder. She slammed the door shut, walking resolutely towards me. For a moment I considered ducking into a side street and allowing her to pass, so that I would be able to shadow her, but when she had come a bit closer, and I watched her long hair light up under the yellow streetlight, I was so sure it was the alabaster-skinned girl that I calmly waited for her to reach me. I took off my plastic raincoat, rolled it up and put it in my carrier bag. The girl who was nearing me naturally saw my light-brown muskrat jacket. It evidently didn't disturb her; on the contrary, she picked up the pace, came up to me and said: 'Hey, is it you, Mrs Kuyper? How did you get here so fast? Saw you cycling by the canal a while ago. Were you on your way over here?'

'I followed you here,' I said. 'I wanted to know who was driving Rose's black Saab.'

'Oh, that's dead simple. It's Fiona. But surely you already knew that? Passed you in Wassenaar, honked horn at you, you were on the bicycle path to Den Haag.' She gave me a friendly smile.

I stared at her, feeling bewildered. 'How did you find out Rose was dead, Fiona?'

'Heard it in the hospital. Was there for out-patient surgery.'

'How come you're driving Rose's Saab?'

'Rose used to say: if I die, you can have my Saab.'

'Yes, but how…did you fetch it from Katwijk?'

'Took the bus to Katwijk after the funeral service, thought it was okay then. After all, Rose was gone forever.'

'You knew where it was parked?'

'Yes, had come along often enough when she went sunbathing, she always parked in the same spot; could find it almost without looking that Monday evening.'

'How did you get hold of her car keys?'

'She had given Fiona the second set. In case she died suddenly. She kept thinking she would die suddenly, and in that case Fiona wouldn't be able to get her keys.'

'But the car isn't registered in your name. The other day I got a photo-radar speeding ticket in the mail. That caused a big hassle.'

'Oh, sorry, know where that happened.'

For a while neither of us said anything. The best thing seemed to me to talk with Graafland before I discussed with her how we should proceed. As far as I was concerned, she could have the Saab; but then the ownership had to be transferred to her, and what effect would that have on the death duties? Or would I have to give it to her, after which she would have to pay any gift tax that was due? Anyway, we could cross that bridge when we came to it. First I wanted to know why she had frightened me out of my mind at two in the morning and why she had given the *Poseidon* as her address in the condolences register.

'What brought you to my door in Grimburch Estates at two a.m.?'

As if it were the most normal thing in the world, she said sweetly: 'Was broke and thought: will give Rose's Bible a good shake. She doesn't need it any longer herself, anyway.'

'Why did you give the *Poseidon* as your address in the condolences register?'

She looked at me with her innocent eyes as if to say: what kind of weird question is that?

'That figures, doesn't it, was there so often with Rose.'

'Do you live here on Waard Island?'

'No, Fiona's father lives here.'

'Oh, so you're on your way to his place?'

'If that were only true. He won't admit he's Father. Mother worked in the lab for a while, got pregnant by him then was dismissed. Rose really took that to heart. Rose a big help to Mother. Rose thrashed Father regularly, but he never wanted to admit that he and Mother… He still doesn't want to admit it. Rose kept saying she would force him to acknowledge Fiona. She would apply pressure, she said, she knew all kinds of things about him, she said, things the public were not supposed to know.'

'So from his point of view it was convenient that she had sunstroke.'

'You bet. Right away said: Father did it, and wanted to go to the police.'

'Why didn't you do that?'

'Can't turn in own father, can you?'

'So you think your father…?'

'Thought so, but…'

'But what?'

She didn't answer that but said sombrely: 'Hoped that after the service ended he would…but he saw Fiona and vanished… You're wearing one of Rose's jackets, looks good on you, she used to say you were her sister.'

'And you were supposed to be her cousin.'

'That's right, was her cousin, so is also your cousin.'

'What are you going to do now?'

'Go watch Father, am a stalker, in fact. Whenever possible Fiona goes to his house. Mostly he's working in the sunroom; can see him, sitting in the light, through the windows, from the path in their backyard. Come along, you can see him too, if you're Fiona's cousin he must be a relative of yours in some way.'

'I think it's weird to…'

'Not weird at all. Come, walk with Fiona for a bit, he won't see us anyway. Fiona a stalker, yes, but doesn't want to push. Rose used to say that if he weren't married, he wouldn't treat Fiona so badly. It's because of his wife that he doesn't want to admit he has a daughter, that's the reason.'

We walked to the far end of Waard Island, found ourselves in a narrow lane between high hedges. A bit farther on, one of the hedges was somewhat lower, and we could look over it.

'You see,' she said. 'There he is. It always makes Fiona very happy when he sits there. It looks very peaceful. He works, he writes, he studies, it's just like everything is fine then. Sometimes his wife joins him, and then he snarls at her. A pity he has her for a wife. If she wasn't there, Fiona could sit by the lamp in the sunroom with him. But she was a doctor once, so he always has a physician nearby. Practical.'

'She was a doctor once? She studied medicine, and she also worked in the lab. I doubt that she ever practised medicine.'

For twenty minutes or so we stood there, silently watching. The river babbled restlessly, the ducks nattered loudly and indignantly because of the cold. In spite of my warm jacket I started to grow cold too, but I kept my eyes fixed on the man in the sunroom. The girl was right. The sight of the Professor, working calmly in his lighted sunroom, was cheering. Now and then I cast a glance at the alabaster-skinned girl, who spoke so disconcertingly of herself in the third person. She looked at Eduard with a high degree of concentration. She didn't resemble him in the slightest. Perhaps she was lying to me, or perhaps what she had told me was part of her delusional world. I had never heard about her or her mother, even though I had been involved in everything that happened in the lab for more than twenty-five years, closely at first, through Thomas, more distantly later, through Rose. I could check whether Fiona's tale was true, but what did it matter? If madness was at issue here, then this manifestation of madness had a certain attractiveness. There is no such thing as madness; in fact, there are only people who don't understand the condition. As a rule, the logicality of delusions is astonishing.

'Very soon he'll go walk the dog,' she said. 'Must go back, wouldn't like it if he saw Fiona.'

As we were walking back, she to her car, I to my bicycle, I asked: 'What do you think? Was Rose murdered?'

'Rose was murdered,' she said gravely. 'That's certain.'

'You thought your father had done it?'

'Yes, Rose used to say that Father might do some strange things if he were driven into a corner. So that's why...yes, he may be the one, but it may also have been someone else. Rose often said there was somebody who really loathed her.'

'And who was that?'

'Rather not say. Is extremely dangerous to know.'

She smiled enchantingly, then said: 'Dead all of a sudden...then *you* can have the Saab.'

'Why would you die suddenly?'

'Suspect, maybe even know, who did it. If you knew, you might die suddenly too, so it's better for you not to know.'

'Even if I were to keep my mouth tightly shut?'

'Whoever knows is on guard,' she said solemnly, 'and whoever is on guard behaves accordingly. And thereby betrays that she knows.'

Back at the Saab, she looked at me sadly with her big eyes.

'Fiona doesn't want to betray anything, so she has lain low ever since. So it's better to get into the car now. You get on your bike and go in the other direction.'

She got into the Saab, started it and drove off. I walked over to my bicycle, reached into my pocket for the key to the lock then thought: why not see how he reacts to the sight of me?

I walked back to the Professor's house and hid on the porch of another house some distance down the street. I took off my gloves and put them into a jacket pocket. My hands were cold, but Rose's flaming nails had already misled more than one man. I was fairly calm as I waited. I felt like a flasher. Except that instead of a penis I had ten fluorescent Nebuchadnezzar nails at the ready. I heard a door open and close. I couldn't see him, but I heard him coming nearer. Just as he was going to pass me, I stepped off the porch.

I should not have done that. Never in my life have I seen anyone take such terrible fright. He turned ashen and seemed to shrivel up. The small dog began barking furiously, launching an attack on my black boots.

'Rose,' he said. 'You're here…' And then shook his head in great confusion.

'Please excuse me,' I said. 'I am…' Then I stopped, because what I heard was not my own but Rose's deep alto voice. It seemed as if he had been waiting for that voice. He passed out in the same way Bas had, but, unlike Bas, he did not get up again within a few seconds. On the contrary, he lay there motionless. I stepped over him, ran to his house and rang the doorbell. An emergency lamp of at least three hundred watts came on. His wife opened the door, saw me in the bright light, evidently took no fright at all and said in surprise: 'What's the matter?'

'Eduard passed out.'

She spotted him lying there, walked resolutely over to him, almost managing to hide the fact that a nervous condition she had compelled her to use a curious shuffle. She half-lifted him.

'Give me a hand,' she said. 'Then the two of us can carry him inside.'

A moment later he was lying on a sofa, his head on a pillow. The dog regarded him with large concerned eyes, occasionally snarling in my direction.

'I think he must have fainted,' his wife said, 'but let me listen to his heart just to be sure. If you'll loosen his shirt and tie, I'll go get my stethoscope.'

She left the room. Carefully I loosened his tie. Then the struggle with his shirt buttons began. Oh well, fortunately with long nails it's easier to undo buttons than to do them up, so by the time she returned the job was done, thank God. I saw the upper part of his bare chest; saw the creepy-looking black hair. He was the man in the photo.

'When he comes to, please tell him I'm terribly sorry,' I said.

'Sorry? Sorry for what?'

'That I gave him such a fright.'

'Don't blame yourself, he can't take anything these days. The merest breeze and he keels over.'

'I must be going,' I said.

'So soon? Too bad, we haven't seen you for such an age. Please give the cats a hug for me.'

'I'll do that,' I said.

24.

After I had given the cats their Sheba and had eaten my own meal, a casserole of onions, garlic, mushrooms, leeks, carrots, celery root and quinoa, that fantastic high-protein supergrain from the Andes that the Incas regarded as holy, I took the book from the State Herbarium library out of the freezer. More than a week had passed since my expedition to Waard Island. I had wanted to go through the book as soon as I had borrowed it, but when I opened it in the living room that day a horrid little brown insect shot out. Maybe it was a bookworm. So I had put the book in the freezer compartment of the fridge. Before I read it I wanted all creepy-crawlies dead.

On a frigid page thirty-four I found a report about the Black Datura that read as follows: 'Baden-Powell alludes to a series of samples shown in the Lahore Museum as illustrative of the criminal methods of using the drug in Upper India. He says (quoting from a report of these written in 1863): "The series consists of the seeds of the plant in their raw state, seeds roasted, essence of the seeds, *atta* (flour) drugged with the poison, sugar ditto, and tobacco ditto." He then remarks that this is the agent used by the "Thugs" to stupefy their victims. "Both kinds of the dhatura, the white and the purple, are used, but the white [sic] is considered the most efficient. For poisoning purposes the seeds are parched and reduced to a fine powder; thus it is easily mixed with sugar, tobacco, &c. Also the professionals distil the seeds with water forming a powerful essence; ten drops of this is sufficient if put into a *chillam* of the *huka* to render a man insensible for two days. The taste is acrid and bitter, and soon followed by a burning suffocating sensation. It is very difficult to detect in a post mortem examination. The victims are usually discovered in a state of insensibility, and breathing hard and heavily; if removed, care should be taken not to expose them to the heat of the sun, which is fatal. The action of the poison is quicker in hot weather than in cold; much, of course, depends on the individual constitution of the victim, but usually in hot weather it begins to work in five minutes, coma supervening within the hour.'"

Undoubtedly more had become known about the Datura since 1863. Nevertheless, what I was reading sounded familiar. Riet had drawn her information from this book. Her assessment of the story told by Claire's husband, namely that it was full of holes, struck me as exaggerated. It seemed likely that Rose had been poisoned with powdered Datura seeds. Wouldn't Rose have noticed an acrid or bitter taste in her coffee? The freshly made coffee at the Pharmacological Laboratory was always super-strong, bitterer than lima beans that had been left on the vine too long. Rose had always taken her coffee black, and coffee has an acrid taste to begin with.

All that remained was the problem of how the murderer had managed to get the poison into her mug undetected. Solving this one was as easy as tailing a Saab from a bicycle. Instead of sugar, Rose put artificial sweetener in her coffee, in the form of tiny pills. She kept those pills in a pocket of her white lab coat. All you had to do – and pharmacologists were skilled at that kind of thing – was to make small white combination pills containing Datura-seed extract in addition to the sweetener. You would have to put them in her pocket while removing the genuine sweeteners. Since Rose took off her unflattering lab coat many times in the course of the day, only to put it back on later, the murderer had undoubtedly had an opportunity between morning coffee and lunch to effect the switch. When Rose went to the washroom, for example, because in that case she quite understandably took off her lab coat.

What to make of the fact that the poison normally seemed to work so fast? Sometimes it took only five minutes. Had the murderer been able to alter the poison in some way, so that it only began to work after a couple of hours? Could be, there must be techniques for doing that. It just depended on what group of drugs Datura poison belonged to. Maybe it could be attached to molecules that retarded the absorption rate through the wall of the intestines. All the expertise needed to produce something like that was available in the lab. Perhaps the evildoer had first carried out experiments on the white rats that, since time immemorial, were kept available in the catacombs for research purposes. But in that case the murderer had gone to work systematically and purposefully. Or could it be that somebody had accidentally come across the Baden-Powell quotation and then had carried out a few simple experiments, purely out of curiosity, because one of those Indian Daturas just happened to be growing near the sundial in the quad, and he wanted to find out whether that amazing story from 1863 was true?

Who could it have been? All the faculty members were full of scientific curiosity, and all of them were keen to discover something sensational, something about which they not only could publish articles but that would also make for heated discussions of the carefully prepared papers they would be presenting at the next pharmacological conference. Most faculty members were fully occupied by their own research and simply didn't have the time to study Datura poison on the side (although you never knew), but the Professor Emeritus, who no longer laboured under the burden of having to do targeted research that must be published, was of course an obvious candidate. The alabaster-skinned girl had told me that, aside from her father, someone else might have murdered Rose, but she had also told me that Rose had pressed him to acknowledge a child born out of wedlock. Who knows? Rose might have threatened to reveal what she knew about fraudulent research. As the girl had said, Rose knew things the public were not supposed to know. And perhaps the girl had told me that someone else hated Rose because she wanted to shield her father, whom she suspected of being the murderer but whom she would never turn in.

At least once a week the Professor Emeritus came to the lab to do some small experiments, as he himself described his activities. If he had investigated the way the Datura poison worked, Rose, and no one else, would have helped him. But Rose wasn't around to be asked whether she had reduced Datura seeds to a powder and done research on it. From the fact that she had taken a petal to Ici Paris, I could perhaps infer that she had also been interested in the plant on professional grounds.

After I had been sitting by the big living-room window for a long time, gazing at the Big Dipper in Ursa Major and musing about the Baden-Powell quotation and the pharmacologists in the Institute, it hit me: *if* one of them had carried out research on that stuff and had tried it out on rats first and had subsequently administered it as a delayed-action drug disguised as a sweetener, it was almost unthinkable he would have stayed in the lab that afternoon. A scientist would have wanted to be where it was happening, both to observe how the experiment was coming along and to see whether it was a success. In that case he had been on the beach at Katwijk too, he had walked right by her, he had been there among the spectators as she was being lifted into the ambulance.

So I engaged in another bout of freestyle wrestling with the VCR, the booklet of instructions for which I still hadn't managed to locate. The copy of Mastenbroek's tape was a smidgen less clear than the original, but the last thing I wanted was renewed contact with that creep.

Again I saw pretty well the same shadow fall over Rose twice, and since I now was practically certain the murderer was walking there, I became very anxious. Among the spectators before the arrival and after the departure of the ambulance (while the ambulance was being loaded no spectators were visible, because Mastenbroek had zoomed in on the ambulance workers) I once again spotted the slender figure I had taken to be little Fiona, as Fred had called her. Now that I had seen and spoken with her I wondered how I could have identified the person visible on the tape as the alabaster-skinned girl. They didn't look like each other at all. How easily one can be mistaken! Then I thought: I am *such* a dimwit, all this time I've been annoyed because everybody standing there is just about naked and has a hat and sunglasses, and so is almost unidentifiable, but her 'slave' in the photo is naked too; all this time I could have been checking whether the old Professor was there on the beach among the spectators. Why didn't I do that before? I got out the photo, and I looked and looked, hit play, hit reverse over and over again, kept seeing annoying flashes off sunglasses that messed up the image, saw not one, but two men standing there who were just as hairy as the old Professor. If there had been just *one* man, I could have concentrated on him and might have been more sure of myself. I was almost convinced that one of the two was Wehnagel, but 'almost' is not one hundred percent, and certainty was impossible precisely because both men were candidates. Both wore big straw hats, both were partly hidden behind other spectators. Also, the image wasn't sharp; otherwise I might have recognized the Professor anyway.

I stopped the tape. It had grown late: time to go to bed. I picked the State Herbarium book off the windowsill. When I was in bed I wanted to look into it once more. The borrower's slip fell out again. Before putting it back in I glanced at it. What a lot of data! On the narrow left half I read: borrowing date, transit point, borrowing location, call number, title, author, volume information, volume barcode, due date, type of loan, instructions, borrower's name, borrower's barcode. I turned the slip over and looked at the broad right half. The first thing I noticed was the name of the borrower: Eduard Wehnagel. I look at the due date printed to the right of the fold: July 14 2000. July 14? Return by July 14? So when had he borrowed the book? Three weeks earlier on June 23. He had taken the book out roughly six weeks before the day of the murder. Ample time to harvest some Datura seed, test it out on rats and make a pill that combined sweetener and Datura powder.

I went to bed and tossed and turned for hours. All kinds of thoughts and suppositions rushed like wolf spiders through my brain. Around three a.m. I became somewhat calmer. It all seemed crystal clear at last. I got up, walked over to the VCR, wearing my – or rather Rose's – beautiful, expensive, silver-coloured baby-dolls, turned it on, looked at the shadows, which of course did not tell me anything this time either, saw the ambulance drive up, saw Rose being lifted into it, saw the spectators standing around, all jumbled up. Saw the wickedly flashing lenses of the sunglasses, as big as fists, with nothing above them but straw hats and nothing below them but the near-naked bodies of male spectators, with women wearing sunglasses hiding behind them, saw the two hairy men again. Both were possible candidates, and for that reason doubt gnawed at my mind. Nevertheless, after seeing that borrower's slip I really could not be in doubt.

I got back into bed, dropped off at last, thank God, and slept until all hours. The feverish certainty I had felt at three a.m. turned out to have vanished while I slept. Unfortunately that often happens. When morning comes after a refreshing night's sleep, the appealing fantasies of the night before seem like ghostly castles in the air. I got dressed and paced through the living room, with Tiger constantly on my heels. 'What should I do, Tiger, my little Tiger, tell me, what should I do? I don't know what to do. I could go to the police, but what evidence have I got?' They would laugh at me if I said: "Everyone who knew Rose well is a bit shocked when I go around looking like her, but *he* practically had a heart attack, so…" "Yes, so what?" the police would say. "It was dark. You came off a porch totally unexpectedly. That by itself would be enough to frighten anyone out of their mind." And then think of the rest: a jacket he knew well, a fur cap he had seen before, flaming nails that no woman but Rose had ever sported.

A borrower's slip, accidentally left in a book, would that make an impression? An exotic Datura had been flowering in the quadrangle. Because of that, the Professor had very naturally borrowed the book. No big deal.

Properly considered, I had nothing concrete other than the astonishing intuitive certainty that had come to me in the middle of the night: it must have been him. I couldn't even supply a credible motive. Fear that he might be revealed to have cooked up the results of scientific research? Suppose that Rose had threatened to reveal this if he continued to refuse to acknowledge his daughter, how would she have done that? Send a note to a leading pharmacological journal? Suppose that, untrained as she was in such matters, she wrote something of that nature, would anyone believe her? A research assistant who had never published a word on her own? Of course she could have taken the matter to a newspaper, but what could a newspaper have done with information like that? Confiding in Claire would have been a possibility, and it was conceivable that the Professor, when he heard that Claire was coming to work in the lab for a while, had taken appropriate measures.

Could scientific curiosity have been a contributing motive? In his case, yes: perhaps he had even tried the stuff on rats. That could have yielded interesting results that he might have been engaged upon when I saw him working so serenely in his sunroom.

He might also have been jealous. He had been in a relationship with Rose for many years, almost from the day she had put a ten-cent piece on its side in his office, or so Thomas had repeatedly told me. Even back then Eduard apparently already had some unusual sexual preferences, and Rose had been willing to indulge him. Subsequently he had seen that Rose had relationships with other men as well, with his successor Bas, for example. He had sent somebody to tail her to find out whether she was moonlighting in a secret laboratory where Ecstasy or comparable drugs were manufactured. That had yielded nothing, Riet had told me, but perhaps he hadn't told her that he had learned *something*: in the *Poseidon*, Rose dripped hot candle wax on the backs of driving-school owners, auto wreckers, and fire-fighters and emptied her bladder on a scrawny contractor.

Had he come to hate her over the years?

Could a decent person kill simply because of hate? If I had the know-how, and something like Datura powder came my way, could I bring myself to kill Marjolein?

I could go to the lab at the high point of the day, the morning coffee break. Over a cup of bitter coffee I could confront all those jerks who begrudged me Rose's apartment and clothes with what I knew and suspected. Then they in turn might be able to tell me a few things that would confirm my suppositions. It would be even better to go there on a day when Eduard was at the lab too. Then I could shout my theory at him, and perhaps he would become so discombobulated that everyone would be able to see that he had killed Rose. But he might also say: 'We have a VCR here, why don't you run that tape?' and then I would be nowhere. *Two* hairy men instead of just one. He was one of the two, I was pretty sure of that, but a sceptic might see it differently. And they were all seasoned scientists over there, so they were sceptics to the core.

I could take Fred along to intimidate him, but Fred was a loose cannon: he would simply roar and thunder. For some mysterious reason I had the power to silence him, provided I used Rose's voice, but not before he would have spewed out words that had never been spoken at the lab. There was also the complication that, although I had always disliked the old Professor, I felt deeply ashamed about having frightened him so badly. If he had actually killed Rose, he didn't deserve any better, but still I couldn't stop seeing that ashen face before me.

If I had been one hundred percent sure of my case, I would have resolutely gone to Pharmacology at the high point of the laboratory day, even if only to warn the others. Be careful, I would say, he's doing research on powdered Datura seed. You mustn't believe that it works only when the sun is shining; he may be trying to discover what the LD 50 is on overcast days. I could quote Riet: 'A story about a dash of powder in the coffee…come now, things would never be done that amateurishly in a place like this. You wouldn't even know the LD 50 of such a substance.' Well, you wouldn't know that after just one experiment on a sunbather either. But perhaps he had been able to determine the LD 50 – the lethal dose at which half the subjects die – by experimenting on rats. There were more than enough rats there, hundreds of rats, they were available on order in multiples of ten.

Unfortunately I was *not* sure of my case. Worse: as the morning went on and, imperceptibly as always, gave way to the afternoon, and the afternoon likewise gave way to the evening, my doubts kept growing. I had been guilty of jumping to conclusions before. On the flimsiest of circumstantial evidence I had assumed that Rose had been manufacturing Ecstasy on a blacked-out houseboat, while I could or should have inferred from those 'ten tiny little lanterns that were hovering over the water' that they might be used to bring about ecstasy, but not the ecstasy of Ecstasy.

What might count in mitigation of that huge blunder was that I had been premenstrual, and that was not the case now or in the near future. But this was no guarantee at all that I wasn't making another mistake. And yet, as I thought over everything one more time and took into account Riet's report of phoned threats, I could hardly escape the conclusion that he had killed Rose.

What should I make of the fact that he had been so frightened? How would *I* react if I saw someone whom I knew to be dead appear so suddenly? Bas too had fainted; the porter, a student, and Mijna had all been startled. Nevertheless when I recalled how the blood had left his face and how he had stammered 'Rose' and then had shrivelled up as it were, only one inference seemed possible: he was tormented by feelings of guilt. He could easily have slipped into the lab by way of the mortuary to replace the sweeteners with his own pills. Since he knew the layout of the lab so well, he would have had no trouble doing that without anyone seeing him. In that gloomy building there were many alcoves and dark corners you could slip into if you heard somebody coming. All the same, it was quite conceivable that someone *had* seen him. I could ask around; but would anyone still remember whether the old Professor had been in the lab on the morning of Wednesday, August 9?

By nine o'clock that evening I was in bad shape, dying for some pill that would calm me down. I put Gerald Finzi's *Introit* for solo violin and small orchestra on the CD player. This serene elegy had always helped me, had always restored calm to my mind. This time not even Finzi worked. In the end the only thing I could think of to bring my nerves back to normal from their state of uproar was to go for a walk. When I got downstairs and opened the door to the outside the freezing cold cut me to the bone. I went back up and said to Tiger, who was glad I had returned so soon: 'This is *force majeure*. I know I shouldn't: I don't eat dead cows, pigs or chickens, I spit on factory farming, I abhor everything that smacks of raising animals for the sake of their fur, but that coat is there, and I want to use it to help calm me down.'

Just putting on her mink coat turned out to be magic. You don't know what comes over you when you wrap yourself in mink. It's like swallowing a benevolent Ecstasy pill. It is as though you're being very gently caressed. When I went out and the cold hardly even bothered me, demonstrating clearly just how wonderful a mink coat is, I knew I had to go back inside quickly. This was unquestionably every bit as addictive as cigarettes or chocolate.

When I got back into the apartment after my brief walk I found the cat odour really offensive. I wrote a postal transfer for a hundred guilders, payable to Respect for Animals, said to Tiger: 'I'll just go put this in the mail,' and, wrapped in her mink, went out a second time. The sky was amazingly clear; it was freezing. I could see Cassiopeia and Auriga sparkle as though they were within reach. When I exhaled, little clouds of condensation appeared. Unlike Rose I was alive, I was still alive, but if it *was* the Professor who had killed Rose, it seemed likely I would be the next test subject in a scientific experiment, having so emphatically fixed his attention on me with my flasher-like behaviour. Could Datura powder also be used to kill people who don't go sunbathing? One thing was clear: I must warn Fred.

25.

'Well, well, it's crowded here during visiting hours. Would you perhaps be Graafland the pyromaniac notary?'

'At your service, Mr Volbeda, isn't it? But crowded? Come now, I am the only one here, anyway, I just g...I just arrived.'

'I could have got here earlier, but I've been looking all over the bloody place, this is not a normal hospital, this is practically a small country. I wish *I* had been asked to put it up.'

'Yes, Leiden University Medical Centre has gr...gr...'

'Were you born that way, or did you have a playground accident when you were little?'

'An accident, Mr Volbeda? How do you mean?'

'You sound like a donkey at death's door every time a "g" turns up. What a fix *you* are in, here you've got to bullshit all day long, read documents to people and all that stuff, and each "g" gets stuck in your throat like a fishbone. How did it start? Did you almost choke on a grape when you were a toddler, and so now you can't get the "g" out? I can see it, grape stuck in your throat, your mother asks: "What's wrong?", and you want to say: "Grape in my throat", but you only keep saying: "Gr..." Why not come and lay bricks for me, you'd be a huge help, nobody wants to lay bricks anymore these days; it would be just the thing for you, you spread the mortar on those bricks and you never have to open your trap.'

'I deal with bricks and mortar in a different way; I convey property.'

'Yeah sure, I hear you, Graafland, you're another one who thinks he's too good for manual labour. You can only get immigrants for that nowadays, Moroccans, Turks, all those Koran-readers...there's plenty of them around.'

'You are apparently one of those who thinks the Netherlands is overcrowded.'

'You'd better believe it, much too crowded, filled to the rafters, but not because there's too many of those Koran-readers, they would fill ten football stadiums at most, that means zilch. No, it's overcrowded because there's so many Netherlanders, fifteen million or thereabouts, and that's not the worst of it, the worst part is that all those Dutchmen have grown too damned big for their britches. Just try to find a Dutch craftsman, a carpenter, a plumber, a housepainter. All our own people want something loftier, they look down their noses at manual labour. And they've all got big mouths on them. You go to Aldi, you're lined up at the checkout, wedged between a few of those polite smiling women wearing headscarves, and a Dutchman shows up. Right away there's a big to-do, loud voices, people trying to butt in line.'

'I never shop at Aldi.'

'Too down-market, I'll bet.'

'I wouldn't say that, but...'

'You're right, it's not always top quality over there, yesterday I thought, oh shit, Tiger and Ober and Lellebel must be starving, so at once I head over with a can of cat food from Aldi. They didn't go for it at all. They sniffed at it and looked up at me in disgust. Like I was trying to screw them. Well, praise be, when I want pussy I can get me the real thing. Fortunately they were still perfectly healthy. Only thirsty as hell. It's pretty hard to kill a cat; they even outlive vets, you can look it up.'

'What exactly happened? I heard a few news reports on Radio Rijnland and saw something on TV West, but...'

'I'll tell you exactly what happened. It started when she phoned and said to me: "Maybe I'm shying at shadows, but shouldn't we be taking a few simple precautions?" So I ask: "What kind of precautions did you have in mind?" "I'll give you a key so you can get in here if something should happen to me. And we should have a kind of hotline so I can warn you right away if there's anything the matter. If when I call a voice answers: 'Volbeda Construction', and then I hear: 'No, Mr Volbeda can't be reached just now, can he call you back?' I could be dead before you got back to me." "I'll give you my private mobile number," I said, "and you get yourself one of those damned things too and keep it with you all the time, then you can phone me any time, any place." "Yes, but do you always have your mobile with you...?" "Right next to my heart," said I. She spoke kind of flippantly, but I started to hear alarm bells ring. I mean, this happened to me before, and that was when you came into the picture, Graafland, you suddenly had a lot of work, I wouldn't wish that on you a second time.

'So I called Van Stenis and said: "You owe me one, because you sent two big invoices for a nebbish piece of work, you scumbag, so you keep an eye on her." Fortunately he wasn't very busy, what with Christmas around the corner, so he had all the time he needed to tail her. He soon reported that he thought she was being stalked by some creep from Katwijk, but that was a non-starter. If you read the report he sent to me *with* an invoice just after Christmas, then you'll see that he... Hard to believe...that lamebrain saw exactly what happened. He should have raised the alarm right away, but when I phoned him about it yesterday he said: "You see it so often. Someone looks in someone else's shopping cart and thinks: hey, those mushrooms look better than mine, and when the other one's back is turned to get something off a shelf, the first one quickly switches the boxes. Women especially are really good at that."'

'So the poison was in the mushrooms?'

'You got it in one, Graafland, in the mushrooms. No better place for it. They're poisonous to start with.'

'They can actually be pretty tasty.'

'Tasty? Mushrooms? Even rabbits won't eat them. Sure, Leonie's crazy about them, I figure she must have eaten them with every hot meal, that's why it was so damned clever to put the poison there. The first time we went out for dinner she ordered mackerel filet with some kind of porcini mushrooms. She just picked at that crappy mackerel, but she tucked into the mushrooms like they were tiger shrimp. Porcini mushrooms, hard to believe... If you served mushrooms to guys doing hard time, nobody would steal anymore.'

'Leonie prepared those mushrooms at home?'

'Yes, fortunately not all of them, she left half for Boxing Day, otherwise we still wouldn't know that's where the poison was... I mean, injected into the mushrooms with a thin needle, go figure...so in the morning you buy a box of mushrooms, you dissolve the poison in water, you fill up a hypodermic needle with that solution, and you inject it into each of the mushrooms. You put the see-through lid neatly back on the blue box and carry it to the supermarket in a bag, you wait calmly until there's a box of mushrooms in someone else's cart, and then, when the other person isn't paying attention or moves away for a moment to get something, leaving the cart unattended, you use the crowd as cover and quickly switch the boxes. It happened on

Saturday afternoon, December 23, so Digros was chock-full of people, it's almost a miracle Van Stenis saw it at all. Or maybe you have to say it was professional. So I guess I'll just have to pay the extra invoice that prick sent me. Even though of course it's unforgivable that when the two boxes were switched that way, with him standing just about right next to it, he didn't push the alarm button at once. I think I'll knock ten percent off the invoice after all.'

'So at the end of the afternoon she prepared the mushrooms...'

'Yeah, it went into another dish with...with...I knew the name, but I can't remember it, something from the Indians, I believe.'

'Qui...qui...qui...'

'Oh, so you can't get that out either. If that was all there was to your stutter, you'd be sitting pretty, nobody would ever need to know how badly handicapped you are.'

'Quinoa.'

'Great, how come you can say it now?'

'Because her eyelids flickered.'

'Like I haven't seen that already, my friend; she's going to make a full recovery, one of those white coats told me. Mostly I believe bugger all of what those guys say, but in this case I've decided to make an exception...where were we? Oh yeah, she fries those mushrooms to go with the quinoa, she eats from it a bit later, and because she's been on her guard for some time she notices right away there's something wrong, that she has swallowed that crap. So she calls me, I go over at once, but when I got there she was already in a coma. So I phoned for an ambulance and the police. They got her to the hospital here at record speed, stomach pumped, and since then she's been here, no Christmas celebration, and that while I'd actually persuaded her to come to the dis...what's the matter now, my friend? How come you look so pissed off? Jealous? Hey, guy, you're at least ten years younger than her.'

'When I telephoned to let her know we had to talk about the inheritance she showed up riding her bike. Without any fuss or hoopla. Mostly you see dollar signs in their eyes the moment you tell them they've inherited a lot of property, but she...not even *once* did she ask me how much it would add up to in the end. That's always the first thing the heirs want to know. Gr...gr...avarice, it's really quite incredible, people are so avaricious. And later, with those shares...someone else would have wanted to know immediately how many and what company and what the market was, but she just wanted to g...be done with them. They were sold while they were at the peak, since then they've g...dropped like you would not believe. When she's better, she can retire on the proceeds. It's too bad, I would have loved to have her working in my office.'

'In your office? Pouring coffee for some notarial loose change, I'll bet. Get out of here, Graafland, she can work in my place too, no problem, in PR, she'd earn a whole lot more, because in construction you can cut corners and pad bills, especially on government contracts. Well, well, so you have the hots for her just a little...'

'Yes, I...right away I...I...yes, no, well, all right, there is...*ach*, it's true; I'm already married...'

'Me, I'm divorced. I've got two broods and a third one on the way, I don't want to think about it; but you don't have to tell *me* she's one you wouldn't mind getting down on your knees for, though I wouldn't want to live with her, mushrooms every day... Goddammit, and at first I thought: what the hell is she trying to prove, making such a big effort to look like Rose?'

'That's my fault, Mr Volbeda, I told her the cats needed things to look as though their mistress were still alive.'

'Oh, so it was your idea...anyway, that too will pass, and it must be said, all those beautiful clothes of Rose's look fantastic on her, especially now that she's lost a few pounds, it's just that I get a lump in my throat every time she wears something of Rose's; and there *is* something a bit ghoulish about it...'

'But what I still don't understand is how the police were able to arrest the one who did it so soon.'

'I come running up, open the door, see her lying there, call for an ambulance and call the police. I say: "She's been poisoned, and I'm almost certain who did it." So I tell the cops who they should go after, but, well, they wouldn't believe me. So I call Van Stenis on his mobile...that bandit had already taken his entire family to a resort, and I ask: "Did you see anything unusual today?" So he says: "In Digros a woman in glasses exchanged her box of mushrooms for one in Mrs Kuyper's cart." "Bingo," says I. But I had to talk until I was blue in the face to get the cops to go there right away. In any case it took a lot of searching to find her address. She had "blom" in her name, that I *did* remember, but the rest of it I had wrong, I thought it was "mispelblom" okay, then you can hunt through the telephone directory until hell freezes over. So I keep looking, and the cops keep saying: "it can wait, it'll keep over Christmas." "But then four-eyes will have a chance to poison ten more people," I said. "Peace on earth, goodwill towards men, and ten more shepherds are offed in the night." I said to them: "if you don't so something at once, I'll show up with my biggest hydraulic shovel and demolish that new police station of yours; I put it up so I know exactly where the weak spots are." They had a good laugh about that, but finally, after phoning headquarters, they picked her up after all, and they started in on her on the way to the police station in one of those white Porsches. But she didn't flinch, she denied it every which way, which stands to reason, but a few nights in jail and she'll talk all right...'

'Do they have any idea why she...?'

'The way I see it, she wanted to make a pill you can use to do in people you can't stand without anyone being the wiser. And that you can use to off yourself when you don't feel like going on. It's not such a crazy idea either, I'd know what to do with it, a pill like that. When you're hogtied like me because you've got to cough up cash for alimony every month, you can certainly find use for such a murder pill. You drop by for a moment, you say with tears in your eyes: "I miss my little guys so much," you have a cup of tea with your ex and on the sly you drop a tiny treat in her cup...yeah, I'm absolutely convinced the human race is begging for a pill like that. I only hope that when it does come along they don't make it too expensive. Because of course it's also a solution when you don't feel like going on with life yourself. You take it, you go sit in the warm sun, you feel it caressing your eyelids, you get dopey, and before you know it you're on the other side. Calm, painless, peaceful, bye-bye flowers, bye-bye animals, bye-bye people. About eleven hundred people jump in front of trains every year. A pill would be an answer to that, right? And you wouldn't have that bloody mess on the rails.'

'His Holiness the Pope...'

'His Holiness? The guy in the embroidered pool-table cover? His Toothlessness the First can kiss my ass, he's against everything that could do humanity some good.'

'All right, all right, but that pill, what a lot of nonsense, she was...'

'That's what *you* say, but when I met four-eyes for the first time – over a dish of mushrooms, by the way – she told me there'd be more demand for a pill like that than for wholemeal bread. Right off I thought that she...I said it in so many words, maybe *you* gave Rose that pill...if people had listened to me...if I had listened to myself...Leonie wouldn't be lying here now. I may not be a star where fractions are concerned, but every once in a while...'

'You have nothing to reproach yourself for, Mr Volbeda. Without you Leonie would have died. But didn't I hear something on Radio Rijnland about breast cancer?'

'Yes, the bitch had heard from her doctor early in the year that she had breast cancer, that she had two, maybe three, years left. She wanted to send a couple of people on ahead to find out what it's like up there.'

'Send them on ahead? Isn't it more likely she was sour and embittered and couldn't stand it that a beautiful woman at her place of employment…because she *was* beautiful, Mrs Berczy, you could even say ravishing.'

'You're telling me. Everywhere she went they had to put up barricades to keep the crowds back. Be careful what you say about being sour and embittered. You're opening the floodgates. Before you know it, people will be saying the bitch was highly moral, didn't like the fact that Rose wasn't all that fussy and therefore wanted to punish her, and Leonie, who was so clearly following in Rose's footsteps, ditto. Then you'll get to hear next that she hated Rose because Rose had screwed around with all her male colleagues, who wouldn't have got it on with *her* for any amount of money. Then people will begin to add up all the Christmases and New Year's Eves she spent by herself, eating chicken drumsticks. If you go down that road, they'll bring in the shrinks, and then everyone starts to wail: "Oh, how pathetic", and she'll get sentenced to 240 hours community service, washing the floors in that lab just to make it easier for her…while as far as I'm concerned she should be strung up right away, today if possible. I'll put the noose around her neck, they don't even need to pay me, I'd gladly shell out for the pleasure, no, wait, don't hang her, they should inject her with that crap, and then we'll take her to a tanning studio, and we'll watch her croak, just as she watched Rose croak on the beach, that bitch, that battleaxe, that scumbag, that nasty, dirty, filthy, miserable…'

'Stop talking, please, Leonie's trying to say something.'

'Right. You know what she's trying to say? She wants to say: "Stop that."'

'You have g…sharp ears.'

'Yes, when I was a kid my mother often said so too. *Ach*, yes, and so we're sitting here around a hospital bed.'

'You see how your number can come up at any time. I told Leonie: drop by my office to draw up a will. When she has recovered, perhaps she'll be more receptive…'

'Graafland, you dirty old man, you! You want to entice her into your office again! Oh, what fun, just the two of you in a small room, ripping open little bags of coffee creamer between working on some boring conveyances and…'

'You're always welcome to come along, Mr Volbeda. Do you have a will?'

'Me? What the hell do I need one for? I haven't got a penny to my name, let alone any property to leave to anyone. What I get I spend at once, otherwise sooner or later it'll end up in the claws of my two exes.'

'Still, believe me, a last will and...'

'Man, piss off, if you start on this once more, I'll hit you so hard they'll have to dig up *your* last will and testament out of a drawer somewhere. Because I assume *you* already have one.'

'Absolutely.'

'Hey, look...! No...too bad, I thought she was coming to, but apparently we'll have to wait a bit longer; hey, here comes a white coat.'

'Good afternoon, gentlemen, the State Herbarium people have faxed me some additional information about the Datura. The substance it yields turns people into zombies who are completely conscious but can't even lift their eyelids. The major component of the substance is scopolamine. Now that we know that, we are a good deal further along where therapy is concerned, we can target the treatment more precisely.'

'Target more precisely: you mean you have an excuse now to pad the bill a bit?'

'Please mind your manners, sir, otherwise the doorway is over there. I've come to give her an injection. I'm pretty sure we'll have her back on her feet by the end of the week.'

'Great, then she'll be home in time for New Year's Eve; I'll buy some champagne and put it in the fridge.'

'She is also most welcome to come and celebrate New Year's Eve at my place.'

'I'll bet, but if she gets that idea, Graafland, I shall remind her gently that I...'

'Only because she phoned you. She could also have phoned me, then I could...'

'You? Guy, give me a break, if *you* had dialled emergency, you'd have said: "Please send an ambulance to Gr...Gr...Gr..." and then at emergency they would have thought there was a dog on the line and sent the animal ambulance. Quiet: did you hear that? Somebody else is coming, another white coat, no.... So who do we have here? What brings you here?'

'On Radio Rijnland I heard, on TV West I saw...I called all the hospitals, I was told she was here.'

'And then you thought: "Come on, I'll go pay her a visit? I'll take my camcorder along..." Hold on, maybe you're that beach guy...yes, of course, you're that beach guy…you dummy, you asshole, you clodhopper, you film the whole damned thing, and you manage to leave that bitch out!'

'That remains to be seen. I saw an old woman come by the afternoon of the sunstroke, I remember it very clearly because she was just about the only one that afternoon who was in street clothes.'

'So why didn't you say anything?'

'Nobody asked me, did they?'

'So you should have filmed her, dammit.'

'Should have? I do have her on tape, I'm 110 percent sure of it. There's an old lady with glasses among the spectators. Okay, she's slight, and she's pretty well hidden by all the others, and she's wearing a big sunhat, but you can see her gleaming lenses very clearly because the sun gets reflected off them.'

'Then take good care of it; let's hope they'll accept it as evidence. If by accident you were to film a murder, I'm willing to bet that one of those clever lawyers, one of those shysters, would be able to fix it so that your tape would not only be thrown out as evidence but would also have to be destroyed at once. I just don't know where it will all end.'

26.

I heard waves murmuring softly and smelled the ocean. A male voice sang: 'The sun burns bright. A friendly garden offers welcome/and shelter from the glowing heat.' Then, sung by four voices, came the sweetest, profoundest, most heart-warming little melody I knew: 'Father amid the angel-rows/Look down with favour on the man/Who was the founder and sustainer/Of our cherished institute!' It was just as if the melody wanted to lead me back to life, but it ran squarely against another Schubert melody that also kept running through my head, pom, pompom, pom. I wanted to open my eyes but couldn't do that yet, although it did seem that, after an unbearably long period of time in which I had been on standby, as it were, I was going to re-emerge as a human being with normal consciousness. I had simply registered everything that had taken place by my bedside and every sound that had passed over my head without being able to react to it or think about it. It was just as if I had been completely petrified – incapable of any thought or action at all. I had not even been able to sleep. How remarkable and disturbing it is to be outside your body, as it were, and still be alive. As though you were an appliance with a small red light indicating how to turn it on by remote control. Apparently a human being could be turned on the same way. Only instead of a remote I evidently needed an injection, which had just been administered to me in the presence of Fred and the notary. In the meantime they had left. Were visiting-hours over already?

I tried to think but without much success, because right through Schubert's *Cantata in Honour of Joseph Spendou* I now heard the Christmas carol that had flowed out like Muzak over the customers at Digros on Saturday afternoon:

191

Come and stand amazed, you people,
See how God is reconciled!
See his plans of love accomplished,
See his gift, this newborn child.

When I was little, I had always found this very beautiful, perhaps because in the Christian Reformed Church my parents belonged to we were not allowed to sing it. Come and stand amazed, you people. Strange that this carol was so doggedly trying to break through the Schubert. Could it be because *I* was amazed? If only the explanation were that simple! No, I was not amazed, I was beyond amazement. I was stupefied. Apparently they had arrested Riet. The idiots! The person who killed Rose and who wanted to kill me was still at liberty, could appear at my hospital bed as easily as Fred or the notary or that creep Mastenbroek, to finish the job.

What also amazed me is that, although I was desperately worried, the smell of the ocean continued to visit and console me.

Whatever I had been injected with was finally beginning to take effect. It was as if my whole body had received permission to relax and all my muscles had loosened. I seemed to be sinking away, as if into death, although I hoped it would be nothing more than a deep sleep. That sinking feeling was absolutely delightful, and I hoped I would come out of it to the sound of that ravishing little melody by Schubert.

No matter how blissful that sinking feeling was, though, I nevertheless fought desperately against my drowsiness. Never had I battled such a masterful crushing sleepiness. I had to stay awake, wide-awake, because the real culprit could appear at my bed at any time to finish me off. After all, it had become known via radio and TV that the attempted mushroom poisoning had failed. I was almost certain that the person who killed Rose knew I was still alive. I had to hope she hadn't noticed that I had recognized her, shuffling around Digros, almost perfectly disguised with wig and glasses, although I stupidly hadn't realized it was *me* she was there for. In any case she could not know that the scales had fallen from my eyes as soon as I had seen her, mostly because of that oddly flickering pair of glasses, jaunty hat and oversized coat. Of course, the slender figure on Mastenbroek's tape who had struck me as so familiar each time I saw her and who on that occasion too had disguised herself in an effective, if not very summery, way that was her and no one else. Why hadn't I seen that before? Because of the disguise? But then why did I see through it at Digros? Because I saw her in the flesh and not on a grainy TV screen? Or because of that peculiar shuffle? Years and years ago, while we were washing dishes in her kitchen, she had snapped at me: 'That bitch is screwing my husband,' and then had slapped the dishwater so hard with her brush that it had splattered my face. She had waited for her opportunity patiently. Last summer opportunity had knocked, thanks to the thorn apple bush. Eduard had borrowed a book that she had in all probability looked through as well. And no doubt she had seen the Datura in bloom in the quadrangle, because she visited the lab almost as often as her husband. Just like that, an exuberantly growing and flowering plant, right there in the quad by the sundial, with seeds that she could easily harvest and work with, could even save until Christmas, and that could be made into a small tablet that looked like artificial sweetener or could be used to produce an extract that could be injected into mushrooms. She had the necessary know-how; she had worked in the lab for years before her marriage. It must have seemed to her that last summer everything had succeeded beyond expectation, but then I had shown up one winter evening and she, grossly overestimating me, must have thought I knew too much. Even though I had stupidly focused on her husband and no one else. But I had been just *one* step from the truth. And of course she had known that Rose could tell tales about fraudulent research, she had also known that, if Fiona was to be believed, Rose had used this knowledge in an effort to force Eduard to embrace the girl as his daughter. Add to this that she hated Rose bitterly. I tried to recall what her facial expression had been when she found me on her doorstep, dressed like Rose from head to foot, brightly illuminated by a bulb at of least three hundred watts. She must have nerves of steel, because she had given nothing away. If she was surprised, she had been able to hide it in masterly fashion. But maybe she hadn't been surprised at all, quite likely she had heard weeks earlier that I was wearing Rose's clothes and nails, and had my hair cut in her style. Or maybe she had, by murdering Rose, appropriated her spirit much more effectively than I ever could, had merely laughed at my primitive attempts to look like Rose. This much was certain: I had sealed my fate by ringing her doorbell, and it was a safe bet that she would have another crack at getting me out of the way.

Thank God, I was still alive, I could shout from the rooftops: 'Let Riet go at once, she's got nothing to do with this!' Provided I stayed awake.

How strange it is that, after the fact, you can never remember the moment you fell asleep. When I woke up, the only thing I knew was that I had slept the sleep of the blessed for hours on end. I felt much better, could even open my eyes. When I did so, cautiously and rather slowly, the first thing I saw was the flash of glittering glasses. My whole body shuddered, I wanted to scream, but my fear was so great and my shout so wild that it got stuck in my throat. Oh my God, there she was, now she would…oh, oh, then who would take care of the cats?

'Quiet, child, it's me, no need to be afraid.'

I opened my eyes wide.

'You here?' I asked, flabbergasted. 'So they let you go?'

'Yes, because Van Stenis didn't recognize me, he took a gander at me through the one-way glass and then said with malicious pleasure, loud enough for me to hear it too: "Oh no, you've got the wrong one, the mushroom lady looked like a slender dwarf, and this one is a hefty witch, no, once again you guys have screwed up royally."'

'But why did they wait so long to have him identify you? Why not right away on Saturday afternoon?'

'Because at that point Van Stenis had already left to celebrate Christmas at a holiday resort with his wife and children.'

I sighed heavily then said: 'Will you please take care of Rose's pussycats if anything happens to me? And make sure they play "Soave sia il vento" by Mozart and "Dies Natalis" by Finzi?'

'It's a promise, but why should anything happen to you?'

'The mushroom lady is bound to know by now that I'm not dead, and she'll be looking for a chance to finish the job.'

'That crossed my mind as well,' said Riet. 'And that's why I came here at once and am now sitting here as your unpaid bodyguard. Because it's dead quiet here, between Christmas and New Year more than half the staff are away, and every patient who's not at death's door has been sent home. Anybody with evil intentions can walk right in, and so…'

'Do you have any idea who…?'

'Of course. I had all the time in the world to think about it while I was locked up. I spent all of Christmas in a nice warm nest. It was really quite cosy over there…food and drink right on time, and you don't have to worry about a thing. Otherwise I would have been all alone at home, and this way I had one conversation after another; I had a good time.'

'You kept a stiff upper lip.'

'Could be…fortunately when those guys came to the door I had the presence of mind to grab my disc player and all of Beethoven's piano sonatas, played by Richard Goode…that cheered me up enormously… But I was convinced that in time they'd let me go, even though I didn't have an alibi for that afternoon. How would I have been able to come up with one? I was out shopping all over the place, just like everybody else.'

'I heard something about breast cancer. Is that true?'

'That's such a crazy story, I don't understand how that got started, but consider: when you witness an event and later read a news story about it, there's hardly a detail that seems to square with what you saw.'

'When they were interrogating you, did you tell the police who you thought the mushroom lady really was?'

'No.'

'Why not?'

'Because I kept thinking she'd arranged it all so cleverly and perfectly that if there was ever a trial she'd get off for lack of credible evidence. You can report her all right, but you can't prove a thing; I think the police would laugh at you.'

'The only thing is that Van Stenis may be able to identify her.'

'I very much doubt it, it's a safe bet she was extremely well disguised, she was good at that, years ago…I still recall…'

'Yes, you're right, she was in disguise. I saw her moving around in Digros.'

'How did you recognize her?'

'By that peculiar shuffle.'

'Yes, that's hard for her to hide, as you know she's suffering from a nervous disorder, she probably doesn't have all that long to live. I think maybe the disease has affected her brain. How else to explain that she, who used to be such a highly moral person, is now willing to resort to murder?'

'But her brain still worked well enough for her to carry out a perfect murder.'

'Get out of here! She was always such a perfectionist. And so amazingly smart. Much smarter than Eduard. She could have gone a long, long way. But no, she got married, had children and was lost to science.'

'How would she have known I was going to be at Digros to buy mushrooms on Saturday afternoon?'

'She knew you were a mushroom addict, everybody at the lab knew *that*, maybe she trailed you for a couple of days with those mushrooms, or she simply took the chance that you would be there on Saturday afternoon…it makes me think of her experiments years ago…everything was put together so intelligently, so well thought through. And you can bet she worked on the assumption that you wouldn't use all the mushrooms at once. Whatever was left over is bound to be useless in a criminal investigation by now; I can't believe you'll find any trace of Datura extract in those mushrooms now.'

'If her mind isn't...if she...you understand what I'm saying, she killed Rose in cold blood...oh Heavens, we're sitting here talking like it is something quite ordinary...while...'

'Yes, child, I agree it's simply dreadful, but we've got to face matters squarely, and maybe the best thing is to talk it through calmly...but what were you going to say?'

'She hated Rose, so...but why did she want to kill me too? Why me, for God's sake?'

'Maybe she was afraid you had gradually come to know too much.'

'I have to confess something,' I said, and I told her about the evening on Waard Island, avoiding an explanation of exactly how I had frightened Eduard out of his wits.

'Well, well, so you met Fiona too...very sweet girl, no question, but Eduard's daughter? Don't make me laugh; anyway, that's another story. I wish I'd known, when I was in jail, that you had ended up on Waard Island, now I understand better why she... So you showed up. A dead ringer for Rose. What could she have concluded, if not that you were appearing as a sort of Nemesis disguised as Rose because you had come awfully close to the truth? And that was in fact the case, one small mental leap, and you would have known who had killed...it's hard to believe, someone I've always known and valued enormously, that's why I didn't think even for a moment... But still, my father...a perfect gentleman...when he was suffering from Alzheimer's, he once emerged from the washroom carrying his turds, which he then generously handed out to all and sundry.'

'*She* doesn't have Alzheimer's, does she?'

'No, but there is certainly something wrong up there.'

'Something wrong? If she thought I knew too much and it would be better to...I mean, that's plain, old-fashioned logic, isn't it? On the other hand, what did she have to fear from me? Even if I had gone to the police...she wasn't in that much danger, I mean, she'd killed Rose in such an awfully clever way.'

'An almost perfect murder, you can say that again. I myself never suspected her, I was even convinced it *was* sunstroke...still, look, although she might have got out of it because of lack of evidence, she would have had a lot of trouble. Not that I think it would have bothered her much, knowing her, but

I do think she'd prefer to spare Eduard the trouble of a trial and all the miseries that come with it...plus everything that would be revealed about the long-standing relationship between Rose and the Professor, maybe even details about...about...well, it doesn't matter...'

'About SM practices,' I said.

'Oh, you got that far too...you dug that up as well...be that as it may, I think she got into a panic above all because you seemed to know too much, and so for that reason...she happens to be crazy about her husband, always has been, that's where it all stems from. Even though I think murder is a dreadful thing, I can see why she hated Rose so much. For years he was madly in love with Rose, it was only that Rose never wanted anything more than a casual relationship, otherwise he would gladly have left his wife for his little Rose. Maybe that would have been better...the way things were, year in, year out, she had to watch him cheat on her with Rose. If you think about it a bit, it's a mystery why she didn't kill her sooner... Anyway, let's drop the subject, I have a plan.'

'What kind of plan?'

'In my view it makes very little sense to share our suspicions with the police. Even if they do arrest her, they'll very probably have to release her. If they don't release her and the case goes to trial, then I feel sure she'll be acquitted for lack of evidence. You're going to say: "but shouldn't she be punished for that so-called sunstroke and the poisoned mushrooms?" What *I* think is that punishment, which would surely be a long prison sentence, is ridiculously primitive and hopelessly ineffectual. Does it help to change the behaviour of your fellow humans? Hardly. So what is it, beyond simple revenge? The way I see it, you should never repay evil with evil. That's horribly uncivilized; it's nothing more than a glorified desire for revenge. In this case retribution seems to me to be completely out of place. This woman's life has been a hell on earth because her husband quite openly and for years had an affair with his research assistant. What we've got to do is this: prevent her from trying something like this mushroom stunt again. Hence my plan.'

'Tell me.'

'I'll go to her place and say to her: "They arrested me, and while I was in jail I thought very carefully about things and reached the following conclusion: they should have come for you instead. For that and that and that reason. Aside from me, there's not a soul who suspects you in any way. I've got no intention of ever telling anyone that you killed Rose, on one condition: from now on you keep your hands off Leonie. All the more so because Leonie, contrary to what you seem to think, doesn't have the faintest idea that you killed Rose." And then I'll tell her how, trailing behind that goose Fiona that evening, you ended up on Waard Island quite by accident, and that this really had nothing to do with any possible suspicions you may have had.'

'There are two catches to this plan,' I said.

'What's the first?' asked Riet.

'The moment you let her know you're fully aware of all the ins and outs you run a big risk of being hit by something like sunstroke too.'

'I gave some careful thought to that as well. Yes, I do run a risk, but it's not especially big and besides, she has always liked me a lot, and over the years she has cried on my shoulder dozens of times. Be that as it may, it's a risk I am prepared to take...and she doesn't have long to live, so if I do run a risk, it's for a year or two at most.'

'Yes, but maybe you'll be dead by then.'

'That would be too bad. In that case please make sure they play Beethoven at my funeral service, opus 109, last movement, performed by Richard Goode. But people don't just die, it won't come to that, we've been adequately warned, and I'm going to equip myself with an antidote to Datura pills and extracts. You should have some around the place too; I'll get it for you. My God, this all seems so far-fetched...what matters most is your safety. If I can convince her that you don't have the faintest idea who was responsible for Rose's sunstroke and your mushrooms, that's bound to do the trick. But how do you feel about this? Maybe you think it's so dreadful that someone has tried to murder you that you want to pay a visit to the police no matter what. After all, most people would do that in an instant.'

'Oh no, I don't...I...no, I just want to get back to my pussycats...I want...'

'You're actually speaking with Rose's voice...those cats are in luck...who's looking after them right now?'

'Fred, I hope.'

'Is he the fellow who came barging in when I was eating that luscious quiche at your place?'

'Yes.'

'Oh. Anyway, you mentioned two catches. What's the second?'

'Even if we don't go to the police, there's bound to be an investigation, and then they can...I mean, it's all amazingly simple if they think it through...'

'I gave some thought to that too while I was locked up. Yes, an investigation strikes me as unavoidable, although I did hear a police chief say on the box the other day: "We're up to our eyeballs in work right now. Even serious cases we can't get to anymore. If it's not immediately obvious who the culprit is, we won't touch it." We'll just have to wait and see…if we both keep our mouths tightly shut, and you don't tell them you saw her shuffling along the aisles in Digros on Saturday afternoon… Frankly they *are* rather dim over there in the police station… That interrogation was laughable…two of those guys…one moment they're shouting and stamping their feet, the next moment they're sweet as spun sugar…you should have been there, it was so easy to lead them astray. They thought they could intimidate me… That was a lot of fun; I really enjoyed that. As an academic I'm definitely used to a different level of intelligence. Well, it stands to reason, if you're really intelligent, you go to university and you don't end up with the police. They really aren't…the sharpest knives in the drawer they are definitely not, which is rather a shame, by the way. All the same, if they do investigate, then she'll come into the picture as a suspect, that's a certainty. All the more reason why, even if she does remain at large, she'll think twice before… True, you can never rule anything out completely, all of life is, in the end, a form of uninterrupted risk-taking. In any case I shall do my best to protect you. After all, I'm very much an interested party; I want you to live. Because if you die, I'm going to have to take care of those cats.'

'Maybe there's another interest at work besides,' I said ironically.

'Another interest?'

'I don't imagine you like the idea of the lab being talked about because of a trial.'

'I freely admit that's a consideration too. The lab has an excellent reputation internationally, even if those bastards in Montreal are trying to smear us…anyway, you know all about that. A rumour-producing trial: *that* we don't need. And I'll add in all honesty: I'd feel terribly sorry for Eduard. I would be very glad if he were spared this sort of misery, it would be the death of him.'

While I lay there listening calmly to her, I thought: she hasn't come to the hospital to guard but to manipulate me. Her objective is not to protect me; she wants to protect the lab. Thomas used to say about the way the lab was run: 'Eduard proposes, Riet disposes.' Now she wants to dispose of the possibility that a trial will take place. Maybe she'll succeed, maybe she won't. The question is: do I want to cooperate? Rose was murdered, I was almost murdered, should that go unpunished because of the scientific reputation of a laboratory and of a Professor Emeritus? Because she had failed to kill *me*, maybe some day I could forgive her, a hundred years from now perhaps, for wanting to kill me with poisoned mushrooms, although I must add, quite frankly, that I don't really know what meaning to give to that Biblical word 'forgive'. Never mind all that, I had deserved punishment, although not the harsh one she had meted out, for scaring her husband out of his wits. But I would never be able to forgive her for killing Rose, even if there *were* mitigating circumstances.

What should I do? I lay there and saw small waves on the water of a ditch, glistening in the summer sun. My brother had pushed me into that ditch and then pulled me out in a panic, scared silly because I had gone under. After I had climbed out and stood there, sopping wet, he had pleaded with me not to tell our parents, and we had sat down in the sun a bit farther on so I could dry out, and there, beside the ditch, I had been consoled and caressed by the sun, and I had watched the small waves make little ripples of light that glided soundlessly along the bottom of the shallow ditch. I couldn't remember any longer whether I had already fully realized at the time that punishment can never undo what has happened, but whenever I thought back to those constantly advancing ripples of light and then to the fact that he too had passed away in the noontide of his days, I was deeply thankful that I hadn't told on him back then.

So I said: 'The only thing that matters to me is that, whatever we do or anyone else does or doesn't do, Rose is never coming back. So why not do whatever you think best? Only Fred will go ballistic if the police don't pursue the matter.'

'Fred again,' she said grumpily.

'What have you got against Fred?'

'That hooligan set those ill-mannered louts in their Porsche onto me. That's lost him every ounce of credibility with the police, by the way. You should have heard what they said about him when they had to let me go, no, I'm not worried about Fred… Oh, why did Rose have to hang around with someone like that, and now you too?'

'He seems like a bit of a Neanderthal, but he's actually quite amusing,' I said, 'very genuine, completely different from the uptight academics you and I spend our time with, but, sure, he is very hot-headed, as you have noticed; in many ways he's just a big child.'

'Just like most men.'

'I'm feeling great. Why do I have to stay here, lying on my back? Could you have a look, please: are my clothes in that corner closet?'

'They won't let you sign out just like that.'

'I can simply sneak out, can't I?'

'I'm not sure whether that's a good idea... Wait a minute: seen in the right light, it is. You're not safe here, certainly not while they have hardly any staff on duty, any vagrant with evil intent can walk right in; and it would solve a problem for me too. I wouldn't have to do guard duty. Since there's hardly anybody here, we should be able to leave without being given a hard time. And because there's lots of parking available today, my car is parked right by the entrance; so we can get out of here at once.'

When I had got dressed and started walking I turned out to be weaker than I had thought.

'Yes, what do you expect?' said Riet. 'You haven't eaten anything since Saturday. But not to worry, there are plenty of wheelchairs in this place.'

Moments later she was pushing me cheerfully down one long corridor after another. We met no one along the way; we went past the porter without any problems. While she was returning the wheelchair, I made myself comfortable in the passenger seat of her beige Toyota.

While I was alone in the car, I suddenly wanted to shout with joy. I was still alive, I was still around, and I was on my way back home. 'And then my soul was spreading/Its wings out far and wide/Flew through the silent regions/As if 'twere flying home.' Softly and contentedly I hummed Schumann's immortal song.

'You know something?' Riet said after she got in next to me and we drove off without anyone stopping us. 'When we're in Rose's...in your apartment I'll phone her at once and ask to meet her, today if possible. I've still got to figure out how I can get to speak with her without Eduard being there. But I'll think of something.'

Even Lellebel came to greet me with waving tail when I hobbled into the living room and collapsed on the couch. Riet had already keyed in the number and apparently got Eduard on the line. She said 'yes' a couple of times then put down the receiver.

'Eduard says she's got the flu. He told me she went into town for a while on Saturday afternoon. She came home exhausted and has been in bed ever since. Very convenient: I can go visit the patient tomorrow. I'll be up in their bedroom, sitting at her bedside, while Eduard will be downstairs, working away in the sunroom. She's ill, seriously ill! What happened on Saturday must have hit her hard too, maybe her brain is less affected than I thought... In that case it's all the more likely I can persuade her... And for now you have nothing to fear from her.'

'*Ach...*' I said.

'I'll be going now, if that's all right with you. Drink tea, eat fruit, fruit is the best medicine of all; do you have anything to eat in the place?'

'I think so. There should be half a box of mushrooms in the kitchen.'